A FUGITIVE ENGLISHMAN

Edwin James reaches the height of his professional career in law when, on the brink of being knighted, legal scandals and debt force him to flee England with his new bride and attempt a new career in America. He finds himself recruited into Colonel Lafayette Baker's Secret Detective Service investigating Fenian activity in New York's hell-hole, the Five Point. Forced to work with corrupt judges and policemen in New York he becomes involved with the most notorious fraudsters of the day, and in the background the shadows of his scandalous past threatening to rise up and engulf him once more...

A FUGITIVE ENGLISHMAN

A FUGITIVE ENGLISHMAN

by

Roy Lewis

Magna Large Print Books
Long Preston, North Yorkshire,
BD23 4ND, England.

British Library Cataloguing in Publication Data.

Lewis, Roy
    A fugitive Englishman.

    A catalogue record of this book is
    available from the British Library

    ISBN   978-0-7505-4046-9

First published in Great Britain 2014
Buried River Press is an imprint of Robert Hale Ltd.

Copyright © Roy Lewis 2014

Cover illustration © Mohamad Itani by arrangement with
Arcangel Images

The right of Roy Lewis to be identified as the author of this work
has been asserted by him in accordance with the Copyright,
Designs and Patents Act, 1988

Published in Large Print 2015 by arrangement with
Robert Hale Limited

Magna Large Print is an imprint of Library Magna Books Ltd.

Printed and bound in Great Britain by
T.J. (International) Ltd., Cornwall, PL28 8RW

PROLOGUE

You know, Joe, the first thing I noticed about President Lincoln when I met him at the White House was the piercing intelligence in his dark, deep-set eyes.

After your mother and I retired last night, I was talking to her about him, and we fell to reminiscing about life in New York in the 1860s. She was already living in the city when I arrived there in 1861, but I guess you must have been away at that time, learning seamanship on your first voyage to Australia, while your father cavorted around pretending to teach cavalry techniques to New York volunteers in preparation for Civil War battles to come. He was always a boastful, preening sort of charlatan.

What? Yes, of course, back to Lincoln...

I was invited to the White House within weeks of my arrival in the United States. My reputation had gone before me and the invitation to meet the president was not unexpected. Certainly it was not something to be ignored: after all, I needed to carve out a new legal and political career for myself.

As he advanced along the line at the *soirée* in Washington that evening, greeting his guests, I was aware of his tall, ungainly shamble of a walk; my excited, newly acquired wife Marianne nudged me nervously at the sight of plump Mrs Lincoln, all frills and unsuitable furbelows, affecting a haughty, condescending air but betrayed by the obvious pleasure she took in presiding over such a distinguished gathering – the cream of Washington society, judges, senators, foreign ambassadors and Mr and Mrs Edwin James.

It was probably the ultimate height I achieved in my marriage, attending the president's *levée* that evening. Marianne was delighted and excited and proud. For me also, it was a most pleasurable experience. President Lincoln advanced towards me, Secretary of War Stanton just behind him, and when I was introduced the president nodded, moved on and then paused. He hesitated, turned back, and held me with that keen glance of his. Then, to my surprise, he spoke directly to me, in words that I immediately recognized.

'*Tell the prosecutor that the verdicts of English juries are founded upon eternal and immutable principles of justice! Tell him that no threat of armament or invasion can awe you! Tell him that though six hundred bayonets glittered before you, though the roar of French cannon thundered in your ears, you will return a verdict that your own breasts and consciences will sanctify*

8

and approve, careless whether it pleases or displeases a foreign despot or secures or shakes and destroys forever the throne which a tyrant has built upon the ruins of the liberty of a once free and mighty people!'

I stared open-mouthed at the president, almost unable to speak. At last, awestruck, I managed to mutter, 'My speech in defence of Dr Simon Bernard, when he was accused of involvement in the assassination attempt against Napoleon III... I am, sir, *astounded.'*

'I read that published speech with interest,' President Lincoln said with the hint of a smile on his gaunt, lined features. 'And parts of it I committed to memory.'

'I am flattered, Mr President. *Overwhelmed.'*

Amusement glinted in his deep-set eyes. 'I am aware it was a rabble-rousing speech, Mr James. Nothing to do with the law in the case, of course. But a speech that struck a chord with the jury. A speech that over here the Confederacy might have approved of. But here you are as my guest ... so you are for the Union, it seems!'

'Certainly, Mr President,' I affirmed stoutly as Marianne pressed my arm in excitement. 'The Union and the Constitution.'

A certain grim smile touched the corners of his mouth and his careworn features relaxed a little. He nodded, thoughtfully. 'We appreciate your support, and welcome you to America. I am sure a lawyer of your calibre will do well here. We must talk again, on some other more intimate occasion.'

But we never did. Secretary of War Stanton saw to that, when he involved me in the intricacies of the intrigues that swirled around Washington and New York politics. Marianne was due to be disappointed, of course, but within a matter of months she and I would have our own personal problems leading to her taking drastic action against me and against my fledgling legal career in New York.

What? You're getting confused? But you are right, I am getting ahead of myself again, the perils of age...

So, I suppose I need to explain how it was that I ended up in America, a fugitive Englishman, at the very height of my professional and political career at the English Bar and the House of Commons. I had enjoyed a rapid, dazzling rise and my success resounded throughout England – and even in the States. But the devastating crash when I fell ... that was even greater...

You are wide-eyed! Ah, well, this was the way it was, my boy...

PART 1

1

You know, when I look back, I believe I was at the height of my powers that May in 1860. My rise since becoming a barrister at the Inner Temple had been rapid: from the early, heady excitement of the *Running Rein* case in 1844 when I had made my reputation, to the flood of briefs in sensational cases that drew crowds to the Old Bailey, the prosecution of the poisonous Dr Palmer, my renowned speech in defence of Dr Bernard in the Napoleon III assassination attempt, and all the crim. con. cases like *Lyle v Herbert* when I clashed with Gladstone, the Swinfen inheritance case and the rest of it... Yes, by 1860 I was at the height of my profession, reckoned by Lord Chief Justice Campbell himself to be the best *nisi prius* lawyer in practice at the Bar. He liked my jokes, too.

I had learned from my early days that juries liked sly humour. It was in 1836, I recall, in the *Norton v Melbourne* hearing that I first appreciated the impact an *apparently* innocent remark by counsel can make upon the courtroom. It was William Follett, leading for the prosecution of the criminal conversation case brought by Lord Norton against Lord

Melbourne, then Prime Minister, who showed me how it could be done. I was lucky to get a seat as a spectator in the Queen's Bench court that day – the sensational nature of the case had drawn all the fashionable crowds to the hearing – and I heard Follett state that Lord Melbourne had taken to visiting Caroline Norton in the afternoons when her husband was at work. Follett went on to state, 'I do not know whether much importance in the result may be attached to it or not, but the house had two entrances, one leading from Birdcage Walk – the public entrance – and one in the back from a passage leading off Prince's Court. Lord Melbourne,' he added after a pause, 'invariably went in by the passage behind.'

The court erupted into a roar of laughter – which Follett underlined by an air of presumed innocence of the salacious meaning that could be attached to his words. I noted his performance well, and used such techniques to great effect over the years when I rose rapidly to considerable eminence as a leader at the Bar.

Yes, in those days I walked among legal and political giants: Cockburn, Ballantine, Hawkins, Campbell, Lord Palmerston ... indeed, I *was* a giant. A confirmed Radical in the House of Commons and I was the man the attorneys always sought when they had an important case to win. The *first* man they sought. Take the case I was involved in that May. I was briefed as the leader in the Queen's Bench hearing. I had Roundell Palmer and Dick Bethell as my support. Both men later became Lord Chancellors, Palmer as Lord Selborne and Bethell as Lord Halsbury. As for me that day, I had already been told by Prime Minister Palmerston that he was determined to make me a Law Officer of the Crown, as Solicitor General, as soon as possible, whereupon I was to be knighted and would therefore be on the almost automatic preferment route to Attorney General and then Lord Chancellor. And on that particular day I had facing me both the present Attorney General and the Solicitor General for the defence.

I wiped the floor with them.

The case? Ah, I tell you it had all London buzzing, and New York was alight with expectation also, because it arose from the much-heralded Great International Championship Fight between the English bareknuckle champion Tom Sayers and the American pugilistic hope John C. Heenan, also known as the Benicia Boy. Heenan had not won that many fights, in fact, but he had come up the hard way as a bully-boy in New York, a shoulder-hitter providing the muscle for politicians at Tammany Hall when they needed to persuade reluctant voters which way to vote, but his challenge to Tom Sayers

15

was the talk of England and America too.

Heenan came over from the States that April with Dan Bryant as his second. Bryant was a founder of the black-faced minstrel show, you know, but he didn't black up for this performance! The prizefight took place at Farnborough Common in an open space behind the Ship Inn. Such occasions were still illegal, of course, but thousands turned up nevertheless, to crowd around the roped-off ring. The House of Commons and the Lords emptied. Politicians and judges, the aristocracy, the 'fancy' and the swell mob, dukes and duchesses, they all flooded to the area at the back of the Ship Inn. I caught sight of Dickens there, and Thackeray, as well as the Prince of Wales; Alexander Cockburn was with me, along with Ballantine, and my political supporters Sir James Duke and Lt Colonel Dickson of the Tower Hamlets Militia were at my shoulder: I tell you, it was like Derby Day all over again. I regularly lost money on Derby Day and it need hardly be said I also lost money on the fight … but then, so did most people because it ended indecisively when the referee called it a draw and fled for his life in the uproar that followed. I believe he did *not* lose money on the result.

The fight itself … well, the two pugilists had battled for thirty-seven bloody rounds, over two and a half hours. English champion Tom Sayers was shorter and older, and ended up with a broken left arm, while at the conclusion of the battle Heenan was almost blind. But after two hours, the two fighters were still at it until Heenan attempted to strangle Sayers in the ropes at which point the crowd charged forward in their disputatious enthusiasm. The referee cut the ropes to save Sayers's life and then took to his heels after shouting it was a draw. The two dazed but doughty pugilists continued for another five bloodied rounds but when Sayers finally refused to come up for the mark, Heenan claimed the win amidst a considerable uproar. The trouble was, the referee was nowhere to be found, and controversy started, with both groups of supporters claiming the victory.

The question was then raised: who was to hold the Championship Belt? The referee did not dare to make an award; he was in hiding, under threats to his life by enraged supporters of both fighters. The Sayers supporters claimed Tom had not been beaten so was still champion. The Benicia Boy argued that it had all been a 'fix', that Sayers had not been able to rise from his second's knee to continue the battle, that the ropes had been cut to avoid a decision and so he was entitled to the belt. Newspapers in the States were frantic in their denunciation; they claimed it was all a conspiracy to cheat their champion, and an international incident was threatened.

So Heenan finally decided to have recourse to law ... and who else would he choose in his corner? Naturally, he chose Edwin James, QC, MP. I was to be his champion.

Heenan's long since dead now; he succumbed, I believe, at the age of forty-two after ending his career as a bookmaker, but I can still see him in my mind's eye, seated massively in my chambers at 5 Inner Temple Lane, over six feet tall, a clean upper lip since he had removed his dark-drooping moustache for the fight, shaven-headed, great shoulders hunched and straining in his coat, his handsome face swollen, bruised, battered and yet still imposing even with his half-closed eye. It was our first meeting, but not our last, for our lives became somewhat entwined again later by way of his tavern in New York and his relationship with Adah Menken, the sensational actress who had married him bigamously and who in due course was instrumental in the ending of my own marriage. Ah, yes, Adah... She was the toast of America and England and the whole of Europe ... and J.C. Heenan was the best-known pugilist in England and America. I remember meeting him again at the offices of *The New York Clipper* where I was engaged as theatre critic...

What? Yes, I digress again. Rambling, like

18

all old men, hey? I am sorry. Pass the brandy and water...

Yes, *Heenan v Sayers*, at the Court of Queen's Bench. You know, my boy, it tells you much about the intense interest surrounding the hearing when I point to the fact that the old ogre Lord Chief Justice Campbell himself took the case, flanked by Justices Wightman and Erle. When I took my seat in the crammed courtroom as counsel for Heenan, I caught sight of that old hypocrite Gladstone seated beside the judges, along with my patron, Viscount Palmerston. Lord Alfred Tennyson was up there, wild-haired and heavily whiskered; so was the political economist John Stuart Mill, various dukes and ladies of eminence including the Duchess of Sutherland... It was a glittering, noisy, chattering array surrounding the three judges, I tell you! The Bench was so crowded the judges had difficulty wielding their pens to take notes. And the whole sporting world seemed to be present in court to hear my demand: that the court should make the ruling that John Heenan deserved the Championship Belt that was presently been held back by the referee!

I had been briefed to put up a fight in favour of the Benicia Boy, and I did just that, in my usual manner. A stirring speech, larded with jokes of the kind Follett had been noted for and Campbell enjoyed. But my rival the Attorney General didn't like my quips and sat there writhing as I announced I was representing Heenan as the real winner of the notable battle.

My client, I informed the court, was a 'person of the highest standing in his country: six feet two or thereabouts, I am reliably informed' but the Attorney General then rose to my bait beautifully when I referred to Tom Sayers as the 'late champion'. It was a deliberate needling on my part, of course; Atherton jumped to his feet and protested that since the outcome of the battle had been disputed, Sayers should not be referred to as the *late* champion, he was still *champion*, and it was at that point that the whole court erupted, as I guessed it would.

In the uproar, various insults were thrown by the respective partisans and the Benicia Boy himself was quickly up on his feet, shaking his huge, threatening fist at the Attorney General. He then lunged at that individual, being held back only by his coat-tails by black-face minstrel Dan Bryant. The Attorney General had the sense to cower back behind his colleague the Solicitor General at the perceived threat. As the courtroom resounded with the bellowing of the contending supporters, a regular scrimmage ensued. I was waving my arms about, of course, shouting as I endeavoured to make myself heard above the uproar. I was told later my normally ruddy countenance was somewhat empurpled by the effort. But have no doubt that I was enjoying myself.

I heard Lord Chief Justice Campbell roaring that he had 'never before witnessed such a scandalous scene in a court of justice' and when Heenan was finally dragged back into his seat by Dan Bryant, Campbell fined him £100. It was paid immediately: I had advised Heenan to bring such a sum with him in his breeches against the possibility of such an event. And when things calmed down somewhat I finally proceeded to argue that the court should look at the articles of agreement signed by the two pugilists before the fight. I produced as precedents those agreements that had applied in the notable battles between the Tipton Slasher and the Bendigo Boy, Paddy O'Bralligan and the Hampshire Squeezer and Sambo against the Duke of York. Names to conjure with, hey?

It was a warm Spring day outside, the benches were packed, the graffiti-covered walls streaming with condensation, and the Attorney General was on his feet making his counter-argument when the courtroom windows were opened to prevent the excessive heat overcoming the ladies with their ineffective fans and nosegays. Heenan began to complain that with his shaven head he was feeling the draught. Further commotion then took place when an Inner Temple barrister called Fred Smith handed his bar wig to Heenan – who with a broad smile put it on what the *New York Times* a few days later described as his 'knowledge box'.

The whole hearing descended further into farce when Justice Wightman, himself feeling the heat, left the bench, to be replaced by Justice Crompton – who voted for Heenan to be awarded the championship belt, even though the judge had heard none of the evidence presented – and then that idiot barrister Warner Sleigh jumped to his feet, saying he represented the *Saturday Review*, and wished to be heard.

'I cannot hear you! You have no *locus standi* here,' Lord Chief Justice Campbell snarled, now himself thoroughly overheated and out of sorts.

'I stand on my rights!' Sleigh bawled.

'Then stand on them outside,' Campbell rejoined. 'Officer, remove him!'

Sleigh was hauled outside, shouting and swearing ineffectively; his career as a barrister was always turbulent, as I recall: he never seemed to be out of trouble. He was married three times, divorced twice and bankrupted along the way. And always in hot water with the judges... However, the point is, I won the case for Heenan that day, my fame increased even further, I was named in headlines in the New York papers, and my reputation among the 'fancy' never stood higher. As for the championship symbol, well, in the event Sayers and Heenan were finally each given a belt. The two became friends, and made several appearances on the stage together, reliving their contest in sparring bouts in the music halls in London and Paris, before Heenan returned to America and acclaim from the New York mob.

As for Fred Smith, the now wigless barrister, a subsequent meeting of Heenan supporters in the Blue Boar Tavern in the Haymarket resolved upon a vote of thanks to the Inner Temple man for lending his wig to their hero. They also voted that a copy of their resolution should be sent to Smith's widowed mother in Lincolnshire. I'm sure she appreciated the gesture.

Ha ... yes, May 1860 was the pinnacle of my career, now I look back on it. Professionally, and socially. The legal lion of the day. The darling of society...

That position was confirmed later that week by another invitation from Viscount Palmerston to join him for a Friday-to-Monday at Broadlands. At dinner each evening I was able to regale the aristocratic gathering with my account of the Heenan case and others. By that time I had become a favourite of Lady Palmerston. She had had her own lively past, of course: one of the notorious Lamb family, she was sister to Lord

Melbourne and she had been Palmerston's mistress for years before she was widowed and they were able to marry. Being a husband failed to inhibit Old Pam from continuing his amatory nocturnal amblings thereafter; she knew about it of course, and though she herself was now beyond such caperings, she had early detected in me opportunities for second-hand enjoyment of illicit relations. In other words, she knew my reputation as a *coureur de jupes* and she enjoyed cornering me at her salons for whispered accounts of my escapades, and gossip about others in the Temple. She also liked me seated beside her at dinner, where she was mischievously inclined to indulge in the occasional testicular squeeze; I did not object. It was a small-enough price to pay for political preferment, after all. She had the ear of the Prime Minister, as well as my *co-jones*. Ah, yes … she was a sporty old dame, even at her advanced age.

On that occasion, I recall she asked me again about the eccentric Lord Windham's stained bed sheets in the Windham lunacy hearing and she wanted details of the notorious public copulations on a billiard table by the Reverend Mr Prince after hymns and prayers in the chapel. She was also eager to hear about Sarah Potter's 'educational establishments' in Wardour Street – which I never attended personally since I was never interested in being whipped for pleasure – and demanded to be regaled yet again by my recounting the crim. con. cases in which I had been briefed, notably recalling Lord Cardigan's creaking boots while he copulated with Lady Paget on the sofa, the rocking gondola in the Admiral Codrington case and stories of spyholes bored in bedroom doors, with astonished maids giving witness that they 'had never seen it done in *that* position before!'

My conversations with Viscount Palmerston himself over those few days were of a more elevated nature, of course. We went riding on the Sunday morning, side by side: I was always somewhat stout but I enjoyed riding and accounted myself a tolerable horseman. Always took the opportunity to ride in the London parks at eight in the morning, no matter how late I had been carousing the previous night. On this occasion, as the Prime Minister and I clipped our way along the stoned rides in the Broadlands park and sidestepped under the cool shade of the trees, Palmerston drew rein and took a deep breath.

'It's good, is it not, to get away from the overheated atmosphere of Westminster?'

I nodded. 'Legislature and courtrooms.'

Palmerston laughed. 'Though you clearly enjoyed the Heenan affair. Of course, you've always had the reputation of being a sporting man.'

'It was one reason why the Benicia Boy retained me, my lord.'

'That ... and because he wanted to *win*.' Palmerston paused, took off his hat, wiped a gloved hand over his high, perspiring forehead. He eyed me slyly. 'And you clearly whipped the Law Officers of the Crown. But that would have been your intention, wouldn't it?'

He was aware I was still smarting at being overlooked in favour of Atherton for the position of Solicitor General and knew that in representing Heenan against the Law Officers of the Crown I had another point to make. I made no reply, but merely smiled.

'I also, James, like a winner. It's why I supported your place as election agent at Horsham years ago, approved of your efforts at Marylebone, and since your arrival in the House I have been appreciative of your backing for the Party. I have to admit your radical opinions sometimes cause me a certain uneasiness, but ... well, I know your heart is in the right place, and you are loyal. But that's not enough, at the moment. You're aware I approached the Queen some time ago about your elevation to Solicitor General. I fear Prince Albert was not pleased. He persuaded Her Majesty to reject the proposal.'

I felt as though a dead weight had settled in my chest at the reminder. I had been confident that with Palmerston's support I would get my foot on the ladder of legal preferment at last.

Sourly, I muttered, 'Prince Albert will still be sore about my impassioned defence of Dr Bernard.'

'And what he regarded as support for assassins who would murder the crowned heads of Europe.' Palmerston nodded, reined back his mount as the animal began to skitter impatiently, sniffing the breeze. 'However, your time will come. And soon. Which is why I wanted to have a quiet word with you this morning. Not about legal preferment. About foreign policy.'

It was Palmerston's *forte*, of course: his strength had always been in that area of government. 'I am flattered, my lord.'

'No need to be. As in cricket, James, I like to play to my strengths. I believe you visited Italy in 1848?'

'That is correct, my lord.'

'It's rumoured you met Orsini there,' Palmerston remarked almost casually. 'Was he a committed assassin even then?'

'It was a brief meeting only,' I replied evasively.

'Well, Felice Orsini and his co-conspirator Gomez have paid Madame Guillotine for their failed attempt to assassinate Napoleon III; you saved the other conspirator, Dr Bernard, with your inspired, rabble-rousing speech at the Old Bailey ... which caused me

27

certain embarrassment, I admit, but things move on, James, and we have new preoccupations now.' He pulled his mount's head around and began to move away from under the trees. I dug in my heels and followed him, warily.

'When you met Orsini in 1848, did you also meet Guiseppe Garibaldi?'

'I had that honour. Again, it was a brief conversation only.'

'And you remain a supporter of his efforts to unify Italy?'

'Indeed. I have spoken openly on the matter.'

We cantered towards the longer grass and the dew glittered under the hooves of our horses. It was a fine spring morning and I had the feeling, an exhilarated, excited feeling that something important was about to happen in my life. We slowed after a short while, drew up our horses, allowed them to crop a little as Palmerston sat stiffly in the saddle, staring ahead of him as though peering into the future, lost in contemplation. I waited, silently. At last Palmerston glanced at me and nodded.

'You've spoken of your support for Garibaldi and the Risorgimento. In my position, I, of course, cannot.'

'I am aware, my lord, that as a Minister of the Crown you cannot make pronouncements that might prove embarrassing for government policy.' It hadn't stopped him in the past of course: he was well known for pursuing an independent and forceful line on foreign affairs, whatever others in the Cabinet might feel.

He cleared his throat. 'Exactly. The present situation in Italy is delicate. I cannot openly speak my mind. But there are assurances I would like to make. Privately. To accomplish that I would have need of a person who holds my views, and in whose discretion I can trust.' He turned to hold me firmly with unblinking eyes. 'The Long Vacation lies ahead of you.'

The Long Vacation. My work in the courts would come to an end. Parliament would not be sitting. Lords would be heading for their country seats, young aristocrats would seek the delights of Parisian bordellos, financially embarrassed lawyers like me would scurry to the sea airs of Le Havre and Boulogne, out of reach of dunning creditors.

'I would be greatly obliged, James, if you could find time to go to Italy during that period.'

'On your behalf, my lord?' I enquired, taken aback.

'Not in so many words,' Palmerston replied carefully. 'There would be no diplomatic announcement. You would hold no ambassadorial status, there would be no diplomatic rank conferred on you. But you would go with certain private messages from me, to be conveyed to the leaders of the insurrection in Italy.' He took a deep breath. 'I would like you to meet Prime Minister Cavour, and then seek a private interview with Guiseppe Garibaldi.'

He tugged at the reins, brought his horse's head up and turned for home. I reined in by his side, thigh to thigh.

Lord Palmerston cleared his throat. 'In six months' time I will be presenting myself before Her Majesty once again, with new proposals for the appointments of Solicitor General and Attorney General. And on that occasion I will not permit her, or the Prince Consort, to refuse my recommendations...'

I took a deep breath. An assignment in Italy... It would bind Palmerston even more closely to me. I had won his trust by never uttering a word about his corridor-wandering to ladies' chambers, and he had been impressed by my work as an election agent – and my saving of Sir John Jervis from a claim of corruption – at Horsham in addition to my support in the House of Commons.

'The thing is, James, Garibaldi can be a bit ... impulsive. He needs to know he has my full support in his attempt to unify Italy, but we can never permit a bombardment of Naples, if that is his intention. You can quote me on that matter. Privately. And you should also make it clear to Count Cavour that the

British government will support the annexation of Naples.' He turned his baby face towards me and grimaced. 'I can never make such statements publicly, as you will understand. We cannot be seen to be interfering in the matter of a popular uprising against a head of state. Even such a one as the Bourbon. Imagine what the Queen would say! She hates me enough as it is!'

As much for his scandalous renown as a skirt-chaser as for his politics.

So that's how it came about. My visit to Italy, to meet Count Cavour and join Garibaldi on his march to Naples. Palmerston arranged that I should be accompanied by his Private Secretary Evelyn Ashley – later Lord Shaftesbury, you know – and I carried letters of introduction from my fellow MPs Sir James Duke and Tom Duncombe. So I was well supported. I carried out the planned interview with Count Cavour in Turin and passed on Palmerston's messages, after which Cavour arranged for a Sardinian corvette called the *Authion* to be placed at my disposal. I used it to steam with Ashley to Salerno, and a meeting with Count Arrivabene, who seemed somewhat miffed that proper diplomatic channels were being ignored. And I mingled with the numerous other foreigners who were thronging to be part of the Garibaldian campaign. Alexandre Dumas was there, on his yacht *Emma*, and he invited me on board. He introduced me to the most important member of his retinue: his cook, Jean Boyer, who excelled himself, so Dumas reckoned, by serving us *petites timbales a la Pompadour*, though I'd have preferred an honest steak, or mutton. But Dumas entertained us with his stories, his olive-skinned features sparkling with bonhomie, scratching enthusiastically at his frizzy grey hair, his great *bon vivant* belly spreading comfortably in the massive easy chair at the end of the table. A great entertainer ... but you know, I could never understand how he persuaded Adah Menken to become his lover, some years later. I mean, she was thirty and he was in his sixties... She'd turned me down but then cavorted with Dumas!

What? Yes, all right, I'm wandering again. The Italian campaign. Well, after the encounter with Dumas, we moved on – Evelyn Ashley, Lord Llanover and I – now joined by Frank Vizetelly, sketch artist of the *Illustrated London News* – he published an engraving of me in my Garibaldian costume, complete with a brace of pistols in my belt which I still have here somewhere. Or did I pawn them some years ago? No matter... The engraving caused envious sneering comment at the time in London, but I've always been a decent shot, you know, as well as a competent horseman. However, from there it was on in a commandeered carriage to Eholi where I finally came face to face again with the brave liberator of Italy. I found him in his private room, combing his long, thinning hair before a mirror, in his red shirt and neckerchief, a dirty pair of jean trousers and worn-out boots. I'd first met him in 1848, and he remembered me well.

Ashley and Llanover stood silently by while I passed on Palmerston's verbal messages and Garibaldi then shook hands and gave us permission to accompany his troops. I won't relate the story of my adventures thereafter – they were published to acclaim in *The Times* – but suffice to say I saw action when my carriage, which I was sharing with Frank Vizetelly, was shot out from under me by a stray cannonball that tumbled me into a ditch. A narrow escape! I was also at the retreat outside Caserta when I recommended that some cowardly deserters should be summarily shot ... and I was with Garibaldi on the train that took us into Naples where the whole population seemed to be there to welcome us: bands, banners, *bandiere*, National Guards, carriages, ladies of rank and station in their white dresses adorned with Garibaldian red, pink and white, thousands of *lazzaroni* in procession to the Palazzo d'Angri. Ah, they were great scenes and great days!

And it was in his private chamber that the

tired but happy Garibaldi welcomed me again with a glass of Madeira wine, settled back in his chair and thanked me for my support. We conversed happily for a while, and it was then he gave me advice regarding matrimony.

'You are still a gay bachelor, Mr James.'

'The life suits me well.'

'But I have heard rumours also that you are occasionally short of funds.'

I was silent for a little while, as I sipped my Madeira thoughtfully. Just before leaving London for Italy, I had received a strongly-worded missive from Mr Tallents, the solicitor to the Earl of Yarborough. He was demanding that I gave an account of my indebtedness to his son Lord Worsley. I had not replied to the letter, but I would have to face the situation on my return to England. I had no doubt I could persuade my young acolyte that all would be well, but with the Earl employing his legal adviser I was feeling somewhat uneasy. Garibaldi was watching me with a slight smile on his bearded features.

I shrugged. 'These things happen. To be truthful I have never been free of debt since I was a young man on the stage.'

'Ha, the follies of youth. But your earnings these days, they must be enormous.'

It was true. At that time I was receiving more than £10,000 a year. But the seat at

Marylebone had cost me a fortune, the money I'd got from that fraudster John Sadleir had gone and the damned money-lenders were forever clamouring at my heels...

'You know, James,' Garibaldi said with a twinkle in his eye, 'you have come to me with good recommendations from your Prime Minister. And you have brought me important information regarding Viscount Palmerston's views. In return, the best recommendation I can give you is that you should look to your future. You should seek out a comfortable lady, a respectable lady with a little property, someone perhaps in the lodging-letting way, and marry her, against a rainy day.'

We laughed then... I related the story to Charlie Dickens later, you know, when he consulted me on the dispute between Edmund Yates and Thackeray, and he had the gall to use it when he caricatured me in *A Tale of Two Cities* in the person of the lawyer Mr Stryver. But the advice from Garibaldi was sound. It was still on my mind when I made my way back to England.

Of course, although I was carrying out a diplomatic mission for Lord Palmerston I saw no reason why I shouldn't also take advantage of the opportunity to enjoy myself en route. Politics, blood and the thunder of guns were all very well, but a man requires occasional relaxation. My first stop after leaving England on the way out had been Paris, of course, where I knew a certain lady who lived in the Bois de Boulogne. She was remarkably endowed with the most sensual, supple fingers, ample bosoms and thighs like the haunches of a horse. She had a remarkable capacity for clamping those iron-muscled thighs in such a manner that once in, escape was impossible – even if desired. I enjoyed her attentions for a few days... After Paris, during my peregrinations in Italy I took opportunity to enjoy some of the dark-eyed beauties of Turin and Salerno also, en route to Garibaldi's camp, but from these encounters I emerged with my private parts scarred with red blotches ... not the result of excessive romping but a legacy of the infernal fleas in the beds of the wretched *albergos* frequented by the Italian ladies of the night.

But Garibaldi's words about marriage ... yes, they did come to my mind when I was back in Paris on the way home.

The city was crowded that autumn. When I rode along the tourist track through the Rue Vivienne to La Madeleine and thence to the Champs Elysées I was among a steady stream of tourists, fine, high-stepping horses, flamboyant carriages, well-dressed men and elegant women with twirling parasols. Foreigners abounded, Englishmen in particular but I was headed for a repeated assignation with the lady with the muscular thighs – Henriette, she was named, I now recall. I was meeting her not with a view to marriage, I hasten to add, but my mind was drifting down a list of unattached ladies in London among whom I might find an appropriate mate along the Garibaldian lines. The trouble was, the available ladies back in English society knew me too well, having already advanced to me considerable sums of money during our previous romantic attachments. Gratitude is a wonderful thing as a reward for sexual vigour but even with the most enamoured lady it has its financial limitations.

However, my renewed assignation with Henriette proved as satisfying – and exhausting – as I could have desired and I found it necessary afterwards to relax at the Café de la Paix in the Champs Elysées with a glass of red wine and a biscuit. I was seated there, watching the *beau monde* pass by, a pleasant feeling of satiety in my weakened loins when I became aware that someone was standing beside my left shoulder, and I heard a slight gasp of surprise.

'Mr James!'

I started, looked up and stumbled to my feet, almost upsetting my table. It was Marianne Hilliard.

It's one of those strange things, Joe, but as I told you I'd known Marianne for years and since she had separated from her husband – deceased some years ago now after seven days of *delirium tremens* – I had crossed her path but twice. On each occasion I had become aware of a mutual attraction but was unable to do anything about it; the first time because of Lord Palmerston's nightly corridor-wandering, the second because I was suffering from a dose of Haymarket clap. And here she was again, and I weakened by the rigour of an exhausting romp with the athletic, horse-haunched Henriette!

'Mrs Hilliard! How delightful to see you again!'

She seemed a little flustered, even unnerved. Her glance held mine but a certain anxiety seemed to flicker in her eyes. Her figure had thickened somewhat, naturally enough, but she still boasted a fine bosom, and remained an attractive, bold-eyed, *wealthy* woman. She was protecting her features with a parasol, but her colour was high, and rising. For a moment, the advice from Garibaldi surged from the back of my mind but it receded again when I realized that the lady was not alone. Just behind her stood a middle-aged, stiff-backed gentleman with military moustache, supercilious, hooded eyes, a Wellingtonian nose and resplendent Hussar uniform, albeit somewhat faded in parts.

Marianne Hilliard hesitated, that magnificent bosom heaving unnervingly. 'I did not think to meet you here in Paris! I have heard of your travels, read in *The Times* your stirring account of your recent experiences on campaign with Garibaldi. So exciting!' The officer behind her sniffed, shuffled impatiently and she hesitated, and there was that shadow in her eyes again. 'But I am remiss ... may I introduce you to Colonel Augustus Wheatley?'

The military man edged forward to stand closer behind her, in an almost proprietary fashion, inclined his head slightly, and tugged at his drooping moustache. 'Ah, yes. Mr James. Your name is well known. Renowned lawyer. Haw! Politician. Haw! And now I understand you have experienced the acrid, bitter odours of the battlefield.'

There was a supercilious, sneering, slightly mocking edge to his words. I stiffened. 'I was at Caserta, certainly.'

'And did that officer shoot those unfortunate deserters as you advised?' he asked coolly.

'I do not know. The last I saw of them, they were being imprisoned in a barracks.' I turned away from him dismissively. 'But Mrs Hilliard, it's such a–'

'And I believe you also visited the ammoniac cells of the Prefettura and the Castle of St Elmo,' Wheatley continued aggressively. 'In emulation of Mr Gladstone twenty years ago.'

I bridled at his sneering tone. 'It was not a matter of aping Mr Gladstone. I felt I should learn personally about the reeking abomination of the Neapolitan prisons, in order to make such conditions known to my colleagues in Parliament!'

Marianne was clearly aware of the competitive tension rising between us. She intervened quickly. 'I am now residing at Boulogne ... as is Colonel Wheatley. We are about to make our return there. Colonel Wheatley kindly agreed to escort me on my visit to Paris on business...' She seemed confused, a little disoriented, almost shaky. 'And we must now take our *congé*, I fear. I hope all goes well with you and your family. Perhaps we shall meet again soon, in London, or...'

Her words tailed away. The Colonel's cold eyes were unfriendly; he bowed stiffly and took her by the elbow. Possessively. And yet I noted that she shrugged off his hand as they moved away into the colourful, swirling scene of the pavements of the Champs Elysées.

I left for London next morning.

I arrived at my chambers in Inner Temple Lane late at night. I was tired after my journey and there was a pile of bills, letters and red-taped briefs awaiting me. I ignored them, poured myself a stiff brandy and water, and sat before the fire, thinking back over my adventures in Italy ... and the meeting with Marianne Hilliard. Soon, I drifted off to sleep there in the chair...

At dawn, I returned to my rented house in Berkeley Square. The first letter I picked up at breakfast gave me a jolt. It was yet another missive from Mr Tallents, legal adviser to the Earl of Yarborough. This time, all pretence at politeness was gone: its tone could be regarded as nothing less than threatening.

2

The long vacation was over.

It was a busy autumn for me. The briefs still flooded in from my attorney friend Fryer: I had been forced to allow him to retain many of my fees to balance against the £20,000 he had advanced me by way of loans so I had to turn to others for further advances – at exorbitant rates – to maintain my lifestyle. I dined out at country houses, relating stories of my Garibaldian adventures; I gave a lecture about my experiences at the Marylebone Institute, kept up my attendances in the House and retained the limelight politically by publishing my October correspondence with Count Cavour. And I was still winning cases for delighted clients at all levels of society: clergymen addicted to night-house floggings, pretty horse-breakers seeking compensation from aristocratic lovers, amorous grocers, incontinent admirals and cuckolded magistrates.

But I was becoming more and more harassed.

Young Lord Worsley I could handle. I met him one evening at Brookes'. He was engaged as usual at the tables, his slim young form lolling casually in front of a pile of chips. He hailed me enthusiastically, and told me how pleased he was to see me back from Italy, hale and sound in wind and limb. He'd read my letters to *The Times* – he'd even kept cuttings of them in his pocket to boast of his friendship with me and bask in the reflected glory! I managed to draw him away from the attractions of chicken hazard to a quiet corner, a table where we were served expensive champagne – at his expense, of course.

'I wanted a word, Worsley,' I began as we sipped the champagne. 'I've received several missives from your father's attorney, Mr Tallents.'

The young man sighed, twitched his fashionably luxurious moustache, behind which he still looked absurdly young, and shook his head. 'Dammit, I explained everything to the old man, you know, and he seemed satisfied, but then that damned solicitor advised him, requested that he should be given the task of checking my story ... and he's now been dunning you, hey?'

'His tone has become quite threatening,'

Lord Worsley swore colourfully: I had clearly introduced him to some unsavoury people from whom he had picked up bad habits. 'Tallents, why can't he leave a fellow alone? I'll have another word with the old man. I mean, there's no problem, is there?

You're up to date with the payment of interest on all the due bills, ain't you?'

Now you know, I have to make an admission about this indebtedness. The fact is, it had all started when young Worsley commenced hanging onto my coat-tails during my evening peregrinations around the West End, tagging along like a wide-eyed, adoring sheep. I was able to introduce him to the pleasures of the Haymarket whores, the gaming tables of St James' and also my Cock and Hen Club at the Nunnery, where he became quite a favourite; my bored, middle-aged wives enjoyed the taste of innocent young blood, if you know what I mean. I tell you, some of those aristocratic ladies could be voracious when away from their indifferent husbands – who were off whoring elsewhere. And young Worsley at seventeen demonstrated a real talent for dissipation: he gave evidence of it when I introduced him to Valerie Langdon, who later married Sir Henry Meux, and Bella Bolton – later Lady Clancarty. Interesting thing, that: many of my St John's Wood acquaintances married into the aristocracy in spite of their whoring backgrounds: Rosie Wilson married Lord Verner, as I recall, there was Connie Gilchrist who went off with the Earl of Orkney, and Kate Cook who I imagine laid aside her whips when she married the Earl of Euston. Or maybe not...

What? Ah, yes, I'm wandering from the point again.

Lord Worsley. The fact was, he was an innocent in matters of finance. Money ran through his fingers. And he had no idea where to find tin when he was skinned. As far as I was concerned, the first step was taken when he lost heavily at the tables and was fearful of his father, the Earl, finding out. So he borrowed some money against my signature; he was able to redeem the note when it fell due. But then I made the fatal mistake of asking him to return the favour by putting his signature to one of my outstanding bills. And that's how it started. It snow-balled, in fact. He was so *complaisant*, you see! It was easier to persuade him to sign my bills than to seek out new moneylenders or signatories. And life was such a whirl – my court hearings, sittings of Parliament, rushing down to Brighton to carry out my duties as Recorder, dinners, parties at country houses, whoring in the Haymarket, entertaining at the Nunnery, gambling at Brookes' – I have to admit I lost track of where I was financially. My attorney friend Fryer had by then taken the lease of a house for me in Berkeley Square, and he was always happy to discount my bills as my prospect of becoming a Law Officer of the Crown came nearer ... but I simply didn't keep track!

And there were so many other demands on

my time. Not least from the persistent, stubborn, insistent Colonel Lothian Dickson. In one sense, it was he who started the landslide that finally overwhelmed me that autumn – and it wasn't even a matter of calling upon my professional services!

You see, Lothian Sheffield Dickson had taken it upon himself, along with my friend Sir James Duke, to support me in my bid to become Member of Parliament for Marylebone. Dickson wasn't a politician, of course: he had entered the army in 1825 and saw service in India, Spain and South Africa, but in about 1846 the Duke of Wellington had appointed him Major of the 2nd Tower Hamlets Militia. He became their commanding officer as Lieutenant Colonel some years later. And began to meddle in politics.

To be honest, I never really liked Dickson: he was self-important, dogged, stubborn and, I believe, a strict disciplinarian, an attitude which did not endear him to the officers under his command. Quite why he got involved in my political campaigns I can't say: public duty, he once explained to me with a growl. And when he came to see me ... when was it ... the previous year? Anyway, he came to me aggrieved, with a story *The Times* later described as a 'pretty kettle of fish'.

His lean, be-whiskered features were twisted in distaste as he sat facing me in my chambers in Inner Temple Lane. 'My complaint concerns that notorious whoremaster the Earl of Wilton,' he snarled.

I raised my eyebrows. I was aware the sexagenarian Lord Wilton was his commanding officer. I also knew the description of the Earl was accurate: there were few ladies of the night in London he hadn't sampled.

'I was encamped with the Regiment at Woolwich,' Dickson went on, 'when the Earl arrived as commanding officer. He had with him a young officer, Ensign Beales, and a lady he introduced as the ensign's sister. Wilton asked me to look after Beales, while he himself entertained the young lady.'

Dickson glowered at me. 'He kept the parade waiting thirty minutes while he remained in an adjoining hut with Miss Beales. It was only later I learned the young woman was not the ensign's sister. Her real name was Caroline Cooke.'

I leaned back in my chair, barely managing to conceal my smile. Caroline Cooke... I'd come across her – if you'll excuse the expression – more than a few times in the Burlington Arcade, the noted scene for West End shopping and sex. She was a buxom young woman, never suffocated by her underclothes, if you know what I mean, and before Lord Wilton took up with her she had ridden a number of other aristocratic horses under different aliases. In the clubs she was well known as Nellie, or Lily Cooke. At Long's Hotel in Bond Street she kept an 'entertaining' room under the name of Mrs Murray. At No. 2 Cleveland Gardens she went by the name of Mrs Turner: that particular residence had an accommodating trapdoor communication, as I recall, enabling a client to move unobserved from boudoir to back parlour. Yes, I knew a great deal about Caroline Cooke.

'Moreover,' Colonel Dickson complained bitterly, 'Lord Wilton then inspected the Regiment with this woman on his arm! He visited the mess with her! I must admit I did not think much of it at the time, until some months later I received a letter from Lord Wilton, complaining that his young protégé Beales was being chaffed about his so-called sister! Wilton demanded I stop the badinage, or he would sue for defamation!'

I hesitated. Lothian Dickson's sallow cheeks had reddened with fury. 'So what did you do?'

'I warned the officers under my command, and I transferred Beales out of the Regiment! But that merely served to anger Wilton more. He seemed to think I was behind the gossip. So he trumped up some charges over officer disaffection and unpaid tradesmen and demanded I resign.'

'You did not, of course.'

'I refused. After which I had an unsatisfactory interview with the Field Marshal.'

Viscount Combermere. The doddery veteran of Waterloo, old, deaf, almost senile. I could guess what had been the result.

'The Field Marshal supported Lord Wilton,' Dickson snorted indignantly. 'I have lost my commission.'

'And now...?'

'I want you to act for me against Lord Wilton.'

I should have had the good sense to refuse, since I knew Lord Wilton well, but the brief would bring about a considerable sensation, I guessed ... and I was always one for creating a squawking among the aristocratic hen-houses!

Dickson v Earl of Wilton came on at the Court of Queen's Bench. Lord Campbell presided; the Attorney General appeared for Lord Wilton. And I had a resounding success. I reduced all Wilton's witnesses to petulancy and anger, ridiculed cruelly the ninety-year-old Lord Combermere, playing on his deafness and faulty memory, and even got the Duke of Cambridge, Commander-in-Chief of the Army to admit at one stage: 'I am not much acquainted with militia matters!'

I spoke to the jury for three hours. They were two hours reaching a verdict. They awarded Colonel Dickson £5 for libel and

£200 for slanders issued by Lord Wilton. My work, I thought, was done.

Lothian Dickson thought otherwise, because in spite of our courtroom success, he was not thereafter reinstated in the army as he had expected. Then he discovered the true identity of 'Miss Beales'. He came storming around to my chambers and I was persuaded to continue to represent him.

I have to admit I agreed partly because he had offered me financial support in my bid for Marylebone, and I was finally able to force the Secretary of War to set up a Court of Inquiry. Dickson had provided me with further evidence, a bombshell in fact: Wilton had not only insulted the army in squiring the prostitute Caroline Cooke at the parade in Woolwich; he had also arranged for the young whore to attend the Queen's Ball at the Hanover Square Rooms. She had been admitted by way of a voucher supplied by the Marchioness of Westminster – on the basis of a false representation made by Caroline's lover, the besotted Lord Wilton. A prostitute, in the presence of the Queen!

You can imagine how London buzzed when rumours of the Court of Inquiry began to circulate. The hearing was to take place ... when was it? Ah, yes, I recall, it was due to hear witnesses on 4 June 1859.

And I was then placed in an embarrassing position.

I received an invitation to visit Lord Wilton at his town house in Grosvenor Square. He explained to me that if the inquiry went ahead, and matters were made public, the Queen would be very upset. He suggested he was looking for a skilful negotiator who could persuade Dickson to drop the whole matter. And he asked me about my financial affairs, being aware that Marylebone was the most expensive seat in England.

They were in a mess, of course. I had several substantial bills falling due that week so Wilton's proposal came as welcome as a spring shower.

'Look here, James, we can't have Colonel Dickson braying at the Court of Inquiry in this manner. He's blackmailing me, and the Duke of Cambridge, trying to reinstate himself. That's what it is: blackmail! The Queen will be furious if these nasty stories get out.'

'I have already advised him that I think his course is unwise,' I remarked.

'Well, he's got to be stopped! James, I want you to act for me, persuade him to back away from these allegations.'

'I'm sorry, my lord, but I am already acting as his legal adviser—'

'This isn't a *legal* matter,' Wilton blustered. 'It's a matter of conducting negotiations of a private nature! It should never have gone to court in the first instance: the man's no gentleman!' He took a large mouthful of brandy, swirled it around his tongue as he observed me, a cunning glint in his eye. He stroked his long, greying moustache reflectively. 'We were talking about your financial affairs. Don't beat about the bush, James. I hear you're embarrassed.'

I shrugged. 'These things have a way of turning out well enough,' I replied carefully.

'Let's have them do that – turn out well, I mean. James, I'm prepared to cover your present embarrassments. On condition you persuade Dickson to call off the inquiry.'

'I'm not sure…'

'*Be* sure! Do this for me and I'll call off your creditors, hold your paper until you can relieve your financial affairs at some distant time – but only if you persuade Dickson to walk away from that damned Court of Inquiry!'

Well, the offer was too tempting to refuse and I called Colonel Dickson to my chambers next day. He wasn't a happy man. But in the end, when I pointed out that if the story came out in the Court of Inquiry the Queen would never allow him to re-enter the army, he finally gave in.

'But there's one condition,' he snarled, tugging fiercely at his whiskers. 'I'll back away from the Court of Inquiry, but only on condition that Wilton admits in writing that he's done wrong to me and also uses his influence with the Secretary of War to get me reinstated in the Tower Hamlets Militia.'

Well, when I went to see Lord Wilton you can imagine how he reacted: he prevaricated and argued, but he finally agreed to 'use his best efforts' in that respect. And once again I thought it was all over. But later, when I met Colonel Dickson at Westminster he glowered at me and stated he was displeased in that I seemed to be taking Lord Wilton's part when Dickson had considered me *his* friend, but I could bear that. My debts were not called in, Lord Wilton was holding off my creditors and I could get on with my professional life, instead of being harassed over such private embarrassments. Unfortunately Wilton also held off 'using his best efforts' for Dickson.

So, a year later, when I returned from Italy and Garibaldi's camp, there was Lothian Dickson on my doorstep again. Furious, whiskers bristling and mean-eyed.

'Lord Wilton hasn't shifted his mean arse,' he growled. 'He's out of town, don't respond to my demands that he keep to his side of the bargain. I'll have no more of this, James. You can tell him that if I don't hear from him within seven days I'll publish the whole Caroline Cooke story for the world to pass judgment!'

'That would be unwise—'

'Take the message to your master. You've

53

run with the hounds, James, now go back to the hare! I'd considered you my supporter but it's clear now that you've deserted my camp for that of your aristocratic friend!'

I was alarmed, but I was caught between two stubborn, unmoveable men. The upshot was that he received no reply from Wilton, he went ahead and published the whole story from his point of view – and no one gained from it. Wilton became a laughing stock; Dickson was deemed not to be a gentleman by publishing, and as for Edwin James QC, MP, gossip in the clubs began to swirl regarding the part I had played in the affair. Men were asking whose side had I really been on? Had I been behaving properly in the business?

I tried to shrug it off but I have to admit that my reputation was somewhat dented. Again. But let me stress this, my boy: this whole sorry business concerned a *private* matter. I was being criticized, yes, but like the business of the Horsham election in '48 I could not be accused on grounds of *professional* misbehaviour. So I knew I could ride out the storm.

Except that an even bigger tempest was on the horizon. And in it rode the shade of that fraudster John Sadleir, whose supposed corpse I had identified in the Dead House with Dr Wakley, four years earlier.

3

Herbert Ingram always boasted that he was the son of a humble butcher, but over the course of the years Ingram himself had become a very wealthy man. He founded the *Illustrated London News*, you know, and it became a massive success, selling 300,000 copies a week. He used the newspaper to promote his candidacy for Boston, and he became MP for that constituency in 1856. But I tell you, my boy, acquired wealth did not improve his personality. He was arrogant, and coarse, both in manner and speech. He was a sexual predator – there was a hushed-up scandal about his regular and excessive attempts to seduce his own sister-in-law – and he was a man of bullying tendencies. But like all bullies he was also a coward: a coward, and a greedy fraudster.

In spite of his considerable wealth, he could not resist shady dealings. So when the Irish banker and fellow MP John Sadleir approached him with a proposition that was likely to make them a considerable sum of money, Ingram swiftly agreed – even though it meant the swindling of another of our fellow Reform Club members, Vincent

Scully MP.

Sadleir owed Scully £9,000. He approached Scully and suggested that he, Sadleir, should buy the Castle Hyde estates in Ireland on Scully's behalf at an agreed price of £19,000, sell them later through an intermediary in England – at an inflated figure – and Scully could retain the money owed him out of the profits. The intermediary was to be their mutual acquaintance, Herbert Ingram.

Scully agreed the plan and discussed it with Ingram at the club. But when he heard the profit was likely to be only £600 he became wary and suggested that he should retain the property himself. Sadleir and Ingram told him it was too late to change the plan, since Ingram had already purchased the estates – and Ingram would now resell to Scully only for the inflated price of £28,000.

I heard the full story from Scully when he came to my chambers for a discussion. He was disgusted by the whole business and had never spoken to Ingram since that time.

'I've cut him regularly at the Reform, and in the House. But now that Sadleir's dead by his own hand, and all his business swindles have come to light,' Scully said, 'I discover from Sadleir's private papers that those two rogues had conspired against me: Ingram colluded with Sadleir over the Castle Hyde Estates! That damned newspaper proprietor never bought the estates at all! Sadleir had mortgaged the property for huge sums, acquired a profit of £5,000 and had shared the proceeds with that rogue Ingram, leaving me out in the cold!'

My mouth was dry as I listened to Scully's tale of financial woe. You'll appreciate my feelings – I had after all been involved with Sadleir myself. He had financed my election to Marylebone in return for my identifying his 'corpse' at the Dead House. I looked up at the ceiling, pretending to consider deeply. 'What value can be placed on the Castle Hyde estates now?' I asked.

Scully scowled. 'At least £30,000. Ingram was guilty of a fraudulent representation to me; I could have bought the estates in my own name and made a profit from their re-sale, and there's also the matter of the £9,000 Sadleir owed me – and which I'll never now get back since that damned fraudster swallowed cyanide at Jack Straw's Tavern. Blast his dead eyes!'

Not so dead, I thought nervously, not so dead. But I kept my feelings under control.

'So you wish to consult me over the matter of reparations from Mr Ingram?'

'I want the damned cheat exposed as a fraud! And I want damages for his fraudulent misrepresentation in the matter! Ingram knew what he was doing: he was in league with Sadleir. Ingram's a wealthy man

57

– and I intend to see him pay!'

It was difficult for me to refuse to act on his behalf. I felt that I needed to stay close to this business. There had been numerous claims arising out of Sadleir's 'suicide' and I had represented clients in a number of lawsuits regarding his affairs, not least because if I was involved it meant I could keep a close eye on events ... and ensure that no information embarrassing, or dangerous, to myself came to light. The ageing Dr Thomas Wakley, who had also identified the corpse at the Dead House, would say nothing damaging for the sake of his own reputation as a coroner and founder of *The Lancet*, but one never knew what might come out in a court hearing. It was as well for me to be involved, to monitor and control matters. So I agreed to act for Vincent Scully MP in his suit against Herbert Ingram, our fellow Reform Club member.

When the case came on, Ingram naturally denied everything. He pleaded that he was innocent of any knowledge of Sadleir's fraudulent activity. But I saw his nervousness when I rose to cross-examine him on his statements. He was trembling. A bully, and a coward ... and he was terrified of me and my reputation.

He had good cause. He was about forty-seven years old then, a capricious, coarse individual spoiled by his own success and unused to being bullied in his turn. I knew he had come to realize his involvement with Sadleir had been a bad mistake, but it was too late now.

I tore him to shreds in the witness box.

My questions were fierce and insistent as I went over every detail of his behaviour in the Scully affair over Castle Hyde; he began to be flustered and confused, got dates and sums wrong, contradicted himself, and when I ranged more widely he made damaging admissions which demonstrated that the Castle Hyde business had not been unique: he had had other shady dealings with John Sadleir prior to the Scully fraud.

I kept him in the witness box all day and I never let up in my relentless cross-examination.

When the court finally rose, Ingram was sweating profusely, ashen-faced and trembling. He seemed to be having trouble catching his breath. He could not leave the box unaided, and I noted that a friend of his – Sir Edwin Watkins – went to give him assistance. I gathered from later gossip that Watkins had been forced to take Ingram to a room at the Euston Hotel nearby, where the newspaper proprietor could recover and stop his shaking and trembling. Watkins himself told me that Ingram had been utterly broken down by his experience that day in the witness box, that he felt his reputation was utterly destroyed, his honour was in shreds and that suicide was the only road left open to him.

But while Watkins was trying to calm him at the Euston Hotel that day, with numerous glasses of brandy and water, I was summing up for the jury.

We won a verdict of course, but you can never count on the reactions from a jury. They clearly felt the three men involved were a group of rogues, with nothing much to choose between them, and they awarded Scully a mere £300 in damages. I think they might also have been influenced by the newspaperman's popularity for producing *The Illustrated London News*. Or maybe they felt pity for the man in his broken state after I had handled him so roughly.

Scully was reasonably well satisfied, however. Justice had been served, albeit in a niggardly fashion. And as for Ingram, well, I met him a few weeks later in the Reform Club. I went out of my way to approach him. He eyed me nervously as I extended my hand.

'You are well, sir?'

'Well enough,' Ingram muttered. His piggy eyes flickered glances around the room. 'I was taken ill. I have recovered.'

'I heard as much.' I hesitated, feeling I needed to build bridges, much as I disliked this man. 'I hope you feel, Ingram, that there was no personal malice involved in my treatment of you in the witness box. I was simply doing my duty, doing my best for my client. After all, you might recall that before the case came on I did very kindly advise you, here at the club, that it would be sensible and wise to settle the matter before the hearing, reach a compromise with Scully. Court actions are always risky business.'

Ingram took a deep breath, licked his thick lips. 'But my honour was impugned. I'm not sure I can leave things as they are, Mr James.'

'That will be for you to decide.'

He hesitated, and then asked a surprising question. 'I wonder ... perhaps you would do me the honour of dining with me at Swineshead Hall in the near future?'

I was somewhat taken aback, but intrigued. After a certain hesitation, I accepted the invitation. Though I did not realize it at the time, it was an unwise decision on my part, and was to have unforeseen consequences...

This was about the time of my second election to the Marylebone seat, and expenses were devastating. I had long since spent the money John Sadleir had paid me, and I was in desperate straits. However, I won the seat, and I had the favour of Lord Palmerston, enhanced by the success of my mission to Garibaldi's camp, and I knew that if I could hold on for a little while, once I attained office as Attorney General all would go well.

It was only on my return from Italy that I heard of the sinking of the *Milwaukee* on Lake Superior in Canada. It seems that while dancing and carousing was continuing that evening on board, the ship had been struck by a paddle steamer and had gone down in a matter of minutes. Herbert Ingram and his son were on board: both were drowned. I must confess that I received the news with no great sorrow: we had a memorial lunch at the Reform Club and the usual expressions of condolence were sent to his widow Ann, but to be honest with you, the main feeling I experienced was one of relief.

Until the executor of Ingram's estate, his friend Sir Edwin Watkins, turned up at my chambers. Unannounced.

'You are an unprincipled rogue, sir,' he announced coldly without preliminaries.

I have always been a man of cool temperament. I cocked a lazy eyebrow. 'Make a statement like that outside these chambers,' I replied, 'and I'll see you in court. To your considerable cost.'

He was silent for a little while, but there was a cold fury rising in his eyes. I never liked Watkins. He was a railway magnate, MP for Boston, a friend of Ingram's but I always suspected his real attachment was to Ann Ingram: he had always lusted after her.

'I am here in the capacity of executor to

Herbert Ingram's estate.'

'For which I am sure his widow is duly grateful,' I insinuated. 'But what do you want with me?'

'Want, sir? I *demand!* Repayment of the money you extorted from Ingram.'

I observed Watkins carefully. He was middle-aged, bulky, and short-tempered at the best of times; now he was becoming quite red in the face, and his Dundreary whiskers were quivering with rage. 'I really have no idea what you are talking about, Watkins.'

'You forced him to lend you money for your damned expenses of the Marylebone election!' Watkins exploded.

I rose slowly from behind my desk. As I stood, so did he. My breathing was regular, his was excited. We remained like that, glaring at each other. My tone was icy. 'I think you should leave now, and make no more such statements. You're on dangerous ground, my friend.'

'Not as dangerous as you, James! I'm acting on behalf of the widowed Mrs Ingram, and I've gone over Mr Ingram's papers and I've come across proof of a scandalous debt. Two and a half thousand pounds, to be exact! It belongs to the estate. It belongs to Mrs Ingram. And I'm here to collect it.'

I smiled confidently. 'I'm sure you think you're acting in Mrs Ingram's best interests – take her my condolences by the way, for I hear you're much in her company these days. Comforting the grieving widow, hey? But I've no recollection of any such debt, and I'm certainly not interested in boosting Mrs Ingram's already considerable fortune, attained as a result of her husband's unfortunate death.'

Watkins was almost spitting with fury. Unrequited lust can do that for a man: destroy his judgment. He wanted justice for the widow, as he saw it.

'I have the *proof*,' he snarled.

'I'll say goodbye,' I retorted. 'My clerk will show you downstairs.'

Instead, to my surprise, Watkins slowly sat down and looked up at me, containing his anger with an effort, but suddenly more dangerous in my eyes for his control. He hunched his shoulders, still glaring at me.

'You almost ruined my friend Ingram that day in court. You broke his health. He contemplated suicide. He felt he had lost his honour as a result of your attacks upon him in the courtroom.'

I nodded. '*Scully v Ingram* was indeed one of my more effective performances. But as I later explained to your friend, I was merely acting with professional objectivity for my client. He accepted that with good grace. He knew there was nothing personal involved.'

'So I've been led to understand. He accepted that statement for what it was worth. Mrs Ingram tells me he even extended an invitation to you to dine with them at Swineshead Hall.'

'That is so,' I replied carefully.

'But then, some months later, you acted for Vincent Scully again, when Ingram decided to appeal the verdict at the first trial.'

He was calmer now, but there was still a vicious glint in his eyes. I sat down also, and nodded. 'I did. The hearing was before Lord Chief Justice Cockburn.'

'From whom you requested a meeting in chambers after the opening of the trial.'

'That is not unusual, or sinister. It is normal practice when the parties do not wish to proceed. A compromise was being sought.'

'And a compromise was thereafter effected.'

'A *compromise*,' I said coldly and confidently, 'in which Mr Ingram, his counsel, Lord Cockburn, Mr Scully and myself all concurred.'

Watkins was silent for a little while, but his eyes never left mine. At last, he snarled, 'How was it that during the first trial you humiliated and almost destroyed Mr Ingram, but during the second trial you let him down easily?'

'It wasn't like that,' I stated firmly. 'I was acting on instructions on both occasions. And the verdict regarding damages in the first hearing was upheld: on the appeal, the Lord Chief Justice merely pronounced that Ingram's honour was not impugned, and that allegations of dishonest practices and fraudulent misbehaviour were to be withdrawn. In spite,' I added casually, 'of your friend's well-known propensity in that direction.'

He took the bait. He crashed a fist on the table between us. 'Damn you, James, the man is dead and you still impugn his character! But *you* are the one who shall be on trial over this! Mrs Ingram has told me that she personally will be satisfied by repayment of the money Ingram gave you, but I shall not be so easily bought off!'

'I do not impugn his character lightly,' I replied, becoming more heated myself by his threats. 'Ingram was a rogue and you know it. He was a lascivious bully and a fraudster!'

'And he bought you off!'

I clenched my fists, and brought myself under control. I needed to know what was behind this attack by Watkins. 'You had better explain yourself.'

'I intend to do so. Not merely to you, but to the Benchers of the Inner Temple. I'll see you destroyed, James, before I'm through! But first, I want that two and a half thousand.'

'A figure plucked out of thin air.'

'No! A figure stated in writing, by your hand!' Triumphantly, he thrust his pudgy fist into his coat pocket and drew forth a piece of paper. He proceeded to read the words written on it. '*I must make the sum two thousand five hundred and fifty pounds. Please send me cheques for five hundred pounds for Monday and seven hundred and fifty for Monday week.*' Watkins grimaced sourly. 'You signed this note! He sent you that money against the security of an insurance policy you gave him. Now I demand you repay that debt to his widow.'

I took a deep breath. 'You can tell Mrs Ingram I shall always be grateful to her deceased husband for the support he gave me regarding my election to Marylebone. But he was not alone in that. Sir James Duke gave me financial assistance. So did Colonel Dickson, and others who believed in the principles for which I stood. Reform. And the money you're talking about was duly repaid. There is no debt outstanding to Ingram's estate.'

'There is no evidence of repayment! That money was *never* repaid, and you damned well know it! Moreover, you got it from Ingram by clear extortion!'

I had had enough. 'I think this conversation has run its course, sir,' I said firmly.

'Extortion, I say! What you do not know, James, is that after the first hearing of *Scully v Ingram*, when I took my distracted friend to the Euston Hotel, he was in a state of shock. Some weeks later, when he was somewhat recovered he told me he had to pay you some money. I replied I saw no reason why he should do so. His reply was: "I must. I am so afraid of him. I must do everything he asks and I must give him the money he asks for."'

I felt as though a knife was turning slowly in my gut. But I remained outwardly impassive. 'I doubt that conversation ever occurred. And I am sure you will be unable to provide any corroboration of it. As for the letter ... I have already told you Ingram was merely one of many others who gave me financial support at Marylebone. He asked me how much I needed. I told him.'

'But you were in a special relationship with Ingram when you took that loan! You can't compare him with Duke and Dickson and others – you were not acting as an advocate against those other *supporters*, as you describe them! This was extortion, James, and you know it. This was a payment made under threats ... and the evidence is that you did not repeat your devastating performance in the second hearing. You didn't, because Ingram had paid you to go easy!'

He stood up, and walked towards the door. 'You may argue about the repayment – and there is no record of it among Ingram's papers – but you will not be able to escape the consequences of your behaviour. You dined at Swineshead Hall with Ingram. You knew he was terrified of you, afraid to face you again in the courtroom. And you made it clear to him that if he did not lend you his financial support, you would tear him to shreds again! That's why he lent you the money. It was not to support you in your damned Reform ideas, it was to pay you off, to make sure you'd go easy with him in the appeal hearing. And that's precisely what happened. A compromise! No further cross-examination! I know, James, and the world shall know that this was nothing less than professional misconduct! I shall proclaim it and it will be the end of your career at the Bar!'

PART 2

1

I was somewhat shaken, of course, after my encounter with Watkins, but I remained fairly confident of my ability to brazen out the criticism because the *provable* facts were on my side. There had been no particular difference in my tactics in the two hearings of *Scully v Ingram*. True, I had not subjected the newspaper proprietor to a second cross-examination, but that had been because Scully had agreed to a compromise to avoid further costs – Ingram of course wasn't worried about the money he'd have to expend to regain his so-called honour. And my old friend Alexander Cockburn – now elevated to the bench – had agreed and approved of the compromise. So if Watkins was to make a complaint to the Benchers of my Inn, what could they do about his complaint? In my view, nothing. It was like the election at Horsham all over again. The dealings I had had with Ingram – the money he lent me – it was outside the boundaries of their jurisdiction. They could concern themselves only with *professional* matters and, like at Horsham, the relationship with Ingram over a loan to support my candidature at Marylebone was a *private* matter, not a legal one.

Of course, I was still somewhat anxious, with the Dickson pamphlet appearing, consequent muttering in the clubs, and Watkins's threat of a complaint to the Benchers of Inner Temple hanging over my head. But more seriously, there was also the ongoing business regarding the loans advanced to me by young Lord Wilton.

There were other creditors as well, I am forced to admit – several ladies who had enjoyed my favours and I theirs – but these were manageable. A hot thrashing-about between the sheets for instance, often satisfied – or at least delayed – a financial demand for repayment of a loan. And I could also manage young Wilton. He was still taken up with admiration for my talents, swept along by my success in fighting for Dr Bernard and James Anderson...

What? I haven't told you about Anderson? Well, it was another sensation at that time: he was a black slave who had escaped his master – unfortunately killing him in the process – and the Southern states were trying to get him extradited to face trial in America. I took up his case in England, and persuaded the court that Alabama writs could not run in our jurisdiction. I was hailed yet again as a hero, Worsley was much impressed, and continued to be reliant upon me for further introductions into Haymarket nightlife. He

74

still remained open-handed, prepared to back my due bills with his signature; but his father was another matter.

Or at least the Earl of Yarborough's solicitor was another matter.

He was a ferret-faced little man, Mr Tallents. He wore an attorney's black frock coat with no hint of colour in his dress that might detract from his air of purpose. He had bulldog eyes, droopy, pouched, full of unswerving menace behind pince-nez spectacles. His teeth were stained, sharply pointed, as though ready to tear an opponent's flesh, and he assured me that his client had no desire to meet me personally to discuss matters; rather the Earl had full confidence in his attorney, Mr Tallents, to reach a satisfactory resolution in the matter of my indebtedness to his heir, Lord Worsley.

Tallents and I met some months after my return from Garibaldi's camp, at his insistence, in my chambers one Friday evening. I was feeling exhausted after a long day in Queen's Bench protecting the bank account of an amorous pork-pie seller from the financial demands of a Haymarket whore, so I was not at my aggressive best when the redoubtable Mr Tallents launched the first broadside. He started quietly enough.

'You know George Lewis, I imagine.'

'The attorney? Of course. He has briefed me on a number of occasions.'

'He holds you in high regard, profession-ally. The leading counsel in *nisi prius* matters. An opinion also held, it seems, by Lord Chief Justice Campbell.'

'I am happy to be regarded as such by attorneys and judges.'

He smiled; it had an edge that reminded me of an executioner's sword. 'But they don't know the full story, do they, Mr James?'

'I'm not sure I understand what you mean,' I lied.

'An excellent practitioner in the court-room you may well be. But your conduct outside has been somewhat reprehensible. Not least in the keeping of your word. You would seem to regard the giving of a pro-mise as a matter of little consequence.'

'I resent that comment!'

'Resent away, Mr James. I have discussed matters in detail with Lord Yarborough and we are in full agreement. It would seem that the promise you made to Lord Yarborough some weeks ago has not been kept,' he averred.

Nettled, I replied testily, 'I can assure you that is not the case. I wrote to him to assure him that the debts incurred against Lord Worsley's signature would be settled as they fell due.'

'Quite so. But you also *assured* him that you would batten upon Lord Worsley no further.'

'I object strongly to your use of the word *batten!* Lord Worsley sees me as a friend and–'

'And therein lies the problem. His lordship is young, immature and impressionable. His father is of the opinion that he is unable to protect himself against an adventurer such as you.'

'Tallents, I will not take such language from you! I warn you–'

'Oh, come, come, Mr James! I may be a humble attorney in the company of an eminent barrister such as yourself, but I am not overawed by the glitter of your legal reputation or the bombast of your protests. I have been making enquiries. I am apprised of most of the facts. And I have a specific function here today. It is to bring to an end the predations you have continued to make upon the heir to the Yarborough estates.'

It was promising to be a beautiful autumn evening in the Temple Gardens. In my chambers a chill seemed to have settled on the room. I took a deep breath.

'Look here, Tallents, you need to report back to Lord Yarborough that he has no cause for anxiety. The debts shall be paid as the bills fall due. It will not be a problem for me. Don't you know how much I earn each year? In excess of £11,000! Yes, I have incurred debts but I insist they are manageable.'

When Tallents replied, his tone was remarkably mild, with almost a hint of mocking wonder. 'You deceive yourself, Mr James. I have made discreet, but wide-ranging enquiries. By my reckoning you owe somewhat in the region of the vast sum of £100,000. How can you hope to repay such a sum – which I suspect is on the lower side of reality?'

'It cannot be that much,' I blustered. 'And surely you've heard that I'm on the first rung of a ladder which will increase my earnings hugely! I have it from the lips of the Prime Minister himself that I'm about to be elevated to the position of a Law Officer of the Crown! You must be perfectly aware that once I am Attorney General or Solicitor General my earning capacity will increase massively. It could rise to perhaps £20,000 a year. Look at Lord Denman's earnings in past times, and Sir John Jervis's. Look at–'

Tallents held up a hand to silence me. I can see that claw-like, bony structure still in my mind's eye. His eyes were stony.

'Ah yes, to be sure. A Law Officer of the Crown. And a knighthood. That is something else that concerns Lord Yarborough. He knows well enough what such a position can mean to your earnings. And to your future. The next vacant judgeship would be in your grasp. His lordship, I fear, does not view such prospects with equanimity.'

I was momentarily stunned, I tell you. I could not believe what I was hearing; I could not believe the cold enmity in Tallents' tone: It was clear to me he was enjoying this conversation immensely. 'I ... I am not certain ... what are you implying?' I stammered. 'His lordship–'

'His lordship,' Tallents cut in sharply, 'is well aware of the immense earnings that you are likely to acquire in the near future, as a leading member of the Bar. He has no desire to curtail those earnings, provided they can be assigned to the extinction of the debts guaranteed by his son and heir.'

I moistened my lips, somewhat relieved. There would be a certain problem with that, since much of my income was already being grabbed by that damned Wimborne attorney Fryer, in the settling of my debts to him over the lease of the house in Berkeley Square and certain other advances he had made to me. But that consideration could wait. I nodded. 'I feel sure we can come to an appropriate arrangement in that respect. I would wish you to assure Lord Yarborough that it will be my earnest intention to relieve him of all anxieties concerning the bills signed by Lord Worsley.'

'Lord Yarborough,' he replied drily, 'will be grateful for that assurance. Lightly given as it may be. But you have not let me finish. I have not yet expressed to you the remainder of Lord Yarborough's feelings in this matter.'

'You can assure him—'

'He requires *action*, not assurances, Mr James. In the first instance, apart from the early settling of the bills signed by Lord Worsley he requires that you have no further communication with his son and heir.'

'The friendship has been pressed more by Lord Worsley than by me,' I insisted stoutly. 'I have not taken advantage—'

Tallents cut in upon my protestations, raising an admonitory, claw-like hand. 'The Earl of Yarborough has also authorized me to insist upon certain other conditions if you are to be allowed to continue with your professional life. Perhaps you would allow me to detail these conditions?'

I was puzzled, and wary. I had expected Tallents to insist that I stay away from Worsley but that was of no great concern to me: I was becoming bored with the young man's drooling admiration for my talents even if financially the heir to the Yarborough estates had proved a useful companion when the moneylenders called around.

'Conditions...?' I said weakly.

Tallents drew from his pocketbook a sheet of paper which he consulted briefly. I was certain he was already fully aware of the contents of the paper: he was delaying his little speech for malicious effect.

'His lordship considers that over the last

two or three years you have behaved in a reprehensible manner with regard to his son. You have gulled Lord Worsley, dunned him, caused a rift between him and his father, and plunged the callow young man into a morass of debt. These have not been the actions of an honourable man. His lordship therefore requires that as a matter of principle you must make reparation by resigning from your gentlemen's clubs.'

I stared at him for several moments, dumbfounded. 'Resign from Brookes' and the Reform? What purpose does that serve?'

Tallents sniffed loftily. 'Lord Yarborough does not consider you to be a gentleman in your conduct towards his son. His forbearance from your exposure will depend on your resignations.'

An angry heat rose in my chest. In a sarcastic tone, I said, 'I imagine this will not be the last of his lordship's demands.'

'Quite so,' Tallents replied, almost cheerfully. 'He requires also that you resign from your seat in the House of Commons.'

'*What?*'

'You must step down from representation of Marylebone. Lord Yarborough does not consider you a suitable person to represent the people of that notable borough.'

'I feel sure,' I snarled, 'that his political persuasions will have something to do with that demand. I am a Radical whereas his lordship is as far to the right as one could possibly be!'

'I cannot comment upon that viewpoint. I am here merely to follow his lordship's instructions. He further considers–'

'He has more demands to make?'

Tallents permitted himself a thin, malicious smile. He glanced at the paper in his hands, and caressed his wispy moustache. 'The list is not complete, Mr James. In the same manner that his lordship feels you to be unworthy of membership of your clubs and of a seat in the Commons, he is also of the opinion that in view of your general reputation and behaviour, it is highly inappropriate that you should continue to act in a judicial capacity, passing judgment on others ... namely, he insists that you also step down from your position as Recorder of Brighton.'

I was stunned. I slumped back in my chair. I needed a brandy and water. 'This is monstrous,' I murmured.

Tallents was cool. 'No, Mr James. Merely inevitable.'

'But if I am to be allowed to make a living, pay debts when they are due, I need to maintain my practice, my legal standing, the Recordership...

Blandly, Tallents cut in on my protestations. Outside the window of my chambers a late evening thrush was in full song, in sharp contrast to the droning tones of the attorney facing me. 'You will stand down as Recorder of Brighton. But you will continue in practice as Queen's Counsel. His lordship and I have gone into the matter thoroughly: I have prepared for him detailed estimates of your likely future earnings. They will be considerable – no one doubts your ability to earn huge fees, Mr James. At the next election there will be the usual rash of election committees and you have already proved that you are a past master at that game. The briefs reaching your chambers will be numerous and your fee income will rise enormously. Your undoubted success in these issues will enhance your professional reputation and your work at *nisi prius* will no doubt continue to garner much by way of professional fees. By my calculation, during the course of the next five years you should be averaging the princely sum of between twenty and thirty thousand pounds each year. This money shall be assigned to his lordship, and used by him to pay off your numerous creditors who in the meantime will be persuaded to stand back against his lordship's own, personal guarantees. You see,' Tallents added drily, 'it is not merely his son his lordship wishes to protect. There are also the other, numerous, sometimes small creditors whom you have pushed by your extravagance to the edge of penury.'

Grimly, between gritted teeth, I muttered,

'And how am I to live in the meanwhile, slaving in the courts but having my fees taken from me?'

'*Soberly*, Mr James. His lordship will be prepared to make you a small living allowance. But there will be no more Haymarket. No more night houses. No more gambling hells. And no more Friday-to-Mondays at country houses. You will turn aside from society. You will live a productive and restrained life. And in due course, by my calculations, in perhaps five or six years' time the restrictions placed upon you may be lifted. By which time, hopefully, you will have seen the mad error of your ways in the past.'

A silence grew around us for some little time. Even the thrush in the courtyard outside seemed to have been affected: her song had died away. At last I roused myself from my sickened torpor. I shook my head dolefully. 'I don't see how I can concur with these conditions.'

'I don't believe you have any real choice, Mr James. His lordship is offering you the opportunity for redemption.'

'His terms are harsh.'

'But necessary. You are an unscrupulous hedonist, Mr James. Your reputation echoes in the halls of Westminster and the Temple. You are a spendthrift. You are dissolute. You are without remorse in preying upon the vulnerable. You must reform. The alternative...' He paused, and eyed me carefully. 'If you do not agree these conditions, the Earl of Yarborough will be forced to proclaim your disgraceful behaviour to the world.' His thin lips twisted maliciously. 'I have amassed considerable details regarding your debts. These details will be made public. You have shown considerable skill in keeping most of your creditors unaware of the existence of each other. That will change. The result will be the Bankruptcy Court. After which ... there will be no earnings at the Bar. You will be ruined, Mr James. As much an Untouchable as that most degraded section of the population of India.'

'*Reform*,' I sneered. 'You sound like a preacher from Exeter Hall. You sound as though you seek to save my soul.'

'It is time someone attempted to do so,' Tallents replied pompously. 'And Lord Yarborough has taken the task upon himself. Through my agency.'

He passed to me the sheet of paper he held in his hands. I stared at it with dulled senses. It contained a list of the demands being made by Lord Yarborough. It was, in effect, a draft letter that I would have to accede to, and sign.

I had signed many papers in the course of my career. Many had been bills, either in my favour or to assist friends and colleagues in the discharge of their debts. I had witnessed wills of the wealthy, signed certificates of death – including that of the fraudster John Sadleir. But that is all they were ... *signatures* on a piece of paper. At the thought, my spirits began to rise again. The main thing was that I should keep the pack at bay, continue to be able to appear in the courts. Lord Yarborough and his legal adviser were right in that at least. I could still make considerable sums by way of professional fees. That was the important thing; the rest of it amounted to a setback to my political career but it was no more than that. While my practice was still open to me I could get out of this situation. I could recover. I could reach the heights again. I took a deep breath. The important thing was not to panic. I needed to calculate, weigh things in the balance. The Earl of Yarborough could ruin me. But I had to buy time...

After all, who knew what might lie around the corner? The Earl was an old man. He was not in the best of health. He could not be long for this world. And when he died, he would be succeeded by Lord Worsley, and I was convinced that my influence over that starstruck young man could yet bring about dividends. The important thing was to survive.

I looked at Tallents, and I smiled. I was pleased to see that my smile unnerved him, unsettled him, jolted him out of his complacency. I nodded.

'I agree to his lordship's requests. I shall let you have a fair signed copy of the draft agreement in the morning. I shall also send you a draft of the letter I will need to have published in *The Times*. But I also have a condition to impose upon his lordship.'

'You?' he croaked. 'You seek to impose a condition?'

'The condition is a simple one. I will follow his decisions in these matters but in return I will require his personal assurance and yours – that no details of the agreement outlined in this paper shall be published without my specific permission. At any time. In any event.' I folded the sheet of paper and put it into my pocket. 'I believe our conversation has now run its course, Mr Tallents. My clerk will see you out.'

He seemed a little out of countenance when he left.

After he had gone, I sat in the darkening room with the brandy decanter in front of me. I had much to think of and I've always found that a glass or two could help considerably in my contemplation of difficulties, in reaching sound decisions. You see, my boy, I have always been a man of cheerful and optimistic disposition. I had been in many scrapes in my years at the Bar and had managed to survive them – emerging even more strongly as a consequence. And I have always believed in my innate abilities. Yes, I had much to think about. There was no doubt that my resignations from clubs and Commons along with my relinquishing the position of Recorder of Brighton would cause a sensation in the metropolis and beyond – but my creditors would be silenced and constrained and I could concentrate on the expansion of my career.

All, I considered as I sipped my brandy and water, was not yet lost. A setback, it certainly was, but I was convinced a glittering future yet shone before me.

2

A sensation it certainly was.

The *Marylebone Mercury* was beside itself with unsuppressed excitement as was the *Monmouthshire Merlin*; the *Spectator* was full of wild surmise; the *Morning Post* carried a supportive leader, but the *Manchester Guardian* was suspicious and probing for details that might destroy me – the result of its legal correspondent being an old enemy, Craufurd, who had been smarting ever since his parliamentary humiliation over the Horsham election. *The Times* was one newspaper that attempted to paint a broad picture, and even guess at the truth ... what did its leader say? It was something like '*He who starts on a career at the Bar dares greatly in his early days and the daring takes the form of running into debt...*' It was something like that, anyway, and its tone was mainly sympathetic. And more or less accurate.

But while I had never been averse to publicity, since over the years it had greatly enhanced my reputation with the attorneys, this kind of speculation was not welcome. I needed to wait until the hubbub had died down; I needed time to think and plan and scheme my way back to the heights, so I told my clerk to turn away any new briefs for the time being and I scurried off to Paris for a few days, to escape the turmoil and speculation.

My needs were several: getting away from the prurient probing of the press was important, but my nerves were on edge and I needed relaxation of a stimulating kind, if you know what I mean. Accordingly, I spent a few days trawling through various *brasseries á femmes*, you know, the peculiarly French establishments which offer lamb chops and *écrevisses bordelaises* on the ground floor and French tarts on the floor above. My favourite haunt was one operated by a certain Marcel, a pomaded, grubby-collared, plumply self-satisfied Parisian, who proclaimed his establishment as one catering for lovers of *haute cuisine*, but who pimped enthusiastically for the whores on his upper floor. In person, he concentrated mainly upon the food, however, never indulging himself in the carnal delights available above his head: he preferred salivation to ejaculation. He regarded food as a healthy substitute for sex.

I enjoyed both, of course, and, suitably sated after two days at Marcel's, I calmed down and reverted to *langue de veau au jus, huitres* and *entrecôtes a l'Anglais* at Café Lapérousse in the Quai des Grands-Augustins where I could forget my misfortunes and entertain myself by observing the passing scene. I sprawled at my table and watched the passing show; I enjoyed the waft of patchouli in the air as the doll-like *demi-mondaines* with their frizzed hair, frills and furbelows came trit-trotting past, their high heels tapping out unmistakeable invitations. And my other pastime was to watch the *suiveurs*, middle-aged men who spent their time trailing the factory girls and *grisettes* who strolled by on the pavements – men who were too timid or impecunious to approach them, satisfied only with lascivious leering. I despised them: I saw myself as a man of action, both professionally and in terms of leisure pursuits.

To my surprise, one afternoon I thought I recognized one of these *suiveurs*. Stiff-backed, magnificently moustached, he caught my eye as he walked past the café table where I was relaxing with a glass of *vin rouge*. He seemed startled, hesitated, then acknowledged my presence with a reluctant bow before giving up his trailing of a little high-heeled giggler and turning swiftly on his heel to disappear into the thronged street. It took me several puzzled minutes – I was still somewhat distracted those days with a turmoil of thoughts – before I recalled who he was. He had been introduced to me by Marianne Hilliard: Colonel Augustus Wheatley.

The eminent hussar, now a Parisian *suiveur des jupes*.

I smiled at the thought, but soon dismissed the man from my mind. I had a campaign to plan. I had spent five days in Paris; there would have been time for some of the heat over my resignations to be dissipated. It was now time to return, pick up new briefs, charge into the legal fray and work myself to the bone. I knew I had the talent and the reputation; I knew I could get back to my previous eminence; I knew I was the most successful man at the Bar and the attorneys would still be eager to brief me – whatever the gossip in the clubs.

So the next day, I took the ferry back to Folkestone, and the train back to London. Only to find my enemies had already been at work.

Leading them was that weasel Craufurd, backed by the man I had seen as a convenient friend: the attorney Fryer. I returned to find that the sneaky lawyer had entered into my premises at Berkeley Square, taken back the lease, and had put in an attainder on all my plate and other household effects. As for Craufurd, well, he had taken advantage of the situation to obtain his long-awaited revenge: he had issued a formal complaint to the Benchers of the Inner Temple, requesting that they set up an inquiry into my affairs – notably my involvement with Colonel

Lothian Dickson, the entanglement with Herbert Ingram, and the extensive list of creditors who would seem to be clamouring at my door.

Charles Craufurd; I recall I've already told you about him. He had never attained the kind of success I had enjoyed at the Bar. He was an MP and fellow member of the Inner Temple and he had hoped to obtain the post of Recorder at Brighton. When I had been appointed, he had dragged up the stale story of my activities as John Jervis's agent in the notorious Horsham election, had made wild accusations in the House of Commons where he was unwise enough to drag in the names of Sir Alexander Cockburn and Sir John Jervis as co-conspirators, and had been roundly jeered at and criticized by his own supporters. Ever since, he had been seething with envy and burning for revenge. A decade of loathing ... and with the news of my resignations he now felt he could finally obtain vengeance.

A simple seaman like yourself, perhaps you won't appreciate the chicanery, self-serving, vindictive hating that can go on among a group of men who compete for the prizes of the legal profession. Believe me, a brawl in a Marseilles saloon is nothing by comparison. And when Craufurd made his complaint, and I was notified of the list of Benchers who would be making enquiries into my conduct,

I knew I was in trouble. Russell Gurney, John Roebuck, Dr Lushington – they were all men who disliked and envied me. They had been among those who blackballed me when I was first commissioned as Queen's Counsel, barring me from membership of the Bench of the Inner Temple. I could expect little sympathy from these men.

Yet, I still felt confident. In the days that followed, I prepared myself thoroughly for the ordeal to come. I was convinced I was on safe ground. I had thought things over in Paris and I had worked out what I would say – and most of all I knew I would put them on the back foot by my challenge. These matters that Craufurd complained of, what were they to do with the Benchers? They had the right to adjudicate upon professional matters affecting membership of the Inn, but nothing else. Certainly not private financial arrangements I might have entered into: all lawyers borrowed money! And as for the level of my indebtedness, they would never discover the extent of that because I had the word of the Earl of Yarborough that he would not disclose my activities with Lord Worsley. I had kept my side of the bargain by my resignations from clubs, the House of Commons and the Recordership. The Earl of Yarborough, I knew, would, as a man of honour, keep his.

So as I prepared my defence in the days before the inquiry was to be held, I also kept myself busy with briefs that took me to Cambridge, King's Lynn and Oxford, with the occasional foray to Liverpool. It meant late nights but I was used to that, and the challenge of winning cases for my clients kept my wits sharp and stimulated. Then, two nights before the inquiry, I returned to my chambers to find two letters waiting for me.

The first was from France. It was intriguing, to say the least. I can still remember the words...

My dear Mr James
I am informed by Colonel Wheatley that he recently saw you in Paris. Should you think of visiting France again in the near future I should be very pleased if you were to call upon me at my home in Boulogne. I would much welcome the opportunity for a discussion with you, on a matter of business. It could possibly be to both our advantages.

It was signed by Marianne Hilliard.

I sat and thought about the mysterious invitation for a little while, then set it aside. I had too many other things of consequence upon my mind to consider how I should reply. Apart from our brief recent meeting in Paris, it was some years since I had last seen her. I thought back to the occasion when a nocturnal assignation had seemed to be on the

95

cards, not long after she had left her husband, Crosier Hilliard. It had been a disaster, interrupted by the amative nocturnal wanderings of Viscount Palmerston. A disaster, and yet in a way it had also been a useful encounter in that my subsequent discretion had led Palmerston to view me in a friendly light. And offer me political support…

I set the letter aside and picked up the second missive. It was brief, and to the point. It was from Ben Gully. He suggested that we should meet soon, as a matter of urgency.

We met the following day at the Blue Boar Inn in the Haymarket.

I've already told you about Ben Gully. I had used his services for a number of years. Short, stocky, broad-shouldered, he was a man you could rely upon in a tight corner. Fists like hams, a scarred, broken nose and a brain that had locked away most of the secrets of the London underworld. He knew the larcenous families and the forgers, the horse-copers and the swell mob, the coiners and embezzlers and the arsonists. He enjoyed unrestricted access to the rookeries of St Giles and the riverbank hideaways and gained much intelligence from the racecourses and bare-knuckle pugilistic encounters that were frequented by men of high and low station in life. So whenever I needed information for a client – information regarding anything from brothels to bone-breakers

– it was to Ben Gully that I turned. He was a rich mine of information who had helped me crack the mystery of the disappearing Derby winner, Running Rein, back in 1844.

But it was on only rare occasions that he suggested we meet. Such occasions were invariably of some importance.

Do you know the Blue Boar Inn? No? It was located at a short distance from the Haymarket. It was an ancient inn, reputedly the place where Richard III had spent his last night before riding out to his death at Bosworth Field. Its character had changed over the centuries: now it tended to be a haunt of prostitutes and the sensation-seeking swells who came spilling out from the Haymarket Theatre in the evenings. During the day, it still had a certain dilapidated, louche appearance, but under its black-timbered roofs there were dark corners where a man could indulge in discreet discussions: it had its own code with regard to its clientele. Police informers might obtain access but never found it easy to get out again.

Ben Gully was already ensconced in a corner away from the grubby windows. He wore a dark-brown greatcoat which he had opened to display a blue coat with a black velvet collar. I had no doubt that in the depths of the greatcoat pockets he would be concealing weapons of offence. A short club, perhaps, or a pistol. And a knife. He always took precautions when he ventured out into the dark streets of London. I sat down opposite him. I ordered a brandy and water from a sullen waiter, along with a pint of porter for Gully. I had never seen Ben the worse for wear as a result of alcohol. I knew he enjoyed porter, but never saw him partake of more than two jugs.

'It's been a while, my friend.'

'It has that, Mr James,' Gully murmured. His voice was roughened, and there was an odd tension in his tone. 'I been out of town a while ... and you've had no call on my services.'

'That's true. No private enquiries to be made.'

'Eight months, in fact, Mr James. But no matter. I don't doubt there'll be other occasions.' His narrow-eyed glance traversed the room, suspiciously. 'I saw you at the Sayers-Heenan fight. And I read about your showing in the case that followed.'

'Is that why you wanted to see me, Ben?' I enquired as I smiled, and sipped my brandy and water. 'To chat about shaven-headed pugilists?'

'No, no...' He was silent for a little while. He tapped a scarred knuckle on the table in distracted fashion. He leaned back in his seat, his face shadowed from my curious gaze. 'You ever come across James Sadleir, Mr James?'

Something cold seemed to touch the back of my neck and I did not meet Gully's careful eyes. 'Of course. From time to time. He was an MP and a member of the Reform Club, as was I, but resigned from both after the banking scandal of the collapse of his brother's Tipperary Bank.' I shrugged carelessly. 'We were never friends, if that's what you ask. We met occasionally. That's all.'

'He's no longer in London.'

I affected a lack of concern. 'No one seems to know where he is these days. Some say he's gone abroad – though maybe he's back in Ireland, skulking from the blame heaped on his shoulders when the bank collapsed.'

Gully shifted in his seat, took a draught of his porter. 'It was his brother, John Sadleir, who accepted the major part of the blame. Wrote a letter of explanation, before he took his own life at Jack Straw's Tavern on Hampstead Heath. But you would know all about that, Mr James.'

It was a flat statement, and yet it held a hint of enquiry in it. I nodded slowly. 'Yes, of course I knew all about it. I've had more than a few briefs arising out of that business, believe me.'

'But you knew him, John Sadleir.'

'I did. I knew John Sadleir, rather better than I knew his brother.' I kept my tone steady, unconcerned. I had the feeling Ben Gully was fishing for something. 'He also was a member of the Reform Club. But John Sadleir was an unscrupulous rogue and few will have mourned his passing.'

We were both silent for a little while. My mind drifted back to the Herbert Ingram problem: that had all arisen because of John Sadleir's criminal conspiracies and fraudulent activities. Sadleir's shade still hovered over me, even after all these years.

'I think you saw his corpse, did you not, Mr James? And identified it.' Gully said suddenly.

'I did,' I admitted shortly. I had no desire to elaborate further.

Ben Gully nodded reflectively. 'Nasty way to go. Cyanide, I believe. That can do fearful things to a man. Twists his guts and his face. Wouldn't be my poison of choice, if I was inclined to do harm to meself. Not that it's a likely possibility: there's others who would put my lights out quick enough, rather than me doing it myself...'

I managed a nervous laugh. 'So I believe. A man of your talents makes many enemies.'

'As does a man of your high position, Mr James. But this John Sadleir ... when you saw him in the Dead House. Was he really dead?'

'I never saw a colder stiff.' Gully may well have noticed the slight evasion in my reply: he was sharper than a whetted knife, was Ben Gully.

'Yes ... and I understand it was the coroner,

Dr Wakley, who was with you that day at the Dead House. Together you identified the corpse.' Gully paused. 'Dr Wakley's getting old now. Bit doddery.'

'He can still tell a dead man from a live one.' I was suddenly irritated. 'What's this about, Ben? I'm a busy man. I can't waste time talking about events that barely touched me five or more years ago.'

Ben Gully sighed, leaned forward, drained his mug of porter and inspected his broken fingernails. He shook his head. 'You know, Mr James, some people is never satisfied. When a man of consequence passes on, there are always questions, and rumours that fly through the taverns. Take the time Lord George Bentinck died suddenly. There was a lot of talk, some saying he didn't die of natural causes; but it was wild talk. Names were bandied about. He was always a committed enemy of yours, Mr James. I never heard you pass any comment on his lordship's death.'

The coldness at the back of my neck had increased. I had good reason not to recall the mysterious passing of Lord George Bentinck. 'The death was finally determined to have been a heart attack,' I muttered.

'Aye, that's so. But gossip still swirls around, long after such events. Take this thing about John Sadleir. He died a swindler's death, expressin' his remorse in the suicide note. But there's all these cases in the courts, arising out of his swindles – you been briefed in many of them, I know – it means his name never seems to be out of the papers, even after these years.'

I finished my brandy and water. I pushed back my chair, scraping it on the bare boards. 'What's this all about? What's your interest in John Sadleir, Ben?'

Gully scratched his head and grimaced. 'It's not a personal one, Mr James. It's just that I thought you ought to know that apart from all these court cases arising out of the Tipperary Bank collapse, there's also been rumours circulating.'

'Rumours?' My mouth was dry. I raised a hand to the sullen waiter; I called for another brandy and water.

Gully waited in silence until I was served. 'There's them who say Sadleir ain't really dead. Rumour reckons he's been seen alive in South America.'

It would be Valparaiso, in my opinion. I shook my head. 'Rumours only. I saw that corpse. Dr Wakley and I identified it.'

'And there was the matter of the money Sadleir withdrew before his death. Seemed to vanish into thin air. About the time you got elected to Marylebone.'

'*Two years* before I got elected,' I corrected him, impatiently. 'What's this all about, Gully?'

He shifted uneasily in his seat. 'I'm asking you no questions, Mr James. Not about any ties you had to Sadleir. Not about the identification. Not about what happened to the money he drew out, day before he died. I don't want to know no details. And I got no interest in what's happened in the past. There are things I don't pry into. But you and I, we've had a sound relationship for some years now and I've appreciated the trust you've resided in me. So when I heard some chatter recently, well, I thought I ought to have a quiet word with you.'

'About John Sadleir?'

'About John Sadleir and James Sadleir and defrauded investors in the Tipperary Bank and other financial houses.'

I finished my drink in a gulp. My hand was shaking slightly. I could not tell if Gully noticed, but he always had sharp eyes. 'Chatter,' I muttered. 'Idle tavern chatter. What's it got to do with me?'

Ben Gully sighed. 'It's all a bit ... vague at the moment. But you of all people, having handled so many fraud cases regarding Sadleir's activities, you'll be aware that he defrauded hundreds of small farmers and tenants in Ireland, persuaded them to put money into his bank, forged railway shares, played the big man with expensive tastes – while all the while milking the banks for all they were worth. The big London investors, they could handle it. But all those little men in Ireland ... that's a different kettle of fish.'

'I don't understand your meaning.'

'You know, there's all sorts turn up in the London back streets; Wapping and Black-friars, and St Giles, these parts see lots of foreigners coming in, cheap lodgings, criminal intentions, you know how it is. And their numbers include a great swathe of Irish immigrants. From what I hear, that's why James Sadleir has disappeared.'

'I still fail to see—'

'James Sadleir is keeping his head low, probably in Italy or some such place, because he's heard that some of the Irish immigrants in London have come here with a specific purpose.'

'Which is?'

'Repayment ... or revenge.'

I stiffened. I kept my head down, thinking hard. I had known Sadleir at the Reform Club and the House of Commons, and I had acted in numerous cases arising from his death but the only other known link to him was my identification of the corpse. There was the money he paid me, of course, but I had never heard my name mentioned in connection with the missing thousands Sadleir had drawn out of the bank before his death. I couldn't see how I should be in danger from these people.

'Who are these individuals, specifically?'

Gully's face was shadowed as he leaned back against the wall. 'You know what the Irish are like, Mr James. They're all obsessed with their Catholic secret societies. They're always for righting the wrongs done to them in Ireland. If it isn't evicting landlords it's Home Rule; if it isn't boycotts it's hunger marches. And almost always it's directed against the occupying English. The Fenian movement–'

'Are you warning me about the Fenians?' I demanded abruptly.

'Not so, Mr James. But there is a group of angry, bitter, determined men who have sent some of their so-called soldiers to London. A secret society, of course, but with one object-ive only. They are composed of hundreds of swindled men, little men, tenant farmers ruined by the depredations of John Sadleir. They are determined to get hold of his brother James, whom they suspect of having salted away vast sums himself, before going on the run. And once they find him, whether he's got money or not, they mean to murder him.'

'This group ... this secret society, how are they calling themselves?'

'The Cork Revengers.'

I took a deep breath. After a short silence, I muttered, 'You said you wanted to see me *urgently*, Ben.'

He nodded, scratched his scarred, broken

nose. 'It may be nothin Mr James. But names have been bandied about. I can't be certain of anything as yet, but with these people wandering around the rookeries and elsewhere, askin' questions ... well, I thought maybe I should tell you about it.'

'Warn me?'

'That's a bit strong. I have no precise information yet. But there's one thug, a Patrick O'Neill. I'm told he's dropped your name in a couple of taverns ... been asking about you. I can't say more than that. But I thought maybe you should know...'

As if I didn't have enough already to worry about.

3

The three benchers who had been given the task of investigating my affairs began by interviewing Edwin Watkins. I knew what he would be saying: he had already threatened me clearly enough. They then went on to talk to Colonel Lothian Dickson. I made sure that I was provided each day with copies of the evidence that was given to them.

I remained confident, for the reasons I've already mentioned. Even if these things could be proved, they were not matters rightly within the jurisdiction of the Benchers. All I had to do was stand my ground, and challenge them.

That's exactly what I did when I was finally called to make a personal appearance before the three wise men. It was June 12th, a foggy evening along the river, as I recall. I'd had to hurry back from a hearing at Cambridge to face the Benchers and there in the dark, candle-flickered hall of the Inner Temple, I dealt with my accusers. They threw at my head the accusations made by Edwin Watkins, that I had forced Herbert Ingram to lend me money, in return for going easy with him in the second *Scully v Ingram* hearing. I simply denied the inference arising from Watkins's evidence. And I was convincing: they knew they didn't really have a case against me. I named Sir James Duke and Tom Duncombe and other fellow Reformers in the Commons. They had all helped me financially – in the same manner as Ingram.

'Their intention was to assist me in obtaining the seat at Marylebone. The party needed me in the House. As for Mr Ingram, I shall ever regret the indiscretion of accepting a loan from him but there was nothing dishonourable ever intended or thought of by Mr Ingram or myself, either in the offer or acceptance of that loan.'

And I could tell from their glum expressions, at the end of the interrogation, that they were uncertain how to proceed. My challenge as to their authority over my private actions, the support I had received from other fellow MPs, all this undermined the basis of their inquiry. They were suspicious still, but suspicion was not enough. I knew, and *they* knew, that all they would be able to do was perhaps to issue a reprimand and a warning.

I left with my head in the air, after agreeing to a resumption of the hearing in a few days' time. My guess was that they would then enquire into the Lothian Dickson affair – but what did I have to fear from that? Once again, it had not been a *professional* matter. I had merely been acting as a negotiator between two of my friends.

All would have been well, but for the interference of that weasel John Roebuck.

He had been appointed Queen's Counsel in 1843, but had never managed to drum up a large practice. He was a short, apoplectic man of violent speech and manner. He was a Reformer like me, but clearly resented the leading role I had assumed in the House since my election. He was a man of forceful opinions – he always regarded working men as spendthrifts and wife-beaters – and he resented my support of the building trades in London. He was outspoken in his criticisms of Garibaldi: he was a supporter of the Austrian empire. He disliked me intensely.

But he was also cunning, dogged and persistent.

On the second evening, I arrived at the Inner Temple prepared to challenge the Benchers on the Lothian Dickson affair. I began by announcing that they had no grounds on which to make inquiry: the matter was a private one outside their jurisdiction. But then Roebuck surprised me by turning to other matters entirely.

'We have a list of persons to whom you are indebted, James.'

'That is most improper! My indebtedness is a purely personal matter!' I complained. 'It is beyond the jurisdiction of the Inn.'

Roebuck's lip curled nastily. 'One of them is stated to be the Earl of Yarborough.'

I smiled my contempt. 'I have already stated my position.'

'Both his lordship and his lordship's advisers have refused to attend to give evidence.'

'That is their privilege.'

'Do you fear such evidence being given?' Roebuck demanded aggressively. Dr Lushington, at his side, had the grace to look uneasy, while Russell Gurney frowned, but kept his counsel for the time being.

'I have nothing to fear concerning this matter,' I countered angrily.

'Mr Tallents, solicitor to the Earl, is here at the Temple,' Roebuck snarled, 'so if you fear nothing, may we call him?'

I knew the Earl of Yarborough had promised to say nothing unless I gave permission, and the same ties bound Tallents. 'I would have no objection to his giving evidence if the Benchers so desire,' I declared stoutly, calling Roebuck's bluff. I knew where I stood: Tallents would say nothing, even if called.

Hubris is a dangerous mental state, as the Greeks recognized; I was confident, I knew what cards I had and I knew how to play them. But I also knew that in a court hearing, things can change quickly, if one does not remain focused, and retain concentration. I was focused, and careful, when the Benchers called Tallents into the room. Russell Gurney was uneasy, Lushington edgily nervous; but Roebuck was under full sail, and he pressed the attorney hard. Tallents refused to give way.

'The Earl has instructed me not to give evidence, unless Mr James personally requests it.'

And when Roebuck pressed him aggressively, Tallents, thin lips compressed, restated the position. 'My silence is a result of an agreement between myself, the Earl of Yarborough and Mr James. Only Mr James can release me from that agreement.'

It was an impasse, and Roebuck knew it. But he was not about to give up and he demanded that I instruct Tallents to release himself from the promise of non-disclosure. Naturally, triumphantly, I refused. Roebuck was furious, his tone became sharper, he pressed Tallents hard but the attorney remained constrained by his duty, albeit unwillingly. I had kept my side of the bargain: the Earl and his attorney must do the same. Finally, Tallents wavered.

'I will present evidence ... if Mr James so requests.'

'Do you object, Mr James?' Roebuck demanded.

'I do.'

There was an uneasy silence. Dr Lushington sighed. 'It seems strange that you should raise objections to evidence from Mr Tallents. You did, after all, agree to the examination of his lordship's advisers.'

And at that critical moment, fatefully, I lost concentration. The door opened and my clerk came in, requesting permission to approach me. Russell Gurney nodded assent, and the clerk came near, gave me an envelope. I opened it, and read the words written on the single sheet of paper. I stood silent, shaken.

'May we proceed, Mr James?' Russell Gurney asked.

My mind was elsewhere, my senses whirling. 'Of course, of course,' I replied, distracted.

I was barely aware of what was going on. There was a brief discussion between Roebuck and Tallents. The attorney agreed that the Earl of Yarborough would have no objection to his giving evidence. But I had to agree to it. The Benchers turned to me again, and asked if I was agreeable to Tallents being examined on the matter of my indebtedness to the Earl of Yarborough and his underage son.

And I looked again at the note, then crushed it nervously in my hand. A question was asked of me again but I barely heard it. I nodded, agreed, and then too late realized what I had done.

'Now that Mr James has finally given

112

permission, Mr Tallents, we may proceed to the examination.'

I opened my mouth to protest, but it was too late. Distracted, confused, I had allowed my enemies to enter the gates. The questioning began, but I barely heard a word of it. All that I could think of was the content of the note, the words burning in my mind. Ben Gully's note had been succinct.

'*Get out of London. NOW!*'

A few minutes later, to the surprise of the Benchers who were still questioning Tallents, I rose, and without a further word hurried from the hall.

The evening was dark, overcast, with occasional slivers of moonlight slipping past the scurrying clouds overhead. My chambers were close by: I had been sleeping there since Fryer had taken back the lease of the house in Berkeley Square, some weeks ago. I left the Temple, and entered the narrow lane leading to my chambers. Dark shutters were closed against me in the lane and there was no chink of light to be seen. In a courtyard ahead, a pale light gleamed for a moment but I detected no movement. All was silent except for the sound of my boots on the cobbled surface of the lane. But my skin crawled, for I had the overwhelming feeling that I was not alone.

I slowed my pace, moving forward cautiously, and then there he was: he materialized out of a dark corner to my right, at the junction of two alleys. I stopped, my heart in my mouth, the blood pounding in my veins. I knew these dark lanes; I knew the terrors they could hold for unwary citizens. And I had no defences, no knife, no pistol, no cudgel. The man approaching me was big, dark-clothed, bare-headed. I could not make out his features but he came towards me without hesitation, determination in his stride, his boots clanging in the dark alley. I hesitated only momentarily, then turned to flee back towards the security of Inner Temple Hall because I was convinced this man meant mischief. But before I had moved ten feet, I realized it was already too late: my retreat had been cut off. Ahead of me, a dark figure was detaching itself from the shadows of a concealing doorway. I heard a low whistle and then there was a scuffling of boots, a sharp cry.

I spun around, not knowing which way to run, and everything was suddenly confusion, a stamping of boots, a roar of anger, and I turned my head to see that the menacing figure that had first threatened me was now himself under attack. There was a whirling of bodies in the darkness, thudding sounds, the harsh breathing of violent men struggling. It was an indistinct mass of fury and violence, it seemed to rise and flail like some great wounded animal, and I heard another sharp cry.

Then my heart seemed to leap into my mouth as a fierce hand gripped my left shoulder, turned me sharply about. I hesitated, struggled against the restraint, ready to flee, but the fingers that dug into my shoulder held firm. Then a wave of relief rushed over me as I heard a familiar voice.

'Mr James! It's me. Ben Gully.'

I was badly shaken. I could hardly get the words out for a few moments. 'Ben! Your note ... what's happening ... what's this about?' I demanded in a scared voice.

'Wait!'

We looked back to the struggling men: it was almost over. I thought I could make out the figures of two men, holding down another, who was groaning on the cobbles. As I watched I saw a hand raised, heard the crunch of a cudgel against bone. Ben Gully's hand relaxed, slipped down towards my elbow, began to steer me towards a narrow, dark alley on the right.

'This way.' His voice was low, controlled.

We moved towards the alley and as I peered back to the now silent group I saw one man raise his arm, as though in salute. Ben Gully raised a hand in response then pushed me into the alley. 'We can get you to your chambers this way.'

'What's going on?' I gasped as we hurried along.

'We've been watching him. We thought he might try to waylay you. With what object, we don't know – but it was mischief, believe me. So I arranged a couple of outliers.'

They would have been the men who had intervened, the two who had subdued the villain who was about to attack me. Gully released my arm. We were emerging again into Inner Temple Lane. Gully was close beside me, almost whispering into my ear. He had taken no part in the swift battle behind us, but he was breathing hard. 'You need to leave London at once.'

'I don't understand–'

'Leave at once. Take only what you need. But you must get away.'

'What's happened? What's going on?' I asked, half scared, half angry.

Gully took a deep breath. 'I told you there was a man called O'Neill in London. He's been asking questions in the rookeries. And people have been talking. Irishmen. There's gossip of the secret society, a band of committed ruffians, the Cork Revengers. Rumours have been scurrying around like rats. And tonight I heard what O'Neill was after. A quiet talk with you. And I could guess how that would have ended.' Gully stopped, gripped my arm fiercely. 'Look, Mr James, I don't know and I don't want to know what your relationship was with John Sadleir, or with his brother James Sadleir.

But it's come to my ears that O'Neill had questions he wanted to put to you regarding your possible implication in the frauds that Sadleir committed.'

'I was never involved with him in that way!' I burst out, even as I shivered at the memory of the fraudulent identification I had given in the Dead House five years earlier.

We were near my chambers. Gully hurried me along again. 'It doesn't matter what the involvement was. What's important is that O'Neill and the men he has with him are of the opinion you were tied to Sadleir in some way. And they want to talk to you about it. Such a discussion would not have been a pleasant experience, if I know such men.'

We were at the door to my chambers. I stood at the foot of the steps and glared in frustration at Ben Gully. 'O'Neill, O'Neill – what about him? I know no such man! Was that him back there? What does he intend? Those men, they were your friends–'

'*Listen*. Patrick O'Neill intended to question you closely and he had a knife as a persuader. Yes, that was him back there. But don't worry. He'll now be dealt with,' Gully said softly.

'What do you mean?'

'With luck it'll be days before his body will be dredged out of the river.'

'What?' I was shocked even though relieved. 'You're getting rid of him? I don't understand! This man–'

Gully pushed me towards the steps. 'He's a *danger* to you, Mr James. He's been dealt with, now. But he's not alone. The whispers in St Giles are that there's a small group of them, these Irish thugs. You can't be sure he's not passed on his suspicions to his brothers in the society. They'll be after talking to you, particularly once they realize Patrick O'Neill himself has disappeared. It's my view you need to lie low, Mr James. I don't know what this is all about, and I don't want to know. But it's *dangerous!* Ordinary thuggery it's not – these men believe they have a cause! That makes their determination absolute and uncaring. It's my opinion you have only a short time to do as James Sadleir has done. Disappear. Get out of the country. Place yourself beyond the reach of O'Neill's associates: beware of the Cork Revengers! *Get out of London!*'

After the scene at the alley, I was quickly persuaded. I dashed up the steps into my chambers. Ben Gully was still standing guard at the entrance in the lane when I emerged some ten minutes later, shaken, sweating, carrying a miserable bundle of possessions and the last of the money from my sadly depleted war chest, the chest that John Sadleir had once filled to the brim. As we hurried together down to the dark riverside and the

Temple Stairs where he had a wherry waiting, Gully was silent. As I stepped into the boat, he held out his hand. I could not see his face but there was a hint of regret in his voice as he gripped my hand in farewell.

'I think this will be goodbye, Mr James. I wish you well. It's a sad way for our association to end, but ... now, you need to hurry. I've made all the necessary arrangements for you.'

'Gully,' I said, my throat dry and rasping. 'I don't understand... I can't thank you enough...'

His voice also sounded odd. He was affected in a surprising way. 'No need, Mr James. We've done a lot of work together. It's been a privilege for me. But now you need to go. I'll be getting out of London myself, after this charivari, for a while at least. Now, good luck!'

We shook hands for the last time. I can still remember the touch of his hand, the scarred knuckles, the hard grasp. The firm grip of a friend.

At midnight I was on board the ferry to Boulogne.

4

During the following weeks, no news reached me from England regarding the inquiry by the Benchers of the Inner Temple. All had fallen silent, it seemed; no announcement was made by the Benchers after my abrupt retreat from Inner Temple Hall, though there was some speculation in the newspapers as to my whereabouts.

At Boulogne, I found lodgings near the port and spent a few days relaxing in the cafés along the waterfront while I considered what next I should do to retrieve my fortunes. Ben Gully's warnings had been strictly phrased: the Cork Revengers had singled me out because of my suspected links with John Sadleir; O'Neill and his compatriots had been entrusted with a mission of violence. He had paid the penalty for his probing but there would be others like him, thirsting for revenge. For the moment, England was an impossible location for me. As for Boulogne, it was a suitable staging post, I decided. There was quite a group of English people here, seeking a haven from debt, and a considerable group of English army officers on half-pay.

It was that thought that brought back to me the memory of the brief letter Marianne Hilliard had sent me. I checked the address, and thought about it for a while, sipping a few glasses of wine before deciding I had nothing to lose: she had intimated there was some business she would like to discuss. I decided I would visit her and discover what proposition she had in mind for me.

Marianne's eight-room cottage stood in the Haute Ville, behind the thirteenth-century ramparts of Boulogne, overlooking the river Liane. It was a handsome building with a gravelled courtyard and fine views across the sea, close by to the fashionable promenade, the law courts and adminis-trative buildings, but secluded enough to offer a desired privacy. I had hired a carriage to take me up into the Old Town, and I sent in my card.

She was at home.

I was shown into a somewhat faded recep-tion room by a maid and was requested politely to wait: Madame would be there shortly. The maid withdrew and I wandered around the room looking at the French lithographs on the wall and noting some books thrown carelessly upon the settee under the tall window. They were school-books, I was surprised to note. I was slightly puzzled. As I recalled, Marianne and Crosier Hilliard had produced a girl and two boys

121

rather early in their marriage: they would be beyond school age now. And the marriage had ended with the separation of the parents some years ago. Then, in 1852 Crosier Hilliard had drunk himself to death.

I was still mulling this over in my mind when the door opened behind me and Marianne entered the room.

You know, Joe, every time I'd seen her I was struck with the same thought: she was a handsome woman. Not a conventional beauty perhaps, and certainly not your fluttery kind, but a woman with a full, mature figure, intelligent eyes of a startling violet and slender hands. Her bosom was of the kind that could instil raptures in a man; I was always somewhat appreciative of the fuller figure in a woman, and partial to bosoms: they were the key to other intimate delights. Her afternoon gown had an interesting décolletage and she still had a bold eye, and the pressure of her fingers as she took mine was positive and welcoming. She gestured me to take a seat on the settle while she placed herself on the Louis XIV chair facing me, her hands folded demurely in her lap.

I looked about me in the brief silence that followed. Marianne had surrounded herself with furniture of taste, but then, I knew she could afford the luxuries of life. Her father had left her a wealthy woman, and her marriage had caused little depletion in her fortune as a result of a carefully drawn settlement. Crosier Hilliard could have made scanty inroads into that fortune before they separated.

My hostess watched me for a few moments, a slight smile upon her lips. 'I have ordered coffee for us both, Mr James. I hope that this will suit you.'

'Immeasurably.'

She held my glance, one hand now rising to lightly touch her left breast; I caught a glimpse of pale, swelling flesh. 'You have recently arrived in Boulogne?'

'Three days ago. I received your note in London. In view of its contents, I thought it polite to see you soon.'

She nodded gravely. 'It is always pleasant to receive old friends. Of course, I do not lack for visitors – there is quite a community of English people residing here in Boulogne, many, like me, spending most of their time here.'

'Like Colonel Wheatley?' I ventured. 'He is retired, I imagine.'

She raised an elegant eyebrow. 'Indeed. He has been on half-pay for some years.' She paused, reflecting. 'He told me he had seen you in Paris recently. He did not say precisely in what circumstances.'

I was hardly surprised. But I was curious: the gallant Colonel had been ogling a collection of Parisian *grisettes* when he would surely have had better opportunities here in the seaport. Unless Marianne's presence would have inhibited him in pursuit of such pleasures.

'Apart from that brief moment in Paris, it is some time since last we met, Mr James.' There was a challenge in her eyes and I knew she was recalling that occasion in a manner that was provocative. After all, she had been in a state of undress at her bedroom door and I had been about to enter the candlelit dimness of the room until the amatory Viscount Palmerston had disturbed us, inadvertently, in his quest for his own expectant prey.

'And much has happened in the interim,' I admitted.

'Indeed. I have followed your career, you know; I have observed with great interest your ... rise over the years. An acknowledged leader at the Bar; a representative of the greatest constituency in England; darling of the Radicals and rumoured to become, very soon, a Law Officer of the Crown.'

I managed a rueful smile. 'That, I fear, is now nothing more than a vaporized cloud. Things have changed.'

She observed me silently for a little while, then nodded gravely. 'I receive the English newspapers here. I have noted the ... speculation. It seems, Mr James, you have made many enemies.'

'It is perhaps inevitable when one succeeds in one's profession.'

I felt that we were somehow engaged in some kind of fencing, a careful circling of each other, a courtly, polite, elegant dance avoiding subjects which were of greatest interest to both of us. And my pulse had quickened. I had always had that sort of feeling in Marianne's presence: somehow a spark always seemed to flicker between us, an urge that was difficult to qualify. A challenge, almost. I was a little relieved when the door opened and the maid came in with a tray on which she bore a coffee dispenser and cups. Her arrival slackened the tension. We remained silent after the maid had poured the coffee and withdrawn, each keeping our own counsel. I waited. She had invited me to her home for a reason. She would get around to explaining herself soon: I was disinclined to bring up the subject before she was ready to do so.

We continued with politely aimless conversation for a while, about the city and seaport, the famous people that could be met while strolling along the promenade. We talked of mutual acquaintances, her life in Boulogne and Paris, the *cotérie* of retired army officers in the town, the death of her mother some years ago, but I still felt we were circling, wary, uncertain. But at last, she took a deep breath which drew my attention once more to that magnificent bosom, and she came to the point.

'My husband, Lieutenant Crosier Hilliard, died in a state of *delirium tremens*, as you know, some years ago. I was estranged from him by that time, of course, and had already left England when the event occurred. Society is somewhat indifferent to an individual where broken marriages are concerned: few houses in England open their doors to the woman involved. Here in France, things are different. And I am a wealthy woman, I can choose the life I wish, do what I want. Boulogne has suited me well during these last years, but there comes a time when it is important to move on.' She fixed me with her glance. 'As I believe you have now found, Mr James.'

I wondered how much she had believed of the gossip that was swirling in the newspapers about my name. The journals speculated, but published facts were few even though rumours abounded.

'Yes,' I replied slowly, 'I think I must make a decision to – as you say – move on.'

'In what direction?' she asked, smiling slightly.

I shrugged. 'England has become ... uncomfortable to live in. But I have skills, talent, and a reputation which I think could serve me well in a different environment.'

'Such as?'

'Canada, possibly. I have thought of the West Indies also. But aristocratic malevolence can travel far in our English possessions. So, perhaps I should set my sights on the land of the free, where I will not be subjected to aristocratic prejudice and envious rivals. I think I could do well in America: lawyers and politicians can rise to the top in that unencumbered society.'

'So I understand,' she murmured, and her hand was at her swelling breast again. She was nervous, tense. I waited, caught the sparkle of the diamond ring on her finger.

'If you were to go to America there would be certain expenses you would have to face, I imagine. To establish an office, to obtain entry to a local Bar Association, living expenses ... all these matters would have to be taken into account. It would take you time to make your mark.' Her level gaze held mine. 'But from what Dame Rumour suggests you are not in a sound position financially to attempt such a Great Adventure.'

'I have friends,' I murmured evasively. 'Friends, and acquaintances who would be prepared to assist me. And I am not without funds entirely...'

'Of course, and your present debts could not be called in if you were beyond the jurisdiction of the English courts. Even so...'

I was still uncertain what she had in mind. Numerous women over the years had been prepared to lend me money – which they knew they would never see returned – but as I waited for Marianne to continue, I confess I was puzzled. We had seen so little of each other over the years, and though I was convinced that a certain attraction drew us together, I was yet unable to guess what she was about to propose. And I knew some sort of business proposal was coming.

'The status of widowhood can be lonely,' she murmured finally.

'I thought you had a friend in Colonel Wheatley,' I ventured.

Marianne frowned. 'He ... he has been a companion of mine and a good friend for some years,' she admitted. 'But he has become ... shall we say, possessive? He watches over me a little too carefully.'

'Perhaps he is contemplating marriage.'

'There is a problem in that respect.'

He was already married, I guessed. Or maybe she believed he was interested mainly in her fortune.

Her glance was steady and purposeful. 'You have long been a bachelor, Mr James ... have you never contemplated marriage?'

Garibaldi's advice came back to me and my pulse quickened even further. I hesitated, before replying. 'There have been occasions over the years when I have been tempted, but work, politics, ambition, the pleasures of a bachelor existence have intervened. And I have never truly been in love.'

She sighed theatrically. 'Come, Mr James, we are in our forties. Dreams of young love must have long since departed. We are experienced individuals; we know how the world works, and we know that more can be attained by way of business propositions than heartfelt sighing and posturing. There, I have said it. A business proposition.' She paused, watching me carefully. 'You are in financial difficulties. You need to make a new start. I ... I also wish to make a new beginning. I believe ... I believe we could sensibly do this together. Hand in hand, as it were.'

I smiled openly. 'You know, I have never had a woman propose marriage to me before. If that is what you are now doing.'

A flash of annoyance sparkled in her eye. 'Need I spell it out further? Yes, Mr James I am proposing a marriage and alliance, after which we can go forward together. You wish to make a new start in America. I have money. I am prepared to ... not to make over my fortune to you, but certainly to reach an agreement to support you financially until you can reach the heights you have already attained in England!'

I stared at her, somewhat taken aback by her outspokenness, but excited also. She was still a handsome woman, she was wealthy – and I was virtually penniless, burdened by crippling debts. I would perhaps have preferred some insincere, languorous sighs and professions of long-held attraction, but I was nevertheless intrigued and greatly tempted.

'A business proposition,' I murmured. 'I must confess that I am moved. I am sure we could ... do well together. And as you say, we have known each other for many years...' I hesitated, watching her carefully. 'Marrying you offers me great advantages, I see that. But you ... what advantages would you obtain from such a union?'

She frowned. She slowly finished her coffee and we sat in silence for a little while. In the garden outside, a blackbird was singing lustily. I waited, puzzled. Finally, Marianne raised her head, looked me in the eye and reached for a little handbell which lay on the table at her side. She rang it, and then we both waited.

A little while later the door opened quietly and a middle-aged woman entered. She was followed by a girl whom I took to be of ten years or so. She was flaxen-haired, blue-eyed, but somewhat sallow, and she seemed of a certain sullen disposition. She did not meet my glance; indeed, she seemed wilfully to avoid it. I gained the impression she did not want to know me. It was an impression that never left me thereafter.

'This is my daughter, Blanche-Marie. My love, this is Mr Edwin James, of whom I have spoken from time to time.'

There was a brief flicker of the fair eye-lashes as the girl glanced at me. She curtseyed briefly, but said nothing. Marianne watched her for a few moments, then looked up to the woman who attended her. 'That will do, Madame Dupuit.'

The woman nodded, turned away, ushering the girl from the room.

Marianne turned back to me, calmly. 'You needed to know about Blanche-Marie.'

I did indeed. But I needed to ask no further questions. Marianne Hilliard had left her drunken hussar husband, Crosier, about the year 1848. He had died of *delirium tremens* in 1852. I had heard that he had retained control of their children, born in the early 1840s. Blanche-Marie could be no more than ten or twelve years old. She was not the product of Marianne's marriage to her hussar husband. She had been conceived out of wedlock. Probably here in Boulogne, for no whisper of her existence had reached polite society in London.

I now understood the reasoning behind Marianne's proposal. The girl probably bore the surname Hilliard, but was in reality illegitimate. The circumstances of her birth could be concealed in France, but questions would be asked were Marianne to return to England. And, I had no doubt, widowhood could be lonely for a woman like Marianne, and a liaison with someone like Colonel

Wheatley could be unsatisfactory socially – particularly if he was already married. Wheatley ... I wondered whether he really was Blanche-Marie's father. It would account for his possessiveness ... and perhaps the girl's surliness.

'She would come with us if we went to the United States as man and wife,' Marianne stated bluntly.

I smiled. 'I don't see that as a great encumbrance.' I had already made up my mind: Garibaldi had been right. 'So, where do we go from here?'

'A marriage settlement will be drawn up. It will leave me in control of my inheritance, naturally, but I will be generous towards you. There will be conditions, of course: I cannot be responsible for your existing debts – I believe them to be quite staggering – but will support you in your endeavours to obtain a legal position in accordance with your undoubted talents. Am I to assume that you would be agreeable to these arrangements?'

'I think we can be of good accord,' I said, rising.

'Then you may now kiss me and seal the bargain,' she announced with a smile.

You look somewhat shocked and do I detect a certain disbelief in your eyes? A woman behaving in such a wayward fashion? Well, it is a remarkable story, but you know it wasn't all just *business*, if you know what I mean. There was a practicality behind it, of course, but there was more than that: Marianne and I, we had always had a certain ... regard for each other. It had flickered into life from time to time but circumstances had prevented the achievement of our desires. Anyway, the situation was quickly resolved. During the next few days, a marriage settlement was drawn up. My brother Henry came over from London to act as witness to the marriage. On July 9th, a Tuesday as I recall, Marianne and I were married at the British Embassy in Paris with the Earl of Cowley's chaplain officiating. When Henry returned to England, Marianne and I went on to Le Havre while Blanche-Marie remained in the custody of Madame Dupuit.

The honeymoon was spent at Frascati's Hotel.

And you know, my boy, it was quite a honeymoon. The marriage might have been born of a business arrangement, but I was agreeably surprised by Marianne's attitude once the matter was settled. We had always felt a mutual physical attraction, as I've explained, but now she delighted me by demonstrating a voracious enthusiasm for the act of copulation. Our two-day sojourn at Frascati's was largely spent in amatory activity. Perhaps it had been some time since she had so disported herself but it seemed she could not discard her clothing often enough and quickly enough to grapple with her new husband between hastily taken meals. Her favourite positions, I quickly learned, were *à la chienne* and even more often *au hussard* – possibly the result of Crosier Hilliard's and even Colonel Wheatley's cavalry careers. But while accommodating her in these desires, I was also able to introduce her to other more interesting alternatives that I had learned from the likes of Sovrina at Stunning Sam's, the delectable Ying Po at Ah Min's opium-odoured establishment in Soho, and the sometimes astounding variables I had been taught by a Balinese dancer who practised her venereal arts in a bordello on the Marseilles waterfront. I've forgotten her name... What? You've had occasion to meet her yourself, at one of your dockings at that port? Then you know I speak the truth! Ah, the benefits of international travel...

Suffice to say that Marianne responded to all my variables with noisy appreciation. I drew the line at the chandelier trick, however: the decoratively-plastered French ceilings at Frascati's Hotel did not seem to me to be sufficiently robust to support two middle-aged copulating enthusiasts so we never did get around to that athletic delight. However, I must confess to a certain physical relief when we returned to the more constrained atmosphere of Marianne's home in Boulogne where Blanche-Marie sullenly awaited our bleary-eyed, aching-limbed return.

We did not stay long.

Marianne dismissed Madame Dupuit and the other servants in her household and at the end of July we set sail for the United States aboard the steamship *Fulton*. Marianne travelled as Mrs E James; Blanche-Marie as Miss Hilliard. We arrived in New York on August 5th 1861.

The Great Adventure had begun.

PART 3

1

When we arrived in New York the whole country was in a state of turmoil.

The previous April, Confederate forces had opened fire on Fort Sumner and the Civil War had begun. While I was facing my enemies in the Bencher's Inquiry in London, the battle of Bull Run had just taken place and the ragged, demoralized Union Army was falling back on Washington. So all was chaos and New York was in turmoil with war fever and panic. Union uniforms were everywhere. It was still the case when, a few weeks later, our steamship *Fulton* edged its way into the narrow channel leading to New York Harbour. From the deck we could make out the spires and steeples of the city beyond the forest of ships' masts – there were ferryboat sirens, capstans and bells mingling with the hum and buzz of the distant city to welcome us, and we stepped ashore in the sweltering heat of the midday sun. Marianne was as excited as a child; even Blanche managed the occasional smile.

As you can imagine, the next few days passed in a whirl. After taking a suite of rooms at the Albemarle Hotel we made the promenade from the Battery Gardens to Broadway among a swirl of cabs, phaetons, coaches, gigs, and tilburies driven by top-hatted, liveried negro coachmen, and we passed the time of day with ladies sporting silk parasols on the arms of blue-coated Irishmen. The Irish, in fact, seemed to be everywhere – though I was soon to learn that the greater mass of them lived in the slums of the Five Points and Hell's Kitchen.

I do not flatter myself, Joe, when I declare that my arrival in New York caused no small stir, and the doors of fashionable Fifth Avenue mansions were quickly opened to us. The newspapers had been full of the Sayers-Heenan championship fight the previous year, and my part in the courtroom scenes thereafter and my legal reputation was well known. A leader, laudatory regarding my legal prowess, had appeared in the *New York Times* within days of our arrival, and polite society welcomed Marianne and me into its arms: invitations to dinner engagements poured in upon us and we were feted every-where we appeared. Marianne was beside herself with happiness, and showed her en-thusiastic gratitude in the privacy of the boudoir while Blanche continued to sulk elsewhere.

A New York lawyer whose acquaintance I had made in London some years earlier presented himself: Charles Spencer offered to introduce me to influential people who might assist in my projected career and took the trouble to explain how I could take advantage of the opportunities America could offer.

I explained it all to Marianne.

'Spencer observes that practice of the law is the undoubted route to eminence in this country – since the days of George Washington, every president has been a lawyer and almost all the leading politicians of the day, such as Seward, Welles and Stanton, are lawyers! And unlike the system in England I'll be able to establish a legal partnership immediately. A licence to practise should present no difficulty and Spencer has already sounded out some sponsors – Judge Barnard and Henry Webster – who have agreed to promote my application. I need to study the Constitution, of course, and present my patent as Queen's Counsel to the Supreme Court, but the whole shooting match seems nothing more than a mere formality.'

'And what earnings are you likely to achieve?' Marianne asked, a little too readily for my ease of mind.

'Spencer reckons I should soon be earning at least $13,000 a year. I will not be forced to rely upon your generosity thereafter, my dear,' I assured her.

She seemed pleased. I did not of course reveal to her some of the difficulties facing me. Spencer would furnish a certificate regarding my moral character – of which he really knew very little – but I needed to move quickly. If the Benchers of the Inner Temple were to disbar me soon – and I had no information from England on that score – it could raise problems for me with the New York City Bar Association, though I still held my patent as Queen's Counsel. Time was short and so I acted with speed.

I learned my enemies were still active in London.

When I applied to practise my profession in New York, a complaint was immediately lodged by one Daniel Lord to the effect that I had been disbarred in England. I could immediately demonstrate that the complainant had got his facts wrong, however; the disbarment had not been publicly announced and no news of the Bencher's Inquiry had formally reached America, so I called a meeting of the New York City Bar Association at Astor House and put my case in a speech which drew roars of applause every time I mentioned 'freedom' or 'conspiracy' or 'aristocratic envy'. My audience loved the attack I made upon 'vested interests' and Lord's complaint was rejected. Accordingly, on 5 November I was formally admitted to the New York City Bar – two days before the Inner Temple Benchers announced that at a 'parliament' of members of the Inn, my disbarment was confirmed. The news reached New York the following week, but it came too late.

I was in the clear, albeit by the skin of my teeth. Marianne and I fell into a gay social whirl that continued in spite of the threatening conditions of the war, and the way was prepared for my legal career when I took the rental of an office on Broadway. I was described in the newspapers as an 'excellent specimen of a hale and hearty Englishman.' The *New York Times* observed that I was a fluent and impressive speaker, eminently adroit in my management of criminal cases and without doubt heading for the highest levels of the legal profession. Other newspapers scrambled for my services: the *New York Leader* won the race, announcing they were to pay me $2,000 for a series of articles for them, to be entitled *Leaves from the Notebook of an Eminent QC*.

I was invited to call upon Frank Queen, editor of the sporting newspaper the *New York Clipper*. It was on the *Clipper* premises that I first met Adah Menken, the sensation of the New York stage. But more of that later.

First, I must tell you of my trip to Washington and my reception there.

We had been but weeks in New York before the invitation arrived from the White House. Marianne was delighted. On our arrival in

143

New York the doors of society immediately opened, and we were quickly lionized by the high and mighty of that city. We were swiftly invited to dinner at Judge Daly's residence, where we were surprised by the waspish comments of Mrs Daly regarding the president's spouse: she likened Mary Lincoln to a 'vulgar, shoddy contractor's wife' and described her as a 'common-looking country body'. It was clear to me that snobbery and prejudice existed in America as well as England, and it was clear that Judge Daly and his wife had no great liking for Abe Lincoln, nor his predilection for 'indecent' stories and speeches. But I suspected Mrs Daly was also a little miffed when Marianne let drop the information that we had been invited to the White House, whereas she had not. She was never a lover of the Lincolns, but desired the honour of a presidential invitation.

As for me, I was more than elated to be greeted by the president at his Thursday *soirée* and as I already mentioned, Marianne was beside herself with happiness. We stayed on in Washington thereafter for a week, meeting people of importance and being welcomed into high society, but the most important invitation as far as I was concerned came from Secretary of State for War, Edwin M. Stanton.

Stanton had been Attorney General under President Buchanan, but it was whispered that while he flattered Buchanan to his face, it was Stanton who had secretly led the attempt to impeach the president. This piece of helpful espionage was followed by his subversion of the position of Secretary of War Cameron by advising him to arm the negroes in the Union Army. Embarrassed, Lincoln had sacked Cameron and appointed Stanton in his place. I was to discover that the new Secretary for War was a brusque, arrogant, insolent, cruel, conniving man and the most unpopular individual in Lincoln's administration. And he was poisonously unreliable, as I was to learn to my cost.

When I entered the room in the War Department, Stanton made no effort to rise to greet me. He remained seated in a leather armchair, his back to the window, side on to a table on which lay several important-looking documents. Together with the document in his hand, they seemed like stage props to my practised eye.

He was a stocky, balding man, well-bearded, with narrow eyes that glinted suspiciously behind wire-rimmed spectacles. I learned he was always obsequious to those he needed to placate and I felt it was wise to discount his flattery – at which he was a master – for it cloaked a cowardly disposition that could turn to fierce back-stabbing in the furtherance of his designs and political ambitions.

'Mr James,' he said, 'you come to us with an outstanding legal reputation. The president himself speaks highly of you and your accomplishments in England. After meeting you at the White House *soirée* the other evening, he suggested we might be able to make use of your undoubted talents.'

'I am flattered, sir.'

He managed an oily smile and laid aside the document in his hand. He waved me to a seat facing him; I perched on the edge of the seat, not knowing what to expect but with the rising hope of preference in my breast.

'You spoke bravely in your defence of Dr Simon Bernard some years ago with regard to his involvement in the attempted assassination of Napoleon III. And your defence of the runaway negro Anderson was noted here.' He cocked an eye at me, thoughtfully. 'You are in favour of the emancipation of the black man, Mr James?'

'Your Constitution speaks firmly of the equality of man, and I am in accord with that principle,' I answered evasively

He smiled thinly. 'The president also speaks of the Constitution – but is averse to the abolition of slavery in the South. As he is, against my advice, to the use of blacks in the army. It will come, of course: the Union Army will inevitably emerge victorious in view of our greater numbers, unlimited

146

resources, and the blockading which will eventually bring the Confederacy to its knees... But such discussions can wait for another day. I am a busy man ... Mr James, what thoughts do you have for your future here in the States?'

I took a deep breath. Stoutly, I declared, 'First of all I intend to become an American citizen, now I am free of the shackles of aristocratic prejudice in England. I have taken an office on Broadway in New York and intend entering into a legal partnership. I have considerable experience in bankruptcy and criminal law and I am assured that a glittering future could be open to me.'

'Quite,' Stanton observed drily. 'There are many opportunities for criminal lawyers in the slums of New York's Five Points.'

I was somewhat stung by his derogatory tone but remained silent. He watched me for a little while, the fingers of his left hand toying with his greying beard. At last he said, 'A successful lawyer can of course look forward to a judicial position in due course. Would your own aspirations lead in that direction?'

'It is something I would hope to achieve, having had ten years' experience in such capacity in England.'

He shrugged diffidently. 'Things are ordered differently here in America. Judicial appointments are obtained by election, and that can only be achieved by political support. And as for New York politics ... the city is strongly Democratic in its views while we are a Republican administration.'

I waited.

Stanton reached for a snuffbox, took a pinch and sniffed. I assumed it was snuff: I had heard rumours that he was addicted to cocaine. He stretched his eyes, blinked, and fixed me with a sharp gaze. 'The president has asked me to talk with you with a view to government service of some kind. I have thought about the matter, and I believe we can obtain advantage in offering you an appointment ... but perhaps not in the field you envisage. I have looked into your background, Mr James, your support for political assassins, your radical opinions, your championing of the common man ... all admirable traits and well regarded in certain quarters.'

I was beginning to become angry. There was a sneering tone in his voice, a contemptuous curl to his lip as he misdescribed the nature of my legal activities in England. But I was curious also: I could not understand his strategy in speaking to me in this manner. So I kept my temper in check, and made no reply.

I thought I detected a sudden doubt in his eyes, an anxiety that he had perhaps gone too far. As I said earlier, Stanton was always a coward. Now, he placed his hand on the

148

table beside him and drummed his fingers thoughtfully on the documents that lay there.

'The war does not go well with us at the moment, sir, and the president – I speak freely to you – seems indecisive, and does not trust in the ability of his generals. In the prosecution of the war, I must be his back-bone, I must push him in the right direction, and I must drive General McClellan into forceful action against Richmond. But as if this were not enough, I have other problems to deal with. Notably, there's the matter of foreign relations. I need hardly inform you that we understand there is considerable sympathy for the Confederacy in England. And the last thing we would want is for England to enter into an alliance with the Confederacy against the Union.'

I frowned; I still could not see where this was heading, but I deemed it expedient to nod sagely.

He was silent for a little while, stroking his beard. He sighed. 'I believe you were a con-fidant of Lord Palmerston. You will no doubt know his views. I also have no doubt loyalty will prevent you from disclosing those views to me.'

I ignored the sarcasm in his tone.

'But I know you will be aware that rela-tionships between the best of friends can be strained by unexpected events. The president has no wish to offend England. But there is one issue on which I am certain that relationship can be severely damaged.'

'Sir?'

'Canada.'

I leaned back in my chair, confused.

'We are a growing nation, suffering from growing pains,' Stanton mused. 'Take Chicago, for instance. In 1829 there were no more than fifty inhabitants in that city; now there are in the region of three hundred thousand. Canals, the meat trade, the railway depots ... progress has been explosive. *Explosive...* Do you know, Mr James, that this surge has been much supported by an influx of Irish immigrants?'

'The agrarian problems have led to the depopulation of Ireland,' I agreed.

'And they have come to the land of the free with an ingrained hatred of England,' Stanton affirmed. 'Which is where you could come in, Mr James.'

'I don't understand.'

'Have you heard of the secret society known as *Clan na Gael*?'

I shrugged. 'Ireland has always been a hot-bed of secret societies. The Fenians in England are under constant watch by the Government, while their political allies demand Home Rule for Ireland—'

'Chicago houses an active branch – under a man called Sullivan – of *Clan na Gael*, which is devoted to the achievement of Home Rule by violent, not political means. We have our agents who keep us informed of their meetings, we have infiltrated their organization, and we have information that they have been gathering arms with a view to striking at England – not on England's home soil, but at its colonial possessions. They believe that if they cross into Canada with an army of Irish patriots, there will be a popular uprising, the English will be thrown out of Canada and the first step to Irish independence will have been achieved.'

'Pie in the sky,' I observed.

'That is probably an accurate assessment,' Stanton murmured, 'but you must appreciate the problem such an invasion – if it ever comes off – would contribute to the embarrassment of our government.'

'Because the invasion would necessarily have to come from American soil.' I nodded thoughtfully.

'Involving Irishmen who have lived and worked and schemed and armed themselves in America. Such an event could damage our relationships with the British government, it could escalate, it could even draw the English into our own civil conflict. On the wrong side.'

'I can see that,' I replied, nodding. 'But where do I come into this?'

Stanton scratched at his beard. 'You are an

Englishman of reputation. You are known to be a Radical. You have supported political assassination,' he held up a restraining hand as I began to protest, 'and you have declared yourself against oppression, aristocratic prejudice, even to the extent of seeking a new life here in America. Like so many immigrants. I feel it would not be overly difficult for you to persuade these renegade Irishmen that your heart is in the right place.'

I stared at him in astonishment. 'Are you suggesting I should become an agent – a spy?'

Stanton smiled wolfishly. 'Nothing so dramatic. But I think you could act as a political adviser to our own Intelligence Service. And living in New York and being – as I understand from your history – a sporting man who enjoys the manly arts, horse racing, pugilism, clubbing and gambling, in our terms a 'jolly fellow' – you would in New York be in contact with the teeming Irish fraternity. From whom you could obtain information to our advantage.'

I shook my head. I stood up. 'I am sorry, Mr Stanton. This proposal is a complete surprise to me, and one I must decline. I have come to the United States to promote my profession as a lawyer. Working for your ... Intelligence Service, did you call it? I fear this is not at all what I feel to be appropriate for my future success in America.'

152

Stanton held up a hand. 'I think you should take time to consider this matter. I will contact Colonel Lafayette Baker and arrange for you to meet him in New York. The fact is, Mr James, you are green in American ways. You will find great difficulty in achieving your ambitions: a judicial appointment, a seat in the Supreme Court, perhaps? These prizes will never be within your grasp unless you have political support of the most *effective* kind. Let me put it like this, Mr James. With my support, and that of the Cabinet, and of the president himself, your future could be assured. Without it ... in a corrupt Democratic stronghold such as New York...' He spread his hands in a gesture of helplessness. 'But with such support, from a grateful government, who knows what you might achieve?'

Two days later, returning to New York, I was still turning over in my mind the implications that lay behind his offer. And the more I dwelt on the matter, the less outlandish seemed to be his reasoning.

I had opened my office on Broadway and entered into partnership with a law clerk, Thomas Dunphy, who was preparing himself for a career at the New York City Bar as my associate. But Marianne insisted that we investigate all that New York had to offer, and during the next few weeks we toured the city, taking in all the sights as though we were mere tourists. And to my surprise, Marianne wished to experience *all* the sights, including the notorious Five Points area. We joined what were popularly known as 'slumming parties', small groups of ladies and gentlemen who wished to see the notorious slums and rookeries of Charlotte Street and Cherry Street, where we were regaled by our guide with hair-raising stories of the river pirates and the crimps who robbed sailors on the waterfront and shanghaied drunken, drugged saloon inhabitants to service at sea. We were shown the Fourth Ward Hotel, where sailors were enticed inside by waterfront whores, then drugged, murdered, and dropped through trapdoors into the sewers that led to the docks. We learned that nearly every house in the Five Points had a cellar serving as a groggery with a bordello on the first floor, usually family-run businesses, with mother and daughters providing the required services above, while the husband kept order in the saloon. The riots of the 1840s had driven most of the blacks out of the neighbourhood, but the Irish were everywhere, some successful like Barney McGuire, who had begun his career as a fence but progressed to become an owner of opium houses, saloons, hop joints, junk shops and pawnbrokers. Other immigrants from Ireland remained mired in poverty among dirty-faced, ragged children who made a living by sweeping crossing points and picking pockets.

There were also the theatres.

I had always been interested in the theatre, as you know, and with our guide we duly toured some of the more respectable: they did not include Billy McGlory's Armory Hall, which, our guide assured us, was little more than a haunt for thieves, pickpockets, procurers and knockout drop artists. But we were introduced to the Louvre Concert Saloon near Madison Avenue and the cheaper theatres on Broadway, and shown the disreputable dance houses in Water and Cherry Streets. I got to know them more intimately later, without Marianne's company, but that's another matter.

After the tour was over, I received a message at the hotel: when I responded and met Frank Queen, editor and owner of the *New York Clipper*, he offered me an associate editorship of the newspaper ... the idea was that I would contribute articles on sporting and theatrical events. So it immediately became part of my routine to visit the Free and Easy saloon, which was frequented by actors, clerks, bookmakers, theatrical men, journalists – and lawyers. There I could get to know the men who worked in and frequented the stage in New York. And then there were the Bowery theatres. They tended to play broad farces and bloody melodramas, plays involving highwaymen and murderers, and they offered the additional incentives of long bars and huge beer gardens where they offered fiery, deadly liquor served by way of rubber hoses into wooden drinking vessels. It all reminded me of my youth, I assure you! For a few cents, the determined drunkard obtained access directly to the hose and was allowed to swallow as much as possible before he needed to draw breath – at which point another took over the rubber mouth!

I also became aware that most of the saloons, dance houses, brothels, gambling houses and greengrocery speakeasies were operated by Ward leaders backed by the Democratic stronghold, Tammany Hall. Politics and the underworld were closely entwined, each feeding off the other.

I wandered among these haunts, I was soon seen as a 'sporting' man, one of the 'Jolly Fellow' society and I must admit I enjoyed being part of this cultural tradition. Marianne did not of course accompany me on these visits, nor did I take her to any of the numerous gin palaces which appeared on each corner alongside gambling saloons: Madison Square was a notorious haunt for these establishments and provided so-called 'waiter girls' who were scantily dressed, available for assignations, and served excise-free liquor in between the stage shows regularly on offer. I was able to mingle with actors at the House of Lords, run by an Englishman, where they served beer in toby jugs and offered such delicacies as pickled pigs' feet. As for stage shows in the Bowery, Geoghan's was my favourite. Its walls were covered with flash pictures, gaudy decorations and drawings of famous ring battles and was the haunt of the pugilistic fraternity. I had a few months' free enjoyment of these opportunities before Marianne began to question me about my absences and late hours.

Such questions soon degenerated into increasingly bitter quarrels.

2

Marianne.

With no false pride, my boy, I've always regarded myself as an expert in horseflesh and women. True, I never seemed to have much financial luck at the races, but with women, well, I prided myself on my ability to entertain, please, and persuade the ladies at all levels of society. Over the years, I met all kinds, though I disagreed with that impotent fool Ruskin who claimed that a woman's intellect is merely for sweet ordering and arrangement, just as I took issue with that idiot Coventry Patmore, whose poems described the ridiculously pallid *Angel in the House*. No, I'd met fiery women, passionate women like Sovrina and Henriette who were far from the limply bloodless creatures described by the poets. And whether it was at the Cock and Hen Club, or in private town houses when husbands were elsewhere engaged, or in the swirl and colour of the Haymarket after the theatres were out, I found I could handle all kinds of women crossing my amatory path.

But Marianne: I confess she was something beyond my experience, or, let me admit, my control.

We had entered into what was effectively a business arrangement, and once married I had been delighted by her response to activity in the boudoir, but I also quickly became aware of the strength of her character. She had a mind of her own, and she held the purse strings.

'But I assure you, my visits to the Bowery are in the nature of work,' I pleaded with her. 'My articles in the *Clipper* bring in a satisfying income, but they do necessitate my keeping my finger on the pulse of the theatrical world of New York.'

'But the gin palaces and the concert saloons and that appalling De Soto's—'

'You've been misinformed! The dining room is elegant with its chandelier, the broiled kidneys are superior, the cream of the acting fraternity congregate there to gossip and it is there that I obtain my best copy, my love!'

'And Sir John Falstaff's, and Pfaff's—'

'They are frequented by the sporting fraternity, by the supporters of pugilism and horse racing and the theatre – people whom I need to speak with, learn from, understand, in order to produce my articles!'

'I don't like it,' she snapped as she stamped her foot, but she relented, at first.

So for a few months, as she quietly simmered, I continued to claim a legitimate lifestyle in the Five Points and enjoy the company of the Jolly Fellows. That's what they called themselves, you know – it was a sort of culture in masculine New York. The old days of the famous 'Bowery B'hoys' were almost over, but in the saloons one came across the 'shoulder hitters' with their cropped hair, broken noses and thick boots, men who were used at elections to break up meetings of political rivals. Many of them were former pugilists – it was how John Heenan started out, after all – and in the saloons boxing merits were constantly discussed; the same topics of conversation occurred in the grog shops, brothels and gaming hells, where one found a clientele comprising fancy fighters, burglars, street thieves, barroom bullies, drinking alongside lawyers and New York aldermen.

Ah, yes, I felt I was back to the days of my youth! I had known St Cues and the Seven Dials in London, entered the rookeries with the protection of Ben Gully, and seen the dens of thieves and scoundrels – as well as the gambling hells frequented by the aristocracy. But the raucous delights of the gin palaces of the Five Points were different and yet reminded me strongly of a lost, dissolute youth.

But I should not have ignored the warning signs flashing in Marianne's eyes: I was too confident in my persuasive tongue as far as women were concerned. And I had other things on my mind after Colonel Lafayette Baker got in touch with me.

It was shortly after I had attended the Tammany Hall celebrations of 4 July, when my new friend Judge Daly gave the oration, that the messenger called on me with the Colonel's note. It made the suggestion that we should meet at the Union Club on Fifth Avenue: I had already been invited there on several occasions and knew it was a club for highly-placed gentlemen: an entrance fee of $40 was demanded and games of hazard were not permitted. I was met at the entrance by a lackey with trimmed whiskers, black suit with a swallow-tail coat, a white cravat and slippers ... very 'Hinglish' according to New Yorkers. I presented him with my invitation from Colonel Baker.

The powdered lackey escorted me with mincing step through a chandelier-lit drawing room encumbered with heavy dark furniture and a centre table covered with richly bound volumes of American poets. The walls were elegantly frescoed and there was a convenient, wide bay window through which elderly members could ogle female promenaders on Fifth Avenue. We climbed broad stairs guarded by armoured knight sentinels until we reached the smoking room, inhabited only by a wrinkled old naval officer, a short, fat individual I took to be a

161

Madison Square doctor, and a spruce-looking merchant. They eyed me with idle curiosity above their newspapers as the lackey tapped on the door of a private room leading off their den; a short pause followed, then the door opened and the lackey stepped aside after announcing me.

The man who faced me and held out his hand in welcome was a tall, handsome, broad-shouldered individual with dark-red hair and a magnificent, red-hued beard. He was thin as a lath, his eyes were sharp, his forehead intelligent and his handclasp was firm, almost aggressive in its grip. He was dressed in a dark frock coat, white corduroy breeches and military-style boots. He introduced himself as Colonel Lafayette Baker. He waved me to a comfortable seat beside a table on which stood a decanter of brandy. He poured two drinks, then sat down facing me.

'It was Secretary of War Mr Stanton who suggested we should meet. I have taken the trouble to investigate you, Mr James, and I am impressed by your history as a lawyer and a politician. You will know little, if anything, of me so perhaps I should tell you that I am an officer of the Union Army, now seconded to the staff of the Secretary of War. He has asked me to undertake certain tasks ... I seek to root out the corruption in the matter of army supplies among other matters, to ensure the Union Army gets what it has paid for; and believe me, sir, corruption is rife, even extending to senior officers of the army itself. Naturally I do not work alone: I have recruited a number of agents who work for me, report to me, and I report to Mr Stanton. Though...'

He wrinkled his brow and was silent for a while. It seemed as though he was contemplating saying something that might be unwise, or indiscreet, but whatever it was, he kept his counsel. I learned later the reason: he was also keeping a close eye on the business activities of his employer, Edwin Stanton himself, who had his corrupt fingers in a number of company pies...

'The Secretary of War has advised me that we could make good use of you, not in the matter of army contracts, but in relation to an issue that is worrying Mr Stanton.'

'He spoke to me of the Fenians,' I prompted.

Baker nodded, narrowing his ferrety eyes. '*Clan na Gael* ... Mr Stanton seems to feel they can be an embarrassment to us. I am not so sure. In my view they are merely groups of drunken Irish blowhards who call themselves patriots seeking the liberty of Ireland, but while they speechify and drink and sing rebel songs and fight among themselves, I don't believe there's a single soldier among them. But the Secretary of War demands that their groups be further infiltrated so that we may gain intelligence of their intentions.'

'Mr Stanton believes they may be planning an invasion of Canada.'

Baker grunted dismissively. 'A fantasy without foundation, in my view. But it requires investigation. However, to cut to the chase, I would like to offer you a position in the Union Intelligence Service. I can pay you $100 a month, and expenses. All you have to do is mingle with these fellows in their saloons, gambling hells, gin palaces and concert saloons. You'll observe the brawls they call battles; you'll ingratiate yourself with them by singing their sentimental songs and spouting their battle cries – and you'll keep your eyes and ears open, and report directly to me.'

I shook my head doubtfully. 'I'm not sure they'll accept me, an Englishman in their midst.'

'You won't be alone, Mr James. And the company I will provide you will give you an impeccable standing. And legitimacy.' He smiled thinly. 'I believe you already know him.'

And know him I certainly did. My fellow agent turned out to be none other than Carlos Rudio, now calling himself Charles Di Rudio, former Italian patriot and would-be assassin of Napoleon III, now an officer in the Union Army and like Baker assigned to the Secret Intelligence Service.

You don't recall his name? Of course you do ... you surely must! You remember the defence I made of Dr Simon Bernard, charged with planning the assassination attempt upon Napoleon III and his Empress Eugenie? Well, you must recall that while it was Felice Orsini who threw the first bomb that evening in Paris, it was Carlos Rudio who threw the second. They failed in their mission of course: Orsini was guillotined, I saved Bernard in an English court by my impassioned oratory – which even President Lincoln praised and learned by heart – and Rudio, his death sentence commuted because of his aristocratic lineage, was condemned to imprisonment for life at Cayenne, the notorious Devil's Island.

But Carlos Rudio was a great survivor. He was one of the first men ever to escape that hellish prison. I met him briefly in London later, when he made his way there, married, and set himself up as a teacher of languages, but he soon left for America. There he reinvented himself as Charles Di Rudio and was drafted into the army and then seconded into the Intelligence Service.

Now we were to be reunited – as secret agents under the direction of Colonel Lafayette Baker.

I met Di Rudio a week later. He had

changed little since first we met back in 1848; his thick, swept-back hair was a little greyer now and he sported a carefully groomed imperial beard, perhaps in emulation of the man he had tried to murder in 1858. He was a small, enthusiastic, urgent, slim-hipped man with somewhat elfin features and sharp eyes but he was as garrulous as ever; we talked over old revolutionary times, he told me yet again about his escape from Devil's Island – it had been a different story each time – and he even confided in me that he was really an Italian count, not just a low-life Italian assassin. We finally discussed how we were to commence our undercover operations for Colonel Baker.

And so it began. I had already gained a certain reputation in the Five Points as a sporting man; now, in the company of the acknowledged would-be political assassin, the man who had thrown a bomb at Napoleon III in Rue Pelletier, my reputation was enhanced. I had always claimed to be a man of the people, I had fought aristocratic oppression in England and suffered for it, I had defended the runaway slave Anderson and was now seen as the friend and companion of the famous escapee from Devil's Island.

There was initial suspicion, of course, but the lodges of the *Clan na Gael* were manned with simple, uneducated men whose one bond was a common desire to free the 'ould country' from the yoke of English oppression. So we were gradually accepted at the fringes of their drunken, noisy gatherings, Di Rudio and I, we were seen as Jolly Fellows; we were with them when they enjoyed raucous drinking sessions and sang patriotic songs and tickled the waitress girls who edged their half-naked way among the beer-stained tables. We were surrounded by Irishmen: the immigrants – who now in America amounted to probably one and a half million – had flooded into the Five Points and Hell's Kitchen, nourishing their hatred of the English by stories of mass graves, evictions, cruel landlords, and starving peasants; we drank with them loudly to the damnation of England. And they came to tolerate our presence, if not accept us completely.

We drank, and sang, and roared out slogans as lustily as our companions. And we learned almost nothing of note.

Colonel Baker was largely correct in his views: Stanton was concerning himself unnecessarily. He was not alone. The gin-soaked Attorney General of Canada, John McDonald, he certainly feared an Irish-American invasion of Canada, and protested loudly about the activities of American agents who acted as crimps to get young Canadians to enlist in the Union Army. McDonald set up patrols on the frontier to prevent such activities, but as to invasion, well, in New York at least, it was all just talk. A few years later, of course, in 1866 there was indeed an invasion attempt. It involved seven hundred men planting the Irish flag on Canadian soil before scurrying back over the border. It was a mere hiccup of glory.

But for the moment, I took my $100 a month, reported back to Colonel Lafayette Baker and learned precisely nothing.

While my troubles at home multiplied.

I could not, because of the nature of my work for Colonel Baker, tell Marianne why I was spending so much time in the Five Points, Satan's Circus and Hell's Kitchen. I tried using my associate editorship with the *Clipper* to explain away my frequent nocturnal absences, but the story wore thin. She was becoming more and more difficult. And soon the amatory enthusiasm that had so surprised me in the early days of our marriage began to cool. Experimentation ended. Nocturnal couplings became infrequent. And finally, the bedroom door was coldly barred.

It took two unforeseen events to bring matters to such a head. And two women.

The first was a certain Mrs Abigail Grimshaw. Charlie Dickens tended to describe the character of his fictional protagonists by the names he assigned them: indeed, when he caricatured me in *A Tale of Two Cities* he

168

named the character as Mr Stryver, which was apposite enough. I always worked hard, and I always strove for the highest office. Well, Mrs Grimshaw lived up to *her* name. She was a determined, thin-lipped woman of decided opinions and she held a narrowly dark view of the world. Tall, thin, flat-bosomed, voluminously black-skirted and black-bonneted she had a severe tone, a tightly-strapped chest, granite jaw and an iron-hard disposition. Moreover, she had a Mission. Or rather, two Missions.

The first one was the astonishing task of trying to persuade the populace of the Five Points to give up the evils of alcoholic drink; the second was to bring to an end the disgraceful use of women in Hell's Kitchen. Temperance and an end to prostitution! In the most notorious sink-hole in America!

You can imagine where she thought I fitted into this scenario.

She was coldly belligerent towards me from the beginning. Marianne and I had met her shortly after our arrival in New York when we were on our 'slumming' expedition to the Five Points. She was a formidable leader of the American Female Moral Reform Society. On that first occasion, as we made our way past the wooden hovels on the north side of Paradise Square, she regaled us with a discourse on the importance of the Society work, handing out tracts, reading

Bible passages on the streets to the morally degenerate Irish and opium-soaked Chinese immigrants, and urging those who entered brothels to refrain and repent.

I've no doubt she saw me as a supporter of the kind of excesses which she abominated. Though I always suspected she held that view of every man she met. There had been a Mr Grimshaw, I understand, but he lived in India. He'd got as far away from her as he could, I guessed. Anyway, as our little cortege progressed that day from Baxter Street to Bottle Alley and viewed the crazily leaning wooden tenements at Baxter Street and the gap-toothed slatterns in the rubbish-strewn alleyways, she maintained an interminable tirade.

'These hovels, windowless and destitute, house the most degraded of tenants! They are almost all Irish immigrants sleeping here in the most filthy and miserable conditions: fifteen sleeping in one room! You can imagine the depths of depravity to which they sink! They come from the estates of *your* Lord Lansdowne,' she averred, fixing me with a gleaming, furious eye as though the aristocrat and I had been personal friends, 'and Lord Palmerston, who has shipped out his unwelcome tenants to die in these hovels, far away from his gaze! There are young women here who profess to make a living by picking curled hair out of public garbage barrels but

I know they nightly make themselves available to brutal, depraved, degraded men of the most despicable character.'

I began to direct my attention elsewhere as she continued, only picking up occasional comments such as 'damp and filthy cellars ... wretched bunks and hideous beds infernal holes ... horrid stench ... pestilential nuisance ... crimes too horrible to name...' So I failed to pay much regard to her other outpourings. Unfortunately, Marianne did. That evening she informed me she had decided to join Mrs Grimshaw in her Moral Reform endeavours. She intended helping her at the House of Industry and Mission, and to give of her time – and money – to support destitute, fallen women.

Now this was all very laudable, but I was not happy at her giving her money away – except to me, that is. Also, there was a certain irony in the situation, which she herself very quickly pointed out. She was going to spend time doing good works in the Five Points out of a sense of moral outrage. I, on the other hand, was prowling the same streets with different motives.

I protested, of course: I could not tell her about my work for Colonel Baker so I reiterated that I was merely doing work for the *Clipper*, I was writing about the poverty among the destitute even as I described sporting and theatrical events. But Marianne, I discovered, was not easily persuaded. And the bedroom door began to close night after night.

She spent more and more time with Mrs Grimshaw. I was trying to drum up legal business at my office on Broadway and in the evenings joining Charles Di Rudio at various Irish-frequented concert saloons and gin palaces in the Five Points: our regular haunts, I recall, were Monroe Hall and Niblo's Theatre – particularly because of their proximity to opium dens and cheap, Irish-owned saloons. But Mrs Grimshaw's influence became even more malign and Marianne more tight-lipped in her confrontations with me. In desperation I finally committed an egregious error, which was to rebound upon me later with devastating consequences to my legal career in New York.

We were in our private suite in the Albemarle Hotel and Marianne was in a vengeful mood, while her daughter Blanche sat in a corner of the room with cool, watchful eyes.

'It's all the fault of the Irish Catholics and the Jews,' Marianne hissed. 'The immigrants come over from Dublin and think nothing of establishing themselves by taking advantage of later arrivals, skinning them of all they possess, debauching young girls, sending urchins on the streets to beg, prostituting the women so the husbands can purchase grog! Our Moral Reform movement seeks to bring this to an end and to save young children from the pernicious influences of the Catholic Church. This is why the Reverend Pease has begun a campaign to remove young Irish children from their dissolute parents and place them with Methodist families outside the city!'

This was the first I had heard of the Reverend Lewis Pease and his misguided efforts to drag Irish children from their families and the church of their fathers.

'That's probably an illegal activity,' I protested weakly.

'As illegal as it apparently is to preach in the street of the evils of drink!' Marianne countered with the fiery enthusiasm of a convert. 'Are you aware that this afternoon Mr Pease was actually arrested for preaching temperance in Mott Street? He was surrounded by an angry crowd of Catholics–'

Outside Bridget McCarty's whorehouse, I guessed.

'–and when the police arrived, the Reverend Pease was arrested! For *preaching!*' She was silent for a few angry moments, her breast heaving, her eyes flashing fury. 'This cannot be allowed to happen! Edwin ... you must *do* something!'

I held up a warning hand. 'Marianne, one cannot merely walk into a case like this without proper instruction. Mr Pease may well have consulted a lawyer already–'

'Mrs Grimshaw tells me he has not! What can be done, Edwin?'

I sighed. 'Well, clearly a writ of *habeas corpus* could be produced and a demand made for his release, at least on bail. And in this city, I understand getting bail is like being acquitted, because the dockets get filed, the bail is never produced–'

'So you must do it,' she exclaimed enthusiastically and embraced me with something of the old fervour. Blanche sniffed and left the room and I ... well, for the sake of peace I agreed to represent the Reverend Mr Pease.

It was a bad mistake on my part, though I was not to know it at the time.

I don't imagine, Joe, you ever had occasion to enter the police courts of New York when you lived in the city with your mother. She'd have kept you away from such dangers. But the fact is that I was aware that I had all the qualities for successful interventions in the police courts: justice there leaned heavily on stage presence, theatrical performances, and the bail system. Superior oral skills were the key, and I possessed such skills. And as I've mentioned, the bail system was a sham. The police courts were nothing more than un-regulated commercial enterprises riddled with corruption and abuse. They reeked of intimidation, bribery and political influence. And the police-court judges were usually former policemen or firemen who obtained their positions by political influence and barefaced bribery: they had no legal qualifications but were merely pothouse politicians supported by Tammany Hall Democrats.

So I advised Marianne to put up whatever bail would be necessary – she would never have to pay it – and advised Mrs Grimshaw to get her Mission to pay out certain sweeteners to Democrat aldermen while I obtained a writ of *habeas corpus*. And it worked. The Reverend Pease was discharged after my impassioned speech, and no further proceedings were put in place. And I suppose had things gone no further all might yet have proceeded smoothly enough. But Mrs Grimshaw appeared again a week later to seek my further assistance with regard to Mr Pease. This time it was as a result of the Methodist minister's high-handedness – albeit well meant – in once more dragging two young girls from their drunken, disreputable Five Points Catholic parents and placing them with a good Protestant family in New Jersey. Pease was hauled into the police court again and I was persuaded once again to defend him. This time it was to no avail, since despite my advice he refused to return the children to their parents. He was incarcerated in the Tombs, that monstrous, notorious, Egyptian-pillared prison, so I had to make swift application to the Supreme Court for his release.

My application was successful: in a matter of days, the Supreme Court held that the locking-up of the Reverend Pease was illegal on a technical ground. Such a charge could be adjudicated upon only by three justices, not one. The minister was to be released immediately. The police-court justice who had committed Pease to the Tombs was humiliated by this reverse and I saw in his eyes that mine was a name he would remember.

And his name was one I had cause to remember well, later, when our paths crossed again: the police court justice that day was Matthew Brennan, former fireman, ex-police captain, pothouse politician and the darling of Tammany Hall.

Am I wandering again? No, I don't think so. Well, yes, I did say that there were two women who more or less destroyed my marriage. Mrs Grimshaw, as I've explained, in her turning of Marianne's mind and inclinations. The other? Ah well, that was the lady whom I've already mentioned to you, Joe my boy. You'll have heard of her. The sensation of the New World and the Old. The actress who took New York and London by storm. The woman who fascinated Bret Harte and Mark Twain, took Swinburne and Alexandre Dumas as lovers, who married John C. Heenan – among others – bigamously, and who made her name by riding a horse on the stage, apparently in a state of bare-arsed nudity. That's right, the Dangerous Lady, the Queen of the Plaza, the Naked Lady, the Enchanting Rebel … in a word, *Mazeppa*.

3

How did I get involved with her? Well, partly it sprang from my employment by Colonel Lafayette Baker.

'The woman is suspected of Confederate sympathies,' he explained to me. 'We need to find out whom she associates with, and whether she has been secretly passing funds – she earns an enormous amount for her performances on stage, I believe – passing funds to Confederate agents in Virginia, while expressing anti-Lincoln sentiments in private dinner engagements. I believe you have already made her acquaintance.'

I had. I say it was *partly* Baker's suggestion that led me into the association that followed, but I must admit it was not the only reason. No, the other reason was that I had been totally overwhelmed when I made the acquaintance of the actress with the mysterious background – was she of Irish-Cuban origin, a former whore and naked dancer, a woman who had once fought off Red Indians, the actress who had charmed the bohemian crowd at Pfaff's including the homoerotic poet Walt Whitman? Gossip swirled around her. What matter? All I need say is that when I first saw her I thought she was the most exciting woman I had ever met.

That meeting took place in the offices of the *New York Clipper*.

I recall the day well.

I had gone to the building housing the *Clipper* and had a brief conversation with John C. Heenan, who was sitting in Frank Queen's office and seemed delighted to meet me again. Queen was a chubby, excitable little man who was a wild enthusiast for the Noble Art and Heenan and I regaled him with our account of Heenan's battle with Tom Sayers and laughed together when we discussed the famous occasion when I had acted for him over the title-belt business. But when Frank Queen was informed that Miss Adah Menken was below and wishing to see the *Clipper* editor, he bounced up with alacrity, but Heenan turned quite white. He grabbed Frank Queen's arm and begged to be let out of the building, moustache bristling with alarm, by way of a back entrance. The man who claimed to be the pugilistic champion of the world had neither nerve nor desire to see the woman who had married him bigamously. I, on the other hand, was intrigued.

Heenan left, I stayed, and Adah swept into the cluttered office of the editor.

She was not a tall woman but her figure was beautifully proportioned. She possessed large, dark, startling eyes and a full, crimson mouth and that day she wore a simple, dark velvet Byronic dress. Her hair was cut short, a daring fashion for the time, and to my amazement, after Frank Queen introduced us, she took out a *cigarillo*, lit it and calmly smoked it during our conversation. I can't recall, I am ashamed to say, the content of that conversation for that first twenty minutes: I think it was largely about her imminent assault upon the New York theatre world. She was to appear at the Broadway Theatre in her role of Mazeppa. 'You *know*,' she teased me, 'the naked hussy on horseback!'

I was entranced: I had never met such a vibrant woman. She also, surprisingly, seemed attracted to me, a corpulent lawyer/sporting writer in his fifties, while she was in her mid-twenties, sensationally beautiful and the toast of the West Coast. But, looking back, I came to realize it was merely a manner she had cultivated: she tended to 'collect' admirers.

Still, I reacted eagerly to her flirtatious invitation to escort her to the theatre that night. We weren't alone, of course: the famous American poet Walt Whitman turned up – equally dazzled, it seemed, in spite of his penchant for young boys – and we three dined at Pfaff's where she further amazed me by consuming a dish of raw clams, thick chicken soup, a hearty steak and a dish of

180

compote of fruits. I couldn't take my eyes off her, as after such an enormous meal she then requested that Charlie Pfaff also prepare a turkey sandwich to sustain her during the play's intermission!

As for her performance that sensational night, it was witnessed by an audience that contained nine Union generals in full dress uniform, the millionaire Astor and Schuyler families and a packed group of ready-to-be-shocked ladies all agog for the moment when she would appear naked, tied to the back of a galloping steed. I don't believe Mrs Grimshaw was among them. As for Adah, she was superb; she was not completely naked, of course, for in spite of the advance publicity she wore a flesh-coloured body stocking and the steed 'galloped' rather wearily at a walking pace up a sloping frame on rollers, past which mountain sceneries were drawn along in the background. Nevertheless the audience cheered to the rafters and we were all dazzled: Edwin Booth and Ada Clare, then regarded as the royalty of the New York stage, took the trouble to congratulate her, and the newspapers next day were full of her praise.

My presence in her company was noted, as it was when, accepting her offer to show me around the city, I accompanied her on several occasions thereafter. Consequently, the domestic atmosphere in the Albemarle Hotel turned frosty.

'You're making a fool of yourself, Edwin,' Marianne snapped as she paced up and down the sitting room with an infuriated snapping of skirts.

'She's a famous actress,' I protested. 'She provides me with good copy for the *Clipper!*'

Marianne was not mollified. She ranted on and on about my degrading myself by being seen in the company of such a notorious woman. She adverted to my parading with Adah on the new pedestrian bridge over Broadway and Fulton Street, a bridge no *respectable* woman would use because street ruffians below might look up their skirts – Adah was proud of her legs I might add, and would have had no objection to displaying them in such manner. But for the sake of peace I might have stopped the relationship with Adah there, except that a few days later I had the meeting with Colonel Lafayette Baker at which he suggested I should continue to cultivate Adah's acquaintance to determine her Confederate sympathies. So during the next weeks I was often seen in her company.

And Marianne finally exploded.

Unfortunately the quarrel broke out in the crowded public rooms of the Albemarle Hotel. We were coming to the end of our meal and Blanche had already retired sulkily upstairs to our suite. Marianne had been quiet throughout the dinner but I knew she was holding in something, tightly; I knew enough about women to appreciate that a storm was brewing. And when it did, as we took coffee, the storm burst about my head.

'When we made a bargain in Paris, the day of our wedding, I never expected to be humiliated in this manner! Of course I was already aware of your reputation as a *coureur de jupes* – indeed, Colonel Wheatley expressly warned me – and you had long lived a dissolute bachelor life, but I had persuaded myself that marriage would make you change your ways – not least since I would be supporting you financially! Yes, you see, I came into the marriage with my eyes open! But I never expected this treatment! You have been seen everywhere in the company of this degraded woman, this so-called actress, this harlot who has clawed her way up from the streets and who now prances to fame and fortune on the back of a horse!'

I held up a hand. 'Marianne—'

'I see it all now! You will never change! While I have been doing all I can to assist Mrs Grimshaw in helping fallen women on the streets of Hell's Kitchen you have been consorting with the greatest whore of them all! More – you have behaved like this in the public eye! Do you not appreciate what this does to my position in New York society? Are you not aware, as I am, of the snide, whispered comments, the sly glances of contempt behind fans, the murmurings of pity? You are no gentleman, sir, and you have humiliated me!'

There was much more in this vein, and as the tirade lengthened so did the level of her tones as she completely lost control of herself. The whole of the crowded dining room sat silent, wide-eyed, listening to every word. Even the spittoons stopped rattling.

That very evening, the management of the Albemarle Hotel politely requested that we vacate the rooms in which we lived. The affair was reported, as I might have expected, back in England: inevitably, in the *Manchester Guardian*.

I felt frustrated of course by my inability to explain I was acting under Colonel Baker's secret instructions. The situation flayed me further a few days later even when Colonel Baker was sacked, and my employment in the Intelligence Service came to an end – temporarily, at least. Baker's enthusiasm for rooting out corruption had led to his discovery that Stanton himself was receiving kickbacks from army contracts, so the Secretary for War removed him from his situation.

As for me, the domestic atmosphere remained decidedly chilly, even though I stayed away from the Broadway theatre, and Adah herself moved on from New York to play to packed houses in Baltimore – where, incidentally, she got herself arrested by the

Provost Marshall, briefly, suspected of being a Secessionist. She wrote to me about it. She had refused to deny her Confederate sympathies but the authorities let her go anyway: she was too famous to be incarcerated. So Colonel Baker would have got his proof without my intervention. But if I had told Marianne all this, she wouldn't have believed a word of it.

As far as she was concerned, I had broken my marriage vows.

'And I know it's not just a matter of carrying on in public with that disgraceful actress! I am aware that you still frequent the concert halls, the low-down theatres, the gin palaces and saloons, and continue to consort with the tawdry, foul-mouthed, harsh-voiced harlots who each evening throng the sidewalks of lower Broadway. You are an inveterate skirt-chaser, sir, a whore-master, a man whom no decent woman would be seen with – and you are my husband! It is too much to bear!'

I thought I detected the opinions of Mrs Grimshaw in this particular sally.

I reacted as best I could. To be frank, I feared the loss of her financial support. I begged her pardon, assured her I would change my ways, took her to dine at Delmonico's, and the Maison Dorée. I flattered her, cajoled her, bought her flowers and French champagne but I had underestimated Marianne. With the resolute backing of Mrs Grimshaw she was not to be deterred. Both women were convinced I was besotted with Adah Menken. And that I lived a life of wild licence in the stews of Five Points.

What? Did I ever actually become Adah's lover? No, in fact, I did not. True, I was tempted on one occasion. She had invited me up to her rooms so she could read me her poems – she fancied herself as a versifier, you know, and was later encouraged in that belief by that boy-caresser Whitman and that whip-loving degenerate Swinburne. Talking of that little pimp, I never could reconcile myself to the image of Swinburne and Adah as lovers. He was reputed to enjoy being lashed by older women after bathing naked in the sea. Curious fellow... But no, as I say, I did take the one opportunity in her hotel room to press my suit. She read her poems to me, then started talking about love and loneliness, so I naturally assumed an opportunity lay before me. But ... well, to put it plainly she turned aside from my advances. She wanted us to be friends only; even to be a 'brother' to her.

I tell you my boy, that was a novel situation for me!

But to placate the suspicious, edgy Marianne it became obvious to me that I had to buckle down to my legal career and smooth the path of my domestic situation. And for a while things began to go well. Some of the English finance houses in New York placed their prize cases in my hands and I handled such shipping-contract disputes with considerable success. Marianne, Blanche and I were now staying at the Clarendon Hotel but she remained as suspicious as ever each time I failed to return at what she deemed to be a reasonable hour. It was useless pointing out to her that court hearings often took place outside the city, that I had given up my work for the *Clipper* at her behest, and that I was truly a reformed character. From time to time she seemed to be softening in her attitude, but then Mrs Grimshaw would pour some more temperance poison in her ear and the cross-examinations would begin again. But there were times when she seemed pleased, not least when I got the brief in my first big criminal case. It concerned a man called Radetzki, charged with murdering a German called Felimer. It meant my travelling to Freehold, New Jersey to take on the district attorney but I was able to return to the Clarendon jubilant. She even smiled when I showed her the *New York Times* report next day, where it extolled my performance in securing an acquittal for my client and stated there was no reason now why I should not obtain almost a monopoly of criminal business in the state.

But my relief was short-lived. And it all came crashing down within weeks when Marianne discovered a small packet of letters that Adah had written to me from Baltimore. They were innocent enough, but the fact a correspondence had been carried on was enough. Another furious explosion occurred.

Women!

Then a week or so later it all finally boiled over when I was briefed to defend a lady by the name of Mary Real.

You know, forty years ago in England murder by poison was all the rage. I myself handled a few briefs where I demonstrated the white powder had been used as an 'inheritance-hastener.' It was the poison of choice for women. Arsenic was easily available for innocent domestic purposes, of course, as a cosmetic, or wallpaper soaking, or rat eradication. But it was also used widely by women seeking to get rid of husbands or lovers, usually by hiding the white powder in food or drink. Things could be complicated because some men also used it occasionally as an aphrodisiac as well as a murder weapon: there were, as I recall, certain ingenious instances when the arsenic was administered anally – by way of an enema liquid – and even by inserting an arsenic-powdered finger into a woman's cunny after coition as a farewell gift to an unwanted mistress. Indeed, there were rumours that the death of King Ladislas of Naples himself was caused by an enemy concealing arsenic in the king's mistress's vagina. Quite how the lady was persuaded to become an accomplice in this matter has always puzzled me, not least because in due course it killed her as well as the King, but there you are: women can be persuaded to do so many strange things if you use the right honeyed words. Perhaps the assassin persuaded her it would improve her complexion. Or her performance.

I prosecuted the pharmacist-surgeon Palmer, of course, as I told you earlier, but he was one of the few exceptions: male poisoners were rare, and the use of poisons was regarded in England as a peculiarly female method of murder. What's this got to do with Mary Real? Nothing, really. The fact is, Joe, she was made of different calibre: the subtle use of arsenic was not for her. There was nothing secretive about her despatch of her husband: she just flourished a pistol and shot him dead in public. Her husband, Peter Real, was a shopkeeper with a wandering eye. He kept a store at 256 Broadway where his wife Mary resided, but he also supported a mistress glorying in the name of Miss Dorothea Van Name. The suspicious Mary one day trailed him when he left the shop and saw him behaving in an intimate fashion with Miss Van Name, on the Jersey City ferry of all places. She went straight back to the store with her suspicions confirmed, obtained her husband's pistol and when Peter returned she shot him stone dead.

I was briefed for the defence and to me and the larger part of the public it was clear that this was a *crime passionel* – and I had no doubt that with my forensic eloquence I could get her off the murder charge.

I said so to Marianne.

She stunned me with her reply.

'Is she pretty?'

'What? I suppose so, but–'

'No doubt that's why you agreed to defend her! In so doing, do you intend dwelling upon the irresponsible behaviour of the dead man in order to get Mrs Real off the charge of murder?'

Off balance for the moment, almost casually, I confirmed that would be my approach. 'Naturally! I can sway the jury–'

'And I suppose you intend to do so by pointing out the abominable behaviour of the dead man, the kind of behaviour for which *you yourself* have become notorious?'

'Me? Notorious? I protest! Marianne, I really don't know–'

'Let me make one thing clear,' my wife said icily. 'If you enlarge in the courtroom upon the provocation given to Mary Real by her husband's notorious liaison with Miss Van Name, I shall stand up in that same courtroom and publically denounce you for the same species of marital delinquency!'

'This must be a joke!'

'I am adamant!'

'But we are talking about a woman accused of *murder!*'

'There are some crimes more heinous than murder,' she hissed venomously.

'But why ... what is this about ... we had an arrangement–'

'It did not include the frequenting of the infamous houses that you've been attending on the pretext it's connected with your work. It did not include that actress woman you've become infatuated with!' Her eyes were blazing. I knew she was deadly serious. 'I shall be there in court, and if you fail to heed my warning, you shall face the consequences!'

Of course I blustered, talked about the honour and responsibilities of my calling, pleaded with her to think of the unfortunate Mrs Real facing the executioner, but nothing I said made any impact. And she was there, right enough, on the opening day of the trial. Of course I roughly handled the witnesses presented by the prosecution, but Marianne had warned me in advance, and she did not keep her silence. Throughout my perform-ance, when I attacked Miss Van Name with some ferocity, her loud muttering came to the attention of all those seated near her. It unnerved me, I can tell you, so much that

191

when it was time to open the defence I thought it best to let my associate Tom Dunphy take the stage. The next three days were hell; tirades at home followed by caustic comments from the well of the court. I was forced to keep my head down, indulge in no flights of rhetoric and at the end I knew the defence was falling apart. At that point, in desperation, unable to speak of Peter Real's reprehensible character and behaviour, I had no other choice than to change the line of defence, to one of temporary insanity on the part of my client. Even that did not save me. I made the error of using the phrase 'profligacy with other women'. The disturbances from Marianne's muttering became even greater and everyone seated near my wife was much entertained by her comments. I was not.

The misery ended on the fifth day – five days I still shudder to look back upon. Mary Real was found guilty of murder in the third degree. Fortunately the jury, clearly feeling I had put forward a weak defence, made a recommendation to mercy.

For me, there was no mercy, either from a critical press or my wife. When Mary Real went to prison in the Tombs, I had to get on with my next case, in which I had to touch upon the moral lapses of persons placed in high positions in New York society. The advocate facing me found himself the recipient of a deluge of anonymous notes suggesting certain events in my own life which he might use to telling effect. They came from Marianne.

My wife was still staying at the Clarendon with Blanche. I had moved out. Life was becoming intolerable. In a letter to Adah I told her all about it. She advised me to go back to Marianne, make up the quarrel. Even she did not understand. Marianne was like an avenging angel.

I knew the marriage was over, and that November Marianne filed for divorce, on the grounds of my adultery. I denied the charge, of course. But when the issue came up again in January 1863, she named some actresses I had become friendly with in the course of my work for the *Clipper*. She did not name Adah, probably because she thought Adah would give as good as she got. I was expected to put in an appearance to defend myself, denying the adultery. When the day came, I was not there and Judge Barnard gave her the decree she wanted; *a vinculo matrimonii*, freeing both of us from the bonds of marriage. Bonds indeed!

My failure to appear that day was the result partly of my reluctance to expose myself in public to her vituperative tongue; I had also thought hard about the situation over the Christmas period. It was clear to me that there was little point in struggling to hang on to the marriage: the financial support had already been withdrawn by Marianne, and there was little likelihood it would be resumed. So I was cut free, and she and her now smirking daughter could return to England, or France, or wherever they wished to resume their lives.

But the more important reason for my non-appearance at the divorce court hearing was that I had been called to another meeting at the Union Club. Colonel Lafayette Baker had bounced back. It seemed Secretary of War Stanton could not do without his services. The Colonel was being reinstated.

He sat there with a stiff whisky in his hand. He was now clean-shaven – as though to emphasize his determination on reinstatement – clear-eyed and confident. He gave me a flashing smile. 'I am reinstalled as head of Intelligence. We have established a new unit: the National Detective Force. And I want you in Washington, Mr James. I want you linked up with Charles Di Rudio again you worked well together here in New York. You can do so again.'

'Washington? But why–'

Baker smiled in grim satisfaction and his ferrety eyes narrowed. 'I want you there, because a national emergency has arisen. And one of your theatre acquaintances is involved.'

'A theatre acquaintance?'

'Indeed. A man with whom you have trod the boards. One John Wilkes Booth.'

'He's *involved?* In what?'

'It seems, my friend, there is a plot to kidnap the president!'

PART 4

1

She was dead by the age of thirty-two, you know.

Who? Not Marianne – she was a survivor! No, Adah Menken, of course.

Shortly after my divorce in 1863, I saw Adah for the last time. It was not in pleasant circumstances. You could say she was somewhat addicted to marriage, though not divorce. She got married four times, it seems: first to the strait-laced Mr Menken, who objected to her smoking, then to my pugilist client J.C. Heenan, thirdly to the infatuated poet Robert Newell and finally to the rather shady Captain Barklay who turned out to be one of Colonel Lafayette Baker's Secret Service agents, like me. Not that I was aware of it at the time.

What happened was that a pregnant Adah married Barklay, changed her mind after three days and tried to commit suicide. I got a message from her maid – a former actress I knew – and hurried down to her hotel. We pumped the pills out of her, and a few days later I booked her passage to Europe. Never saw her again. But she was a roaring success on the stage in London, Charles Dickens became a friend, that pretentious idiot Swinburne became her lover to much ridicule and speculation about what they actually got up to together in view of his sadomasochistic tendencies, and then she went off to Paris. I saw a copy of the rather risqué photographs of her with the elderly Alexandre Dumas, from which it was clear they had become lovers, and then, just a year or so later, she was dead. Alone. In a Paris boarding house. There was some confusion about the cause of death: some said it was the result of an accident, earlier, when she had fallen from her horse on stage. But it was a low-key funeral, anyway. Apart from the pall-bearers, no one turned up, it seems.

What? The plot against the president? Yes, sorry, my mind has been wandering again, though it's all part of a pattern, really. Time and consequences. Better minds than mine have puzzled over the concept of time – they argue whether it really proceeds always in a forward direction, or whether it can turn back on itself, return to the past... My experience of life makes me believe it's even more complicated – the events in my life have tended to return in a kind of loop to further complicate my existence. Adah, John Sadleir, the Cork Revengers, Mrs Grimshaw and the Reverend Pease, it's all about loops in time and their consequences...

What? Yes, yes, all right, the plot against Lincoln…

I met Charles Di Rudio in Washington and he explained to me what Colonel Lafayette Baker wanted. The former Italian assassin sat there in his Union uniform with his peaked cap placed jauntily over one eye, as he gabbled excitedly in his heavily accented English.

'The Colonel was never very happy about Stanton's concerns regarding the invasion of Canada. He thought we were largely wasting our time when more important issues were raising their heads. Then the Secretary of War got rid of Colonel Baker when the Colonel pointed out he knew Stanton was involved in corrupt military contracts – but now Stanton has had to turn about again. He needs Colonel Baker's skills, and the Colonel needs us to undertake the necessary tasks.'

'Regarding the plot to kidnap the president?'

'Exactly, Mr James.'

'But what do we – what do *I* have to offer him here in Washington?'

Charles Di Rudio calmed down a little, leaned back in his chair and lit his pipe. He had thickened during his years in America: the lean, urgent, impassioned assassin of earlier years had grown into a broad-shouldered, somewhat paunchy Union cavalry officer, with his imperial beard and bushy eyebrows which made up for the receding hairline that had broadened his forehead. He appeared to have softened his political feelings also, though perhaps it was the democratic freedoms that America offered that had brought about the change. This did not mean he had discarded a certain cynical view of life and the impact power could have on an individual's actions, as I was to find out in due course.

'It's your experience and reputation as a sporting man and a jolly fellow,' Di Rudio said, emerging from a cloud of blue smoke. 'It's like New York all over again: the way we worked together infiltrating the *Clan na Gael* patriots.'

'That was New York,' I argued. 'Washington has to be a different case.'

'Not at all! You and I, we saw the Five Points and Hell's Kitchen together, the gambling saloons and cellar dives, the whorehouses, the opium joints and the gin palaces, but believe me Washington is little different even if New York is regarded as the wickedest city in the world! Colonel Baker has given me the list his operatives have compiled. There are one hundred and sixty gambling hells in Washington; there are at least three thousand drinking saloons – in some of them you can get a tin cup of whisky for a dime! The Colonel hasn't even bothered to list the brothels – maybe they're too numerous to count. And then there's the impact photography has had on trade: the president himself recently had confiscated $20,000 worth of vile books, pornographic photographs and woodcuts and ordered them burned on the White House lawn. I think it was Mrs Lincoln who was behind that particular cull: she has something of a small-town mentality, you know, among her other weaknesses. So you see, the work we'll be called upon to do will be in the same kind of *milieu* that we found in New York. You're going to be a jolly fellow again; you and I are going to frequent the saloons and keep our eyes and ears open. And there's the theatres, also.' He drew on his pipe again, exclaimed irritably when he realized the tobacco was no longer alight, and threw it down on the table at his side. 'I am told you are acquainted with the brothers Booth.'

I was indeed.

I had seen the acting brothers on stage in New York in *Julius Caesar*, and had written a review for the *Clipper*. I had been backstage with them, and dined with them. The older, Edwin Booth, was not only performing to considerable acclaim, but was also managing the Winter Garden Theatre at that time, staging mainly Shakespearean tragedies. He was famed for his performance as Hamlet. He was more handsome and much better

203

known than his younger brother, John Wilkes Booth, but I knew them both well enough: I had even at one point shared a stage with the two brothers. I played Friar Laurence, in *Romeo and Juliet*. It was a benefit night, a celebration of the Shakespeare centennial in New York, and my performance was eulogized by the *New York Times*. Acting again? It was not on my part a decision to turn away from my legal career. I had taken the part knowingly: it would have curiosity value and could widen the range of my acquaintances. And more important, I enjoyed it after the inevitable feeling of depression consequent upon my quarrels with Marianne and her courtroom harassment. No, I still knew my best chance of success lay in the courtroom, not treading the boards. I had long since given up that idea and the hope of theatrical fame.

'But what have the brothers Booth to do with our work?' I asked.

'Not Edwin Booth. He's a staunch Unionist. It's the younger one we'll be watching.'

The two brothers, I knew, were not the greatest of friends. On the stage, the younger brother lacked the other's culture and grace – though Walt Whitman thought he had 'real genius' – but they also held different political views. Edwin Booth moved in Judge Daly's circles socially and was open about his Union support. Indeed, I recall attending a dinner party at Judge Daly's when Mrs Daly gushed about Edwin Booth, in the middle of her usual prattling gossip.

'There is a clique of fast young married women here in New York, Mr James. You must have heard the scandal concerning the family of Mr Austin Stevens – his daughter Mrs Peter Strong has been behaving shamelessly with her brother-in-law, while coming and going to evening service no less! And then, I know you as a patron of the theatre and you know our dear friend Edwin Booth. He is so silent, dark and Gawain-looking, don't you think so? He is engaged, you know, to a lady of good family, and only two years after the sad death of his dear wife! You will know his brother too! Quite a different political opinion there!'

When she got on to the subject of Colonel Lafayette Baker, I became uncomfortable.

'Judge Pierrepoint was here and fulminated about Colonel Baker: he claimed the Colonel was arresting honest, inoffensive men and sending them to prison in Washington! We, however, are grateful that he has been getting hold of public thieves and bounty hunters!'

Hastily I returned to the theme of more interest to me.

'You spoke of John Wilkes Booth, Mrs Daly.'

'Ah yes. Edwin supports the Union cause

as we do, but John Wilkes Booth on the other hand is more fiery and headstrong, makes no secret of his Secessionist sympathies, and particularly so when he plays in Albany and Boston, St Louis, and Chicago, where he knows his views could have popular support. Mr Lincoln has always been a president who lacked total support for his war against the South.'

So it was common gossip that John Wilkes Booth often spouted his views in public. He also seemed to be the recipient of funds from a mysterious source, which permitted him to invest successfully in land speculation in Boston. Unfortunately, Mrs Daly offered no gossip on that matter. I learned the truth about that later, from Colonel Baker.

But Charles Di Rudio was telling me that the younger Booth was involved in something more than political ranting. I shook my head doubtfully. 'Are you seriously suggesting young Booth is involved in a plot to kidnap Mr Lincoln?'

'That is the rumour that Colonel Baker is asking us to confirm. Or not.'

'It seems something of a fantasy,' I murmured.

'One attempt has already been made, Mr James.' When my eyes widened in surprise, he went on. 'An announcement had been made that the president was to attend a performance of the play *Still Waters Run Deep* at the Soldiers' Home, three miles outside Washington. It seems the Secessionist group arranged for a look-out while they armed themselves with ropes, rifles and repair tools. They planned to extend the ropes across the road to delay pursuing cavalry after they snatched Mr Lincoln from his carriage, while the group rode on for Port Tobacco. That's about thirty-six miles from Washington. They were going to ferry the president across to Virginia.'

'So what happened?'

Di Rudio's eyes narrowed. 'When they attacked the carriage, they quickly discovered the person inside was not the president. Their plot had been discovered by Colonel Baker. The conspirators fled, and were not caught. But Stanton is certain they hope to strike again. It's to be our task to confirm the identity of the conspirators – and bring about their arrest.'

'But how can we hope to do that?'

Di Rudio smiled and stroked his beard. 'We have an informant. One of the band itself. All we need to do is keep watch on the group, and act when the time is ripe.'

'When will that be?'

'Who can say, at the moment? But we need to become jolly fellows again, Mr James. Eyes and ears open.'

Well, I have to admit it was not an uncongenial task, visiting with some regularity the entertainment centres offered by Washington's sporting life. And that's how Di Rudio and I spent much of our time in the ensuing weeks. And I came up with some surprising information, not least with regard to the security arrangements surrounding the president.

Of course, Colonel Lafayette Baker and his secret agents comprised one level of protection – they had discovered the first plot to kidnap Lincoln, and had foiled it. But there were others charged with protecting the president, men who were not under Colonel Baker's control. There were four personal bodyguards employed by the Washington Metropolitan Police Force.

One of them was a dissolute, unreliable officer by the name of John F. Parker.

I first came across him at a house of assignation controlled by the buxom, bosomy Miss Annie Wilson. I am forced to admit that I was present at her establishment for personal reasons, rather than in pursuit of my investigative duties for Colonel Baker. Nor was Di Rudio with me – he never seemed to suffer from the normal lusts of the flesh that occasionally drove me towards the Miss Wilsons of the Washington underworld. On this particular occasion, I was being entertained by Annie Wilson herself in the front parlour of the establishment, carrying on the

208

kind of genteel conversation that was her normal precursor to an enthusiastic romp in a bedroom upstairs, when the altercation in the adjoining room began. One of the clients had apparently arrived in a state of considerable intoxication, but because of his status as a police officer, no action had been taken other than to put him to bed with a young whore called Miss Elsie Green. But he was still in a wild state and using highly offensive language in describing the character of one of his fellow officers with whom he had quarrelled. He had finally waved his pistol around and then discharged it through the window. Elsie screamed, Annie screamed, my ardour vanished, and I decided to leave the establishment as soon as possible, but was unable to do so before a clutch of constables arrived.

Annie had recovered her poise by then and told the officers it had all been a mistake, but they had recognized their colleague – who was not popular among them – and took him into custody. I learned later that the Police Board had, somewhat mysteriously, thrown out the charge of disorderly conduct in a whorehouse. John F. Parker – it was he who had discharged the pistol – clearly had influential friends.

I thought no more of it at the time until, some months later, I found myself in an opium den run by a Chinese immigrant called Charley Yong. This time I *was* there working for Colonel Baker: I had never been a habitual user of opium. Charles Di Rudio and I had received information via Colonel Baker – presumably from his inside informant – that the kidnap gang included a young man by the name of David Herold. I had made his acquaintance casually, and discovered him to be an unlikely conspirator: he was boyish in appearance, trivial in manner, and almost witless in my opinion. He was of pleasant but trifling disposition, and fond of his drink. He also regularly partook of the recreative drug. I followed him when he entered Charley Yong's opium establishment in Pell Street.

You seem surprised. Chinese dens in Washington? You'll have seen many in the course of your seafaring, no doubt: dens in Singapore and Hong Kong, Marseilles and Sydney, and I've no doubt they'll have been more exotic than those in American cities! But I can tell you that such dens – or 'joints' as they were known in America – flourished both in Washington and New York, and were frequented by a wide range of individuals from all levels of society. Charley Yong himself maintained rooms at two levels in Fell Street and prided himself on the status of the clients who used the more discreet upper floor: politicians, judges, actors, wealthy gentlemen addicted to the pleasures of the pipe. Less well-heeled clients used the lower rooms and the crowded, fetid cellar. Laudanum, tincture of opium, pills and pipes, these were opiates which could induce pleasurable sensations as well as the relief of pain or discomfort: the alleviation of pain was usually provided by pills, while the more relaxing sensations came from smoking the drug. Men, and women – including half-naked whores plying their trade – used the joints and it was not unusual to see convivial little groups, chatting, smoking, whispering, giggling. It was always a scene of relaxation: the drug purveyed in the joints produced a feeling of warm, intimate good fellowship, an opportunity to lie down on a bunk and converse harmlessly with the friend who took a bunk by your side, even if you had never met him before in your life.

But on this particular occasion, while hoping that I might be near Herold and hear some indiscreet comments appertaining to plots against the president, the man I found myself close to turned out to be the police officer John F. Parker. To my astonishment, he rather casually boasted, in between puffs of the pipe, that he had been assigned to the bodyguard staff at the White House, by none other than Mrs Lincoln herself!

As I said, I was never a great partaker of opium and had taken a mere whiff of the pipe provided, in order to keep my wits about me, and as I lay beside Parker's bunk curiosity overtook me. 'White House guard? That must be an enormously important position for you to hold.'

'Aye, it is that,' Parker replied, rolling his eyes at the dark ceiling. 'And that in spite of the bad cess I get from the other officers at the force. I've been victimized, you know; there's them that don't like me, and try to do me down. But I outwitted them. Joe Parker knows his way around, believe me, my friend.'

He took a long draw at his pipe and re-mained happily silent for a little while. But he was keen to continue boasting of his good fortune. 'You'll be wondering how it was I got the attention of Mrs Lincoln herself, no doubt.'

'She is your patron?'

'I got the letter of appointment to the White House direct from her hand,' he announced proudly, with a certain slurring of tone as he waved his pipe airily about him

'Did you provide her with some service while working on the force?'

He chuckled throatily. 'You could say that, my friend. Here, look at this.'

He drew from his pocket a letter. It was on Executive Mansion headed notepaper. I can recall the wording even now, so astonished was I:

This is to certify that John F. Parker, a member of the Metropolitan Police, has been detailed for duty at the Executive Mansion by order of Mrs Lincoln.

The First Lady had signed it with a flourish.

Officer Parker giggled. 'It's me passport, ye see! The draft had been announced, and they was taking officers from the stations to serve in the Union Army, just like anyone else who didn't have three hundred dollars to excuse theirselves! I knew I'd be in the next draft, so I asked her to exempt me, and so she did!'

'But did you know her well?' I enquired, astonished. 'I mean, you're an officer on the beat—'

He chuckled again, evilly. 'It's not that I knew her well – though she's aware of me now! It's the company I keep. One of my drinking friends happens to be a coachman at the White House, and he drives Mrs Lincoln on her shopping expeditions. And he's become friendly, *very* friendly, with one of her personal maids. And do ye know what he had to tell me? Mrs Lincoln, she and her husband have certain points of disagreement, and so she's had occasion to tell Old Abe something less than the truth from time to time.'

I was intrigued. 'She holds things back

from him?'

A haze of smoke was wreathed above Parker's head; he contemplated it for a little while, dreamily, before answering. That was what the denizens of the joints loved more than anything else: the sense of dreaming, refreshment of the soul, escape from the brutal realities of life.

'She's nothing more than a country woman at heart, you know. Clumsy, ill-dressed, intensely jealous of her husband and highly nervous in polite society. But she's keen to make a show in Washington, demonstrate she's the First Lady of the land! It began with the interior decoration of the White House: she spent her Treasury allowance three times over and there was a great row with Old Abe, apparently, when he found out. He insisted she cut back on her expenditure. But she's a flibbertigibbet, don't know the value of money, and don't care much either. From what my friend the coachman told me, she kept shopping and she got deep in debt. Fifteen hundred dollars for a set of china! The woman's mad! And then I was told she fiddled the bill so that it showed the price as three thousand!'

'You're saying she's been defrauding the Treasury?'

'Well, she clearly pocketed the difference and is still thousands in debt. But I learned from what the coachman – and his little maid – told me she was terrified that the president found out what she'd been up to. The sum of twenty-seven thousand dollars has been mentioned. All spent on fripperies – against the president's express injunction!'

I could now guess at what had happened. 'You managed to have a quiet word with Mrs Lincoln.'

'Ha! That's it exactly, my friend. That's how she came to write the exemption letter. I might not be the best copper on the beat, but I'm one of the smartest when it comes to seeing an opportunity. She was quick as a frightened rabbit to call for my appointment to the White House. And, of course, I learned to look the other way when she was off on her shopping sprees. It's about scratching backs, ain't it? Me ... and the First Lady!'

The conversation came to an end at that point, when I saw that David Herold, higher than Haman, was leaving his bunk, weaving his way towards the exit. I took my leave of John F. Parker and at a discreet distance kept watch on the suspected Confederate conspirator. And I made the mistake of not reporting the Parker conversation immediately to Colonel Lafayette Baker.

Who knows what might have happened had I done so?

Most men wish to leave a mark on the world. A name inscribed on a gravestone, charitable foundations in the name of the giver, the erection of an hotel or a palace or a prison. In America, a young, sprawling country, there were many such opportunities for eternal fame. John Surratt took one such opportunity. He did what many did: he built a three-storied house in an unoccupied area, then when others built nearby he caused the group of houses to be named after him, as the first settler.

Surrattsville, some thirty miles or so from Washington.

It was in a house at Surrattsville – Mrs Surratt's own house, as it turned out, since her husband had passed on some time previously – that the conspirators had arranged to meet.

Neither Di Rudio nor I had any indication of how Colonel Baker had picked up this information: he hinted it came from his informant inside the group and seemed disinclined to tell us the identity of the individual. But he was certainly able to tell us not only of the location, but also the date of the meeting when all conspirators would be assembled. He also had their names – it was our task to listen in to their discussions, and confirm the identities. The almost imbecile David Herold was one. The others were a giant of a man called Lewis Paine, a nondescript little man of German ancestry and little breeding by the name of Atzerodt, an Irish renegade called O'Loughlin and a

216

former Confederate soldier who answered to the name of Sam Arnold.

'We've intercepted a letter from Arnold to the leader of the conspiracy, John Wilkes Booth,' Colonel Baker informed us at our rendezvous. 'We now know them, but we need to learn of their intentions. After that, the whole thing can be nipped in the bud. So, gentlemen, to Surrattsville and your listening post immediately.'

And that's exactly what it turned out to be.

We rode to Surrattsville, Charles Di Rudio and I, and stabled our horses at a livery on the edge of the small town. We made our way on foot to Mary Surratt's house where all was dark. As we had been informed, the entrance at the back of the house was unlocked and the house itself was empty. We proceeded, as under Colonel Baker's instructions, to the first floor and entered the room at the end of the gable-roofed property. It was used to store lumber. There was a dirty stretch of carpet in the centre of the narrow room: we rolled it back as instructed and sure enough discovered that two small holes had been drilled in the planking that served as a floor.

We sat down in the darkness and waited for dawn.

After a while, I said, 'I'm not convinced this is a good idea. If we're discovered here, what story do we have to tell? There'll be no escape, certainly.'

Charles Di Rudio grunted and tapped at his belt. 'Don't worry. I'm armed.'

'As am I! But I feel we're being set up here! How did the Colonel arrange all this? Who's his informant? And if Mrs Surratt lets these rooms–'

'Colonel Baker knows what he's doing, James. All we have to do is sit tight and wait.'

The conspirators arrived at ten in the morning.

Mrs Surratt herself had been in the house for an hour, busying herself without climbing the stairs – to my considerable relief, I assure you! Through the spyhole, which gave us a view of the sitting room below, I caught a few glimpses of her as she moved about, tidying the room: a well-built woman in her early forties, I calculated, brown-haired, of a pleasant enough appearance. Charles Di Rudio was at the other spyhole: he made a few notes in his pocketbook. The first of the conspirators to arrive was the man I had been trailing in New York and Washington: David Herold. Mrs Surratt made him a cup of coffee and chatted for a little while, but I thought I detected a certain tension in her voice; Colonel Baker had told us she was a Confederate sympathizer, the widow of an avowed Secessionist, and was lending the safety of her home to the plotting group, but was probably too nervous to become deeply involved. This was confirmed shortly after the second arrival made his appearance.

'George Atzerodt,' Rudio whispered to me.

I could see him when he sat down, a shrinking kind of man, quite unlike the individual who entered a little while later; a big, hulking, confident young fellow who greeted Atzerodt with a slap on the shoulder and for whom David Herold nervously relinquished a chair immediately.

'Lewis Paine,' Rudio whispered, and entered the name in his pocketbook. 'According to the Colonel there should be three more to come.'

They were all in place around the table when Mary Surratt left them to their discussions; Herold, Atzerodt, Paine, O'Loughlin, Sam Arnold ... and John Wilkes Booth.

He was last to arrive, neatly dressed, handsome, swaggering in confidently, clearly regarding himself as the head of the conspiracy and a figure of importance. You know, that was the trouble with Wilkes Booth; he saw life as a theatre, and had always tended to over-dramatize his role in life. He thought he was a man of consequence and boasted of his wealth – though was reticent when it came to disclosure of the sources of his funds. He considered himself to be the leading stage actor of his day – even though he was outshone by his older brother, Edwin Booth.

And he possessed a fatal urge for romantic gestures.

Sprawled upstairs, Charles Di Rudio and I listened silently as the discussions began – first, by way of what nearly amounted to a quarrel over the failure of the attempt to kidnap the president on Tobacco Road. It was Booth who had organized the attempt but who now sought to lay the blame for the fiasco on the unfortunate David Herold – an easy target, a man who was far too weak an individual to defend himself. Lewis Paine took Herold's part, arguing it was the failure of intelligence received that lay at the heart of the matter, and he hinted darkly that in his opinion Lafayette Baker's Secret Service had foreknowledge of the plot, which suggested they had a traitor in their midst.

I shivered at the thought, for it amounted to reality.

Atzerodt had risen from the table, and was pacing the room. He came in and out of my line of sight: he appeared nervous, distraught, excited. It occurred to me that Paine's accusation that the group held a traitor had unnerved him, and I began to suspect that he himself might be the man. I had seen too many men in the witness box, quailing at their own inner guilts, to be far wrong in my assumptions and I glanced at Di Rudio, considered sharing my thoughts but he was concentrating on the scene below.

Booth had called the group to order.

'Recriminations are useless. The past is behind us! What we must do is advance! We are all determined to carry out this kidnapping: it will send a clarion call throughout the Southern States, bring Lincoln's minions to heel, and put iron into the veins of all true supporters of the South! Holding the president will give us a bargaining tool to bring the Union to the negotiating table!'

Herold's tone was plaintive. 'I don't see why we can't stick to the original plan. Since our failure, it seems the president has passed over the Eastern Branch Bridge accompanied by his coachmen and a single guard within the carriage. We can still do it: we need not change our plans!'

Booth made an angry, theatrical gesture, flinging out an arm.

'It's not merely the fact of kidnapping Lincoln that is important! I insist we must do it in a manner that will resound throughout the world! We know of the so-called president's love of the theatre – even if we deplore his low tastes. I believe we must carry out this endeavour in a spectacular fashion: we should seize the man in his own private box at the theatre. I myself shall do it, with Paine's brute strength to assist me! Arnold, your part will be to lower Lincoln, trussed up

221

like a turkey, down to the stage. The theatre will be in uproar but we will succeed. We shall take him to a waiting conveyance, take him south and the world will marvel at our audacity!'

'There will be a guard in the box!' Arnold protested.

'That will be attended to,' Booth replied sternly.

'We'll need assistance from the stage hands—'

'It can be organized! My contacts in the theatre have already been consulted!' Booth insisted, wild-eyed. 'There is a man called Samuel Chester who has agreed to help us. The main regulating valve for the gas in the theatre is located near the prompter's desk. Chester will be on hand to turn it off. Darkness, confusion, uproar – and there shall we be, hurtling into the night, thundering to the South with Lincoln in our grasp!'

I glanced again at Di Rudio, amazed. He displayed no emotion but was riveted to his spyhole. I could not believe he was unmoved by the ridiculous nature of Booth's plan. It was farcical, the product of a monomaniacal mind rooted in theatrical unrealities.

I was not alone in the thought.

A chair scraped back. It was the burly Irishman, O'Loughlin. 'I've heard enough. This is crazy. Booth, you must be out of your mind. An adventure like this might be carried out on the stage, in a melodrama, but what you suggest is utterly impracticable. I'll have nothing to do with it!'

Silence fell. Beside me, the prone form of Di Rudio wriggled uncomfortably. We lay there listening as the argument began. Booth was alone – apart from the uncertain Herold – in his insistence that a grand gesture such as he had described was necessary. It was clear to me that, though he was outvoted by his less romantically inclined co-conspirators, he would not be moved. He sulked, he waved their objections aside, and it was obvious that he would play the game according to his rules, or else he would not play at all.

And when, finally outvoted by the others, he folded his arms across his narrow chest, glared around at the group and made an alternative proposition, silence fell.

'There is another way forward. Assassination.'

Immediately, Di Rudio raised his head and glanced at me. I wondered what he was thinking. After all, he had walked that road himself in his attempt to assassinate Napoleon III in Paris that night five years ago. He had since changed his way of life, become a Union soldier and a spy and now he was hearing another would-be assassin declare his intentions.

The silence in the room below was profound. It was broken at last by Sam Arnold. 'Murder? We've not raised this earlier. I'll have nothing to do with this!'

'It will be a heroic deed carried out on the public stage!' Booth declared passionately. 'Imagine: the large Washington theatre, packed with the great and the good, the best of Northern society, the cream of–'

'Booth, you're a madman!' It was O'Loughlin again. 'Kidnapping, yes: I see the logic of that, the holding of a trump card while the war goes badly for the South, an opportunity to negotiate, to bring about the collapse of Lincoln's government. But assassination, no! I wash my hands of this, Booth. Even if we kidnapped Lincoln, if Lee surrenders, which soon might occur, that in itself will have little practical value. But murder ... there would be nothing to be gained from such a mad scheme! I've had enough. I'm leaving.'

'And I too,' said Arnold.

They moved from our vision, and Di Rudio and I, we heard the front door slam as O'Loughlin and Sam Arnold left the house.

There was little further talk below. A nervous reluctance seemed to have fallen upon Herold and Atzerodt, while Booth seemed almost stunned by the desertion of two of his band. In a little while, the group dispersed with muttered goodbyes. We caught no suggestion of a further meeting. Silence fell upon the empty house, and Di Rudio stretched his limbs; I rose to my feet, stiffly. I could not think of what to say. I watched as Di Rudio pocketed his notes, looked about him at the drifting motes of dust floating in the dim light creeping through the small windows of the old house.

'We'd better leave while we can. The conspirators have broken up early, but we don't know when Mrs Surratt will return. We should go. Now.' He stared at me, his mouth set in a grim line. 'We have a great deal to report to Colonel Baker.'

2

Colonel Lafayette Baker was in a strange mood. While Di Rudio and I sat in Baker's office, the colonel himself seemed unable to remain still. He paraded the length of the room, turned, retraced his steps time and again. He puffed furiously at a cigar, and seemed to be muttering obscenities under his breath. His coffee lay untasted and cold, and he seemed hardly aware of our presence, snorting occasionally in disgust. At last he walked to the window, opened it wide and took in deep breaths of air. We heard the sounds of the street traffic rumbling past, rattling wheels, the cries of vendors, the barking of dogs chasing the snuffling pigs that wandered the unpaved streets.

Colonel Baker turned away from the window and glared at us with undisguised displeasure.

'I read your report on those damned conspirators. I took it straight to the Secretary of War.'

He seemed to be struggling to say more. When the words came they were underscored with anger.

'Stanton dismissed the report with an airy

wave of the hand! He said that Wilkes Booth was nothing but a jumped-up actor of no talent, who dreamed of action but would be incapable of it, was boastful, disorganized – and not to be taken account of!' Baker snorted again, and clenched his right hand in fury. 'I suggested to him that in view of your report, surveillance should be carried out more closely on the damned actor but he waved it aside. I gave him my opinion that the president should be given a stronger armed guard and he announced he had already advised Mr Lincoln on that and the president had refused to countenance the extra expenditure. *Expenditure!* While that damned wife of his fritters away a fortune in public money on unnecessary frills and fur-belows at the Executive Mansion and Stanton himself, to my personal knowledge, is taking kickbacks on military contracts!'

I glanced at Di Rudio uncertainly. 'We both agreed that Booth seemed ... committed. And I've met one of the president's personal guards. A man called Parker. I would not regard him as an able man.'

'Parker? That no-account copper? He's inveigled himself into Mrs Lincoln's favour and it's too late now to do anything about that.' He shook his head, and sighed. 'And there's nothing I can do to persuade Stanton to take your report seriously. When I insisted, he told me coolly that my services – and that means yours as well – are no longer required in Washington. I am required to take up surveillance of the damned Fenians again, in New York. As for you, James, and Di Rudio, you'll receive your stipend for this month and then you can both go about your business. It's back to your New York law practice for you, Mr James! Lieutenant Di Rudio, I've made arrangements for you to join the Ohio cavalry unit which is supposed to guard the president, and you'll act as my liaison with the War Department. I want an eye kept on developments regarding Stanton's activities. You'll report to me. I'm convinced there's something fishy going on, and I don't trust that weasel Stanton.'

He had never previously expressed himself so forcibly in regard to the Secretary of War. But I knew they had a history of dis-agreements. As for me, the New York law practice… I sighed. Tom Dunphy had been holding the fort during my lengthy absences in Washington, but he was not pleased – and not doing well. The shipping firm work had dried up, and echoes of the Mary Real trial fiasco still resounded to my discredit, so little by way of criminal briefs was coming in. But perhaps it was time I stepped aside from this cloak-and-dagger work and buckled down to my true *métier* again.

I arranged to take the same train back to New York as did Colonel Baker. We would be travelling in separate compartments.

My feelings at that time? Well, Joe, I still felt I could make a name for myself at the New York City Bar, and Stanton had promised me he would support me in my candidature for a judicial post if I assisted Colonel Baker. Well, that was over now – I needed to return to New York, enlarge my practice and wait for the next judicial election, when I would call in my dcbt from Stanton.

'But how could the Secretary of War receive our report in such an offhand manner?' I wondered, as Di Rudio and I sat in a downtown saloon later that evening by way of saying goodbye and heading off in our different directions.

The gallant lieutenant shrugged. 'Who knows what makes the mind of a politician tick? He has much on his plate, of course, but the war is coming to an end, General Lee is on the point of surrender, and there is an election looming.'

'Will Lincoln be returned?'

'He is unpopular, but with the war coming to a successful conclusion, I think he will win his second term.'

That evening we parted, expecting it to be the last time we met. That's not how things actually turned out.

My return to New York, and my making use of the contacts I had made in the saloons and bars, brought in some business, but not of the most lucrative kind. My work at the *Clipper* had necessarily come to an end, in view of my absences in Washington. During the following weeks, I had the occasional letter from Adah, who was enjoying a huge success in London and Paris, now counting Charlie Dickens and Algernon Swinburne among her admirers. I was briefed in two murder trials and obtained some publicity in the John Orpen murder case, but it was clear to me now that my chances of reaching the pinnacles I had touched in London were unlikely unless I could get elected as a police court judge. My contacts in Tammany Hall were not proving as effective as I had hoped. So when I was invited back to Washington to draw up a will for a rather acerbic old lady, I decided it was time to beard Stanton at the War Office, to bring to mind his earlier promise to me.

The matter of the will proved to be a rather tricky one. The wealthy old lady in question, a Mrs Van Buren, was estranged from her daughter on account of what she decided was an unwise marriage. The will she asked me to draw up left only a small amount of money to the daughter so I was not surprised when the son-in-law, a Mr Rhea, turned up at my hotel. It was clear he had got wind of what was happening and was incensed: no doubt he had married Mrs

Van Buren's daughter in the hope of eventually coming to share in a fortune.

He sat facing me in my sitting room, a grim-eyed fellow, handsome enough, but with a dissolute mouth marked with discontentment. 'It won't do, Mr James, it won't do.'

'How did you find out about the contents of the will?' I enquired.

'The old lady told my wife. She's always sticking the knife in. She don't like me, that's plain.'

I shrugged. 'I fear there's nothing I can do about that. My task–'

'I got another task for you,' Rhea interrupted. 'I want you to draw up a *second* will.'

'For you? That's no problem–'

'For me? No, damn it! For Mrs Van Buren!'

I leaned back in my chair, folded my hands over my chest and looked him straight in the eye. 'I'm not sure I can do that, Mr Rhea. The ethics of the situation–'

'I ain't interested in ethics, sir! I want only what's right and due for my wife! Look here, you've met Mrs Van Buren. She's a vicious old witch and she'll deal a bad hand to my wife. But she's eighty years old! She can't be long of this world. There might not be time for her to consult you to change her will so I want to make sure that when she nears her end there'll be a document which she's able to sign without the trouble of calling in lawyers again.'

'I still don't see how I can undertake–'

'If she signs the new will you write under my direction, it'll supersede the earlier one, ain't that so? Do it, Mr James, for the sake of my wife's rightful inheritance and there's five hundred dollars in it for you.' He fixed me with those grim eyes. 'And you'll not find us mean-spirited when the old lady's gone. There'll be a further two thousand dollars for you from my wife's inheritance.'

I was silent for a long while. I knew precisely what he had in mind: as the old lady's faculties withered, he was hoping that she could be persuaded to sign the new will, drawn up without her knowledge, for the overturning of her original wishes. I thought about it for several minutes while he waited patiently, like a brooding, narrow-eyed vulture.

I don't deny that the money offer had its effect upon my judgement. But I also reasoned that I would be doing nothing wrong in law, or even ethically. I was merely acting as Rhea's legal representative, drawing up a document in legal form: what he did with it was his affair. I already had Mrs Van Buren as a client, but in my view that did not prevent me taking on her son-in-law as a client in addition. I see you frowning ... well, things were a bit tight at that time, I was in financial trouble again, the practice wasn't going well

– and the developments that Rhea hoped for might never come to pass. So, in a word, I took the five hundred dollars and prepared the second will. After all, it was just a piece of paper, of no legal significance – until the old lady put her signature to it.

What happened after that? Well, the stubborn Mrs Van Buren refused to turn up her toes until some five years later. It seems she did in fact sign the new will, though I don't know how Rhea managed that little trick. Anyway, I later got my two thousand dollars. But Mr Rhea failed in his efforts, finally: the second will was overturned by the courts after a complaint from a distant relative of the family and Mr and Mrs Rhea had to be satisfied with the pittance they received. None of my business of course: I kept my fees – after all, I'd merely been involved as a sort of amanuensis, you might say. There were comments of course, in the press. And I see a frown of disapproval on your face. But I was just acting under instructions, don't you see?

I only mention the Van Buren business, which I see you find disagreeable, because it explains how it was I found myself in Washington on the day General Robert E. Lee surrendered to Union forces at Appomattox. And I was still in the city on the 14 April, 1865.

I stayed on for two reasons: the first was

that the city was celebrating, the end of a long war was in sight and the capital was gaudily bedecked with flags and a grand illumination had been arranged. So much beer flowed in the gutters even the pigs got drunk. As a renowned jolly fellow, I joined in the celebrations in the saloons, but I also had another objective in view. I thought it was now a good time to call on Stanton to fulfil his promise and support my ticket in a judicial election.

So I turned up in the late morning at the War Department and presented my card to a spotty-faced clerk who took it with an undeserved hauteur and sneering eyes behind pince-nez spectacles. I requested that I be allowed to have a private interview with the Secretary of War. The supercilious clerk stared at me in amazement. 'You have no appointment, sir, and it's unlikely you'll get one today.'

Now I have to admit I should have been more sensible, on that day of all days: there was bound to be much coming and going in Stanton's office. But the clerk's attitude annoyed me – I was used to being treated with more deference – and I was also burning with a righteous feeling that Stanton was in my debt after my work for Colonel Baker, and he needed to stick to his promise. So I coldly informed the clerk that I'd wait, while he sent in my card.

He did so with bad grace.

And I waited.

I saw them come and go. General Ulysses Simpson Grant came and went, as did Navy Secretary Gideon Welles. There had been a cabinet meeting that morning and Stanton now held a series of further meetings, clearly discussing the future promotion of the war – he wanted a military territory covering Virginia and North Carolina, I learned later, under his total control of course – but the plan found little support from the others. The president wanted no persecutions, a light hand on the fallen leaders of the Confederacy, and this no doubt angered the disciplinarian Stanton, who wanted reparations, seizures, the ruthless crushing of enemies.

So I waited.

The clerks changed, but attitudes did not. I was there for four hours. And there was no word from Stanton. It was late afternoon when a door opened at the end of the hall and Charles Di Rudio emerged in his lieutenant's uniform. He seemed surprised to see me. I explained the reason for my presence and he shook his head.

'You won't see Stanton. He's already gone home. And there's all hell on.'

'How do you mean?'

'Walk with me, and I'll tell you.'

We left the War Office and found a bar nearby where we settled down to relax with a beer. Lieutenant Di Rudio seemed disturbed.

'You think you know people, by their reputations. Take Grant, for instance. He is reckoned to be a hard, close man. He's never been a parlour politician, always with his men, sharing their hardships, taciturn, in control, a perfect army general. But I suppose we all have our weaknesses. With Grant, it's his wife.'

'I've never heard criticisms of her, or their marriage.'

'Ah, it's not so much about problems within the marriage: Grant is devoted to her and their children. It's that other woman. Mrs Lincoln.'

'How do you mean?'

Di Rudio ran an exasperated hand over his face. 'We know all about the president's dirty jokes, inappropriate language and tall, backwoodsman stories, but Mary Lincoln is insanely jealous and gets into a rage if any other woman is near him. Mrs Grant – who is a wealthy, sophisticated lady – was shouted at by Mrs Lincoln when she was chatting to the president in his carriage, and she has also been denied an invitation to one of those interminable Thursday *soirées* where Mary Lincoln preens herself in unsuitable dresses, and as a result Mrs Grant wants nothing to do with her. It's why Grant was here again, seeing Stanton this afternoon.'

'I still don't understand.'

Di Rudio took a swig of his beer and groaned. 'You've seen the press announcements, surely. The performance of *Our American Cousin* at Ford's Theater tonight.'

'Of course. The president and General Grant will be attending. The theatre is sold out.'

Di Rudio grinned sourly. He put his hand into his jacket, and took out a piece of card. 'Here's a ticket. Exclusive. You can go in my place.'

'I don't understand.'

'Colonel Baker arranged the ticket for me. He wanted me close by, with Grant, in case there was any trouble. But, Grant's not going, so there's no need for me to be present.'

'Not going? Is the General ill?' I enquired.

Di Rudio shook his head morosely. 'No. Believe it or not, Mrs Grant *refuses* to join the presidential party. She doesn't want to be in Mary Lincoln's viperish company. Grant came to see Stanton this afternoon. You can understand his situation: an invitation from the president, to an army man, is the same as a command. He *can't* refuse. But Grant can't persuade his wife; she says she will not be snubbed by *that woman* again. So Grant asked Stanton's advice.'

'And Stanton said...?'

'Unbelievably, he's advised Grant not to

go. On grounds it would be too dangerous –
to have the president and General Grant in
the same box! So Grant should withdraw,
while the president himself goes! What the
hell is going on? Colonel Baker will be
purple when he hears my report. And let's
be clear, you've seen the advertisements put
out by the theatre. Grant's name comes
before Lincoln's. It's Grant the people want
to see: Lincoln is a common sight in Washington. But the crowds have bought tickets
for the theatre performance to see the hero
of Appomattox Court House and there'll be
a stir when he doesn't turn up! And there's
more...'

'Tell me.'

'In the circumstances, the president has
asked for an extra guard for this evening, to
be present in his box. He asked for the muscular Major Eckert. And guess what? Stanton
refused. Said Eckert was busy elsewhere!
What in damnation is going on? Is Lincoln
the Chief Executive or not? He's taken the
matter calmly. I don't think the people will.
Anyway, James, take the ticket. Enjoy the
performance.'

As you'll appreciate, I did not enjoy the
experience. But I took the ticket, went back
to my hotel, changed to go to the theatre,
leaving Di Rudio in the saloon, drinking
himself into steady, morose, Italian oblivion.

So, yes, I was there at Ford's Theater that

evening when the world-shattering events unfolded.

There was the expected buzz of disappointment when the president and his party took their seats in the box just after 8.30 p.m. The audience had wanted to see General Grant, would have been ready to stand and cheer him for his brilliant performances on the battlefield. Instead there was only the president and his wife with a single army officer and his female companion in attendance. The mutters of disappointment continued even after the performance began.

Our American Cousin was never regarded as a distinguished piece of theatre, you know. It had enjoyed a modest run, and that evening I found it not particularly well played. I was bored, in fact: I could have done better myself, in any of the major parts. So when the interval arrived, I decided I would not present myself for the later part of the play. At the intermission, I strolled from the theatre into the street outside, which was still gaily glittering with celebratory lights. There was a saloon near the theatre and I decided to take a drink there, for the night was warm. When I entered, I was met with a wall of sound; all the jolly fellows were enjoying themselves as only they knew how. I began to make my way to the bar but realized I would have difficulty shouldering my way through the mob and decided to leave after all. I turned and as I headed for the doors I caught sight of a face I knew.

Officer John F. Parker, police guard for President Lincoln. He was sitting at a table near the door with two companions, laughing and chattering gaily. I learned later the two companions were Mr Lincoln's footman and the president's coachman. I stood riveted to the spot. What was Parker doing here? He should have been guarding the presidential box ... or perhaps he had been relieved of his duties by a colleague. I stepped out into the street. I will be honest with you, my boy, I cannot say that I had a dreadful pre-sentiment, but I felt a deep curiosity. Stanton had told Grant he should not go to the theatre – which suited Mrs Grant very well – because it would be too dangerous to have both the president and General Grant in the same box. A curious argument, I thought. And now the president's personal guard was not on duty!

So, vaguely disturbed, I went back into the theatre.

I had no problem getting back in. The second part of the play was in full swing. And I had no trouble climbing the stairs that gave access to the presidential box. No one questioned me, no one stopped me. And there was an empty chair outside the box itself. Parker had not been relieved: he had simply absented himself and gone for a drink with his two acquaintances.

Troubled, but more confused than concerned, I reentered the theatre, causing a certain amount of muttering when I disturbed people in regaining my seat. I felt unable to concentrate on the play, but kept glancing up at the presidential box. I could not see Mrs Lincoln nor the army major and the lady accompanying him, but the president was clearly visible, leaning forward, chin in hand, smiling, enjoying the somewhat simple humour of the play. It's a picture that still remains engraved on my memory: my second, and last sight of Abraham Lincoln.

I felt unable to settle, without really knowing why – other than musing over the odd behaviour of Police Officer John Parker. And nothing of interest occurred until the play was well advanced. It was 10.30 p.m. when there were only two actors on stage and the audience were laughing at one of the play's obvious jokes, when the sharp report was heard. I looked up to the presidential box, but Lincoln was not to be seen.

Instead, a few seconds later – I believe the whole event lasted a mere thirty seconds – I caught sight of a man standing on the edge of the box, one hand on the curtain as though to steady himself. It was a theatrical pose, his other hand was raised, and I caught the glint of stage lights on the dagger blade he held. Then, a moment later, he leapt from the box directly onto the stage. It was a dramatic, athletic, stage-worthy entrance but it was somewhat spoiled by the man catching his spur in the flag that adorned the presidential box. He landed on the stage awkwardly, the two players left in confusion, and a general rumble of surprise began to spread through the audience. The man with the dagger stood there on the stage for several seconds, arms held wide, eyes staring, the weapon flourished in his hand. It was almost as though it was part of the drama, something to match Adah Menken's wild ride on her stallion in the role of Mazeppa. But this was no play – though play-acting the man seemed to be.

He stood there, arms raised, staring at the audience and then shouted, almost screamed the lines he had long planned to deliver.

'*Sic semper tyrannis!*'

The actors had already fled the scene. The man with the dagger was hobbling as abruptly he left the stage to plunge behind the billowing back curtains.

The audience was in turmoil after the first stunned murmurs. But I had recognized the man with the dagger. I leapt to my feet.

'*Booth!*' I shouted. 'John Wilkes Booth!'

The man beside me glared at me in brief incomprehension, and then turned and repeated what I had said, until from all corners of the theatre the call was taken up.

'*Booth! Booth! Booth!*'

And yet Secretary of War Stanton did not immediately see fit to name the assassin of President Lincoln: he delayed the announcement until the afternoon papers appeared next day.

3

I returned to my hotel at three in the morning. After the audience had rushed from the theatre and wild rumours were sweeping the city I felt I could not return immediately to my hotel. The saloons and bars – I do not know how many I visited for I was in a state of heightened excitement, and shock – supplied me with all the conflicting news that might be expected. But one certainty was already current: President Lincoln had been assassinated by a shot to the head and the murderer had escaped but was now being hunted throughout the capital. There was no official word of the assassin's identity but I knew who it was, and the name was readily bandied about in the gin palaces.

About half past two in the morning I caught a glimpse of Police Officer John F. Parker in the crowded street. He seemed somewhat dazed, staggering slightly. It could have been the drink, or it could have been recognition of the enormity of his actions in failing to guard the president. He had a woman of the streets in his custody and seemed to be heading for police headquarters. I recognized her: an occasional whore I

244

had myself frequented, by the name of Lizzie Williams. Parker had arrested her: it seemed to me to be a useless attempt by the officer to show that he was still an active upholder of the law, attending to his duties even though he had failed to protect the president. A pathetic atonement for his negligence, perhaps.

Lizzie told me later she was promptly discharged when presented at headquarters.

But when I saw Parker in the street I was exhausted, somewhat inebriated and very confused. I returned to my hotel and went to bed. But I slept badly. Booth ... Mary Surratt's house ... the kidnapping conspiracy ... Booth's suggestion that assassination was a better course. These thoughts whirled in my head. And there was the report Di Rudio and I had prepared for Stanton. The report he had ignored.

And now Lincoln was dead.

I was still in bed at ten that morning when my door burst open. It was Charles Di Rudio, wild-eyed, Devil's eyebrows raised, excited, urgently buttoning up his uniform tunic.

'Get up, James. We've work to do!'

I was bleary-eyed. 'What are you talking about?'

'I've had a wire from Colonel Baker. He's been recalled to Washington again: Stanton wants him back, to head the manhunt for

Lincoln's assassin. Stanton knows he can't do without him. And Baker is putting all his operatives in the field.'

'He ended my contract!' I protested.

'And mine. But now he wants us again.'

'I see no reason why I should go gallivanting about the state simply because Colonel Baker snaps his fingers. I have my practice in New York...'

Di Rudio stood at the foot of my bed, glaring at me, eyes wild. He tugged at his beard in excitement. 'You don't understand! There's a reward been announced for the capture of the killer. One hundred thousand dollars. The whole state will be riding the roads! I've ordered breakfast for you below. Come quickly.'

One hundred thousand dollars. I got out of bed, my head clearing rapidly; the thought of money when you have little can do that.

Di Rudio's time in London had not only perfected his English and improved his accent, it had also taught him what an Englishman liked for breakfast. Not the New York fare of steak and potatoes, grits, hominies and the like, but kedgeree, kidneys, ham and turned-over eggs. As I tackled what was placed in front of me, Di Rudio was busy with a sheet of paper, drawing lines moving out from a central point, writing names beside the lines and grunting to himself. I took a good swallow of the harsh, bitter coffee. I reflected.

'A hundred thousand dollars. And you rightly say the whole of Washington will be on horseback, seeking the murderer. You know it was John Wilkes Booth, don't you?'

'Stanton will make the announcement this afternoon,' Di Rudio muttered. 'Better late than never, but I can't understand why he's delayed identifying the killer. And yes, the militia, the police force, the reserves and half the male population will be out on the roads in force.'

'So what makes you think we could succeed against such competition?'

'When I was in England and working as a teacher of languages I learned your proverb: *Set a thief to catch a thief.*'

I caught his meaning. Set an assassin to catch one: it was a road Di Rudio had travelled himself in Italy and France. He raised his head and looked at me. His mouth was grim but his eyes were sparkling, dancing with excitement. 'It helps to think like a murderer if you must seek one.'

I nodded. 'That's logical. But why do you want me along?'

'Two reasons, James. You know Booth. You've seen him on stage and you've dined with him and his brother. You will be able to recognize him, in disguise or not. And secondly ... if we obtain the reward, you can have half my share as well as your own: I would see it partly as recompense for the assistance you once gave my close and esteemed colleague.'

Dr Simon Bernard, his co-conspirator in the assassination attempt on Napoleon III, the man I had saved from an English gallows.

Di Rudio flourished the paper he held on the table. 'We need to work quickly. Time is not on our side. Stanton has shown a criminal inability to act. Here I have sketched the main roads and bridges out of Washington. Booth will have fled the capital: he will seek friends who will succour him. Colonel Baker has wired me that Stanton has finally ordered a general alarm and the blocking of the roads to prevent Booth's flight. I am told the roads to the north have been sealed and some fool has put it out that Booth is heading for Maryland! But that's Union territory where he can expect no help! Squadrons are out patrolling roads paralleling the Potomac ... here ... and the military governor of Alexandria ... to the south-west here ... has been ordered to send out his entire police force.' He stabbed a thick finger at the sketch. 'But why would Booth go that way – the area is swarming with federal troops! Going straight west would entrap him between Washington and Leesburg and the same applies on the roads to Baltimore, Winchester and Harper's Ferry. Roads, trains, ferries, riverboats, all will now, belatedly, be watched, the roads to

Virginia are barred and the navy is bottling up the Potomac. Stanton has blockaded the whole Atlantic coast from Baltimore to Hampton Roads!'

Di Rudio threw down his pencil. It rolled across the map he had drawn and fell to the floor, where it lay ignored. I sensed a degree of triumph in Di Rudio's glittering eyes.

I frowned. 'You think you know where Booth has gone.'

Di Rudio folded his arms across his broad chest and smiled coldly. 'I have no idea what the strategists in the War Office use for brains, but think about Booth's flight and the likelihood of its success. You know he was injured in his leap to the stage.'

'I believe he injured his ankle. He was limping when he vanished.'

'He will need medical attention at some point. This could have slowed him down. I think he is still not yet in the clear. But which direction has he taken? Stanton is wrong to consider the west because it crawls with Federal troops; the north-west does not lead to friendly territory; Baltimore would provide Booth with shelter but is nothing more than a cul de sac. He will need broad spaces to evade his pursuers.'

'And you think you know the route he would have taken?'

'It is the only likely one, to my mind. The underground railway.'

I had heard of it, of course: it was the road to Richmond which was regularly travelled by Union spies and dispatch-bearers as well as Confederate mail-carriers and dealers in contraband throughout the war. The country thereabouts was full of Secessionist sympathizers, the population was sparse and scattered, the area swampy and networked with bad roads. Colonel Lafayette Baker had himself used the route when entering Richmond as a spy in his early career.

'This is where Stanton should be searching,' Di Rudio snapped. 'Booth could hide there for weeks in relative safety. To close the route would be easy for the War Department – but I have received no information that this has been done. It is the road we must take, James, and quickly if we are to gain the reward. My guess would be that Booth will have intended crossing the Potomac at Port Tobacco, and might well have already done so. The journey would have taken him about six hours and by late this afternoon he could have been safe in Virginia. But what if his injury has delayed him? I know you ride well, James. I have ordered horses. We must go. Time is not on our side!'

We were off within the hour.

We left Washington behind and pushed our mounts hard, pounding through Surrattsville and on to Teebee where Di Rudio had wired for a change of mounts. By mid-afternoon I was tired but still exhilarated by the wild excitement of the ride and the thought of one hundred thousand dollars. I had confidence in Di Rudio's summary of the situation.

'My guess is that from here Booth will have headed for Bryantown and maybe attempted the Potomac south of Port Tobacco,' Di Rudio suggested as we rode on with fresh horses. 'But I'm still thinking of that ankle injury he sustained. And have you noticed something unusual, James?'

I was somewhat out of breath by the hard riding but stammered I had not.

'There should be as many as eight hundred cavalrymen scouring this area – but we have seen not a single patrol.'

He was right. The roads we travelled were empty and unmanned: the underground railway had not been sealed.

It was only when we were allowing the horses a breather near Bryantown that we first set eyes on a detachment of soldiers. Curtly, Di Rudio told me to stay where I was and he rode forward, still in his dapper uniform, his cap with its crossed swords cocked over one eye, sabre at his hip. I watched as he approached the cavalry unit, saluted the young officer in charge, and had an extended conversation with him. Then he turned back to me, while the soldiers went on their way.

'His name is Dana,' Di Rudio explained to me as our horses cropped the grass at the roadside. 'Lieutenant Dana. His brother is the Assistant Secretary of War, and closely linked to Stanton. The lieutenant thinks he's been sent on a fool's errand, to prevent a crossing opposite Piscataway. He has checked the crossing at the Navy Yard Bridge and he believes that the man we seek is still behind us. He's scouring the country we have already passed through. I am not so sure he is right. And he gave me some interesting information, that he himself has not acted upon because of his belief.' Di Rudio's eyes seemed to glow as he stared about him. 'Lieutenant Dana told me he had received a report from a gentleman called Mudd that his cousin yesterday extended hospitality to two strangers, one of whom required medical help.' His eyes turned to me, quizzically. 'I think the young lieutenant has made a mistake in not acting upon that information. I think we should spend the night in Bryantown. Make some enquiries there.'

I was weary, saddle-sore and made no objection.

Bryantown boasted of the best hotel in the district – though it was primitive enough – and we found lodgings there, took a welcome evening meal and visited the local tavern. We were in luck. When we asked about a person called Mudd we were told that Dr George

Mudd was a local surgeon who was accustomed to taking some postprandial refreshment in that very bar, most evenings. We decided to wait. The man himself strolled in about eight o'clock, short, portly, full-bearded. He took a table near the door and Di Rudio, bottle and glass in hand, went across and introduced himself. I joined them as our quarry accepted the offer of a drink, there was a brief conversation about the startling events of the recent days and the information we required was soon obtained. George Mudd was innocently open in his conversation.

'My cousin is a medical man, like myself. I called on him yesterday morning and he informed me that two strangers had visited him the previous evening, stayed the night. He'd had to cut off the boot of one of them and bandage the swollen ankle. The man had broken a small bone in his ankle and was really in no condition to ride in view of the swelling.' George Mudd finished his drink, and Di Rudio offered him another. When Di Rudio went to the bar to procure another bottle, George Mudd confided in me. 'I was concerned about my cousin's behaviour, I can tell you. He's a simple man, has little truck with the world outside Bryantown. I mean, with the news from Washington he should be more careful. Two strangers, one of them injured! And he puts them up for the night! And today there's been talk of that young man in town trying to hire a carriage to take him across the Navy Yard Bridge to Port Royal. He acted suspicious, I've been told. Nervy, scared, simple-minded even.'

As Di Rudio joined us again with the fresh bottle, I said, 'Can you describe this young man more clearly?'

'Slim, boyish, fair-haired, giving the impression he was uncertain of himself. Almost simple-minded, as I said.'

I glanced at Di Rudio; he knew what was in my mind. There was a strong likelihood that the young man seeking transport was one of Booth's co-conspirators. David Herold.

Di Rudio was a fair-minded man. He nodded sagely. 'We met a cavalry unit this afternoon, commanded by Lieutenant Dana. I think your cousin should tell him what he knows about his two visitors.'

'That's what I already told him,' George Mudd asserted. 'And about the boot he cut off. It had JWB carved in the leather.'

I stared at Di Rudio in excited surprise. He kept his own features immobile, as though unconcerned. But when we returned to our hotel he let out a whoop, and that night my dreams were filled with a cascade of dollar bills. We were close to becoming the heroes of the hour, Di Rudio and I. We were about to be the men who captured John Wilkes Booth, the murderer of President Lincoln.

4

The next day proved to be frustrating.

The gossip in town was that Dr Samuel Mudd had indeed now laid information regarding his visitors and that Pinkerton detectives were being despatched from Washington to interview him. We were in no mood to hang about and allow the reward money to be lost, so Di Rudio and I rode out early, ranging the swampy countryside and making enquiries as to the possible whereabouts of the two strangers, who we were confident were the fugitives, Herold and Booth.

It was late evening before we achieved success. Somewhat tired after our exertions, we had returned to our hotel and were stabling our horses at Nailor's Livery when we met the stableman, John Fletcher. He was of the usual grumbling sort, the kind one often finds in the hostelry business. We fell into conversation with him when he arrived in a sweat at the stables, cursing and muttering.

'You gents will probably be needing fresh mounts, the way it looks you worked them today. We can supply them. But I'll be needing a strict arrangement. I just got back from east of the Potomac and I ain't happy.'

255

'What's happened?'

'This young feller came to me this morning, got a horse from me, but he stayed out beyond the time we'd agreed. I went out looking for him this afternoon and damn me, there I saw him spurring the animal hell for leather towards the Navy Yard Bridge! Watching for the horses in my care, it's my job, you know, and I could lose it for the sake of one thieved horse, so I saddled up and went looking for that son of a bitch! And that damned guard Sam Cobb, on the bridge, he told me two men had crossed already, but if I was expecting to go after my horse I could do so, but then wouldn't be able to re-cross the bridge till mornin'. He was closing it, under orders. So I turned back. I'll have to go over in the early daylight to find that damned thief!'

'This guard Cobb,' Di Rudio said quietly. 'Did he ask for the names of the two men?'

'I reckon so. I recollect one of them: Booth. I don't know whether that was the youngster I was after but I'll damn well find out tomorrow!'

We were stunned. Booth had given his own name to the guard on the Navy Yard Bridge! But on reflection, I realized it was in character. Ever the showman, the man who saw drama in everything he did, in his fantasies he still regarded himself as the hero who had committed the perfect crime in the most dramatic fashion, ridding the world of a tyrant. The heroic assassin did not want his name to be lost to posterity. There was to be no disguise of his features, and now no disguise of his name. As for the guard, he had presumably not received the news from Washington – and in any case there was no one to report the matter to.

'What the hell is Stanton up to?' Di Rudio muttered to me after we left the stableman. 'He's not sending out the information, and he's not even closed the underground railway! You'd think he didn't want Booth to be captured! Or else...' Di Rudio pondered, 'or else he wants to make sure the reward money goes to one of his own minions!'

Early next morning, when the mists were still rising from the swampy fields, we rode through fields of cane tobacco. Di Rudio and I were headed for the Navy Yard Bridge and the track towards Port Royal. We crossed the bridge without difficulty, once Di Rudio showed his army credentials, and we then spent the rest of the day ranging along the Potomac banks, checking at farms and mills, hunting through pine thickets and crossing tobacco patches, and forcing our way through cane brakes and marshy, humid land for any sign of the men we were pursuing. We felt sure we were close on their heels. But it proved to be a long, frustrating and sweaty day. There were rumours swirling about: a hired girl was said to have seen two men, one on crutches, beckoning to her from a nearby swamp, asking her to bring food. We followed up that story and were soon joined by groups of soldiers and farmers, all eager to get their hands on the reward money. As were we. The information proved to be false: the hysterical girl was never traced. Gossip. Rumour.

There was another story that a coloured man had seen two men leaving a farm and crossing the river in a small boat that afternoon but that again came to nothing: no one now could even identify the informant. The whole area was now teeming with men searching the dusty roads for sight of the fugitives and time was draining away. We rode back into Port Tobacco late in the day, tired, dusty and hot. I took a bath in the hotel there while Di Rudio went to the telegraph office. He was there for some time, and I was in the dining room, ready for a meal when he joined me. He sat down, ordered a bottle of wine and glared at me.

'I have made a communication with Colonel Baker. He has advised that we need look no further. He is pulling back his operatives, he says, at Stanton's suggestion. But he is angry. And he has assigned his own cousin to continue the search – now that important information has come to his attention.'

'His *cousin!*' I exclaimed.

Lieutenant Di Rudio was furious, and drank down a full glass of wine. He wiped his hand across his mouth, and shook his head. 'This is no longer an attempt to use all means to seize the murderer of Lincoln. This is a naked, greed-driven manhunt, my friend, an opportunity to seize glory as well as money! Two detachments of cavalry have been ordered to return to Washington at once and our *leader* has given the latest information to a member of his own family: Lieutenant Luther Baker will be riding out in the morning before taking a boat down the Potomac. And you and I, we are told our services are no longer required!'

I grabbed a glass of wine and drained it in a similar anger and frustration. I swore. When I looked at Di Rudio, however, I glimpsed a new determination in his eyes. His mouth was set grimly. 'Eat well, James,' he said sternly. 'And sleep well tonight: we will need all our energy tomorrow.'

'We're not going back to Washington as ordered?'

He shook his head. 'We can ride as fast and as far as the redoubtable Luther Baker!'

'But he has information–'

'So do I! I also have read the telegrams from Washington. And Lieutenant Baker is an arrogant, incompetent fool, a hothead. We need only to follow his early trail, to confirm his intentions, and then we can outrun him. We are armed, you and I, we are determined men, and we can find the fugitives quicker than Baker! And once discovered, David Herold will present no problem, thus we need deal merely with a man who can only hobble, not run. And we have the advantage that you know him; you will recognize him; we can be first to seize him!'

And the one hundred thousand dollars would be ours.

I make no apology for the thought, my boy. The prospect of the reward was now driving everyone in the manhunt. That was the reason why it had become almost farcical: no one was giving information to any other group, intelligence was being suppressed, cavalry units, men with dogs, farmers, policemen, detectives were charging about blindly in every direction. The whole area was being picketed and searched but not in an organized way. Every man was out for himself. Luckily for us, Di Rudio had access to Colonel Baker's telegrams from Washington and had seen the way the nepotistic wind was blowing.

Lieutenant Baker's troop left at midday, and we followed their dust. We kept our distance, stopping at intervals while Di Rudio used his Austrian-made binoculars to check the surrounding countryside. He was inordinately proud of those binoculars, you know: some years later he lent them to General Custer on the march to the Little Bighorn, and never got them back. He remains angry about that to this day, I believe. And another thing: Di Rudio might have been an officer with the 7th Cavalry, but he was no expert horseman: several times during our ride following Lieutenant Baker he almost fell off, rolling in the saddle like a drunken sailor as soon as we broke into more than a trot. Some years later, at Little Bighorn, according to his memoirs, he had his horse shot out from under him, which was why he survived the massacre, but I have my doubts. I think it's more likely that when 'Garryowen' was played and the charge was sounded, he just fell off his horse...

What? The pursuit?

Yes, well, with Di Rudio's binoculars we kept the troop within our sights while remaining ourselves unobserved.

'They are heading for the ferry on the Rappahannock,' Di Rudio finally asserted with confidence. He wiped a dusty glove across his forehead. 'We can get ahead of them – look at this map. That arrogant cousin of Colonel Baker has disregarded this track here: he's not even using local maps efficiently. We can get ahead of him, and see what we find.' He stared at the map spread out across his knee. 'There are two farms along this route. The Cox holding, and then, beyond Chapel Point there is Garrett's Farm. This is where we search – ahead of that damned Luther Baker!'

And you know, my boy, he was right. We scouted around Cox's farm – not knowing at the time that it had indeed hidden Booth and Herold for some days – but it was there we made our mistake: we spent too much time searching the fields and tobacco patches in the area, to no effect. In the meanwhile Lieutenant Luther Baker had ridden past – directly to Garrett's Farm. He didn't bother with Cox and Scotia Point: he had received better information than us, after all.

And Di Rudio and I did not reach Garrett's Farm until late that evening. Too late. In the fading light we could see the glimmer of torches, and hear the tumult of voices shouting orders, men running here and there like excited rabbits. The detachment of some twenty-eight soldiers had been deployed: they were surrounding the wooden tobacco shed at the farm. Baker himself was standing directly in front of the barn door, pistol in hand, a candle emitting a feeble light at his feet. It seemed he had finally cornered Herold and John Wilkes Booth.

Di Rudio slumped in the saddle, hugely disappointed. I felt too fatigued after our long days in the saddle to experience much emotion – this had not been like riding to hounds in Norfolk years earlier. This time we were hunting men, and we had failed to be first to reach the target.

Slowly, unchallenged, we rode down from the cane brakes to join the men encircling the barn. All eyes searched the dimness surrounding the structure; no one paid any attention to us. From what we heard, however, it would seem that both fugitives were holed up in the barn.

You know, when Di Rudio and I were at Mary Surratt's house, listening to the conspirators, we had heard John Wilkes Booth declare himself ready to die for the cause. Drama, theatre, monomania – all contributed to his posturing. And now we heard his voice again clearly, as Lieutenant Luther Baker tried to parley with him through the closed shed door, calling for his surrender. The answer was in accordance with all I knew about the actor: I had played such parts myself on the stage of my youth – shaking a fist to the heavens, declaiming death before dishonour, a determination to defy overwhelming odds. In this case, I heard Booth yelling he was determined to shoot it out with his pursuers.

He was alone in that determination, however. A short while later, a shaky David Herold came staggering out of the barn with his terrified hands in the air. And shortly afterwards, the shed was set on fire.

'Are you *mad!*' Di Rudio exclaimed, seiz-

263

ing a nearby trooper by the shoulder. 'All you have to do is wait! Booth is lame, alone, he has nowhere to go, he will have to surrender by morning!'

The excited trooper seemed barely to notice him. He threw off Di Rudio's hand, and concentrated his attention on the blaze consuming the barn. The troops had probably piled some hay at the entrance and the shed was powder-dry in any event, so the fire took hold with a furious rush, outlining the waiting troopers blackly against the roaring red glow of the flames. It was like a scene from Hell, believe me, and all we could do, Di Rudio and I, was watch in frustrated horror.

'Why are they doing this?' muttered Di Rudio angrily. 'Don't they want to take Booth alive?'

We received the answer a short while later.

The shed was beginning to disintegrate. Burning planks of wood were detaching from the walls, the roof was in a state of collapse as red fingers of flame licked about the building and the whole area was lit up like day. Some troops fell back to avoid the stifling heat and a few minutes later we were able to see, through widening cracks in the wooden walls, the figure of the man inside, outlined blackly against the red and orange glow, still defiant, still challenging his pursuers. But finally, it seemed, John Wilkes

Booth came to his senses. He began to hobble towards the door: bowed, half overcome by the smoke and heat, it seemed to me he had decided to surrender. The horrific reality of burning to death would seem to have finally overcome the fantasy of his histrionic stage performance.

He was still some feet from the door when someone fired.

He fell on the porch, just before the sun rose upon the grisly scene.

It's always the same, isn't it: over the years wild rumours spread as they always do when great events occur. It was suggested that the man who died in the burning shed was not John Wilkes Booth, but another who had taken his place. That isn't so. In the chaotic scenes that followed, both Di Rudio and I were able to move close to the body, which was being stripped and investigated by Luther Baker. I got near enough to confirm in my own mind that it was in fact the actor who had been shot there that day. *Why* he had to be shot – and by whom – on the other hand, was something I could not explain. Booth was presenting no danger to the waiting troops. In my view he was about to surrender. But as for identity ... the man who lay there with sightless eyes was certainly the man I had known at dinner parties and on the stage in Washington and New York.

I watched with distaste as Lieutenant Baker searched the body for identification. When he stood up to look more closely at the papers he had recovered, I noticed that one of the items he held in his hand was what seemed to be a memorandum book. He glanced through it, then rapidly thrust it into his pocket. I watched as the body was stripped: a knife, pistols, a belt and holster, a file; one of the soldiers picked up Booth's spurs, a pipe, some cartridges.

We stood disconsolate, unable to do anything and unwilling to take part in what seemed to be turning into a macabre free-for-all, the taking of souvenirs from the dead assassin. 'Come, James,' Di Rudio said quietly at my shoulder. 'There's nothing we can now do here.'

We left, and rode back for the ferry in the growing dawn. We were despondent. Our dream of a rich reward was shattered.

A week later I finally got the interview I had been waiting for with Secretary of War Edwin Stanton.

The most unpopular man in Lincoln's cabinet received me in his office: once again, he did not rise to greet me. He sat there, half-turned away from his desk, peering at me over his wire-rimmed glasses, scratching at his perfumed beard with a penholder, and holding an important-looking document in his left hand. He exuded confidence:

266

brusque, insolent, cruel, he had always held himself in great regard, believing no one could do his work as well as he. He saw himself as a leader among men – one who indeed himself deserved the presidency – and now he was confident he could maintain his status against the already discredited drunken Vice President Johnson, who was presently succeeding Abraham Lincoln as the Chief Executive. But Stanton was also a coward at heart, and could be almost obsequious to anyone who strongly opposed him.

Today he clearly felt on top of the world. It was almost as though a burden had been lifted from his shoulders. He seemed exhilarated. I was surprised, and curious, at his attitude.

'Hah! Our eminent English lawyer, Mr James,' he remarked jovially – though with the hint of a sneer – as he waved me to a chair facing him. 'You have been seeking an interview.'

'For some time,' I replied, and remained standing.

'Ah, well, you must appreciate, urgent matters of state, the conduct of the war, the heavy responsibilities of office; my time has been limited to *important* matters. And then, of course, the assassination of Mr Lincoln ... and the burden of office shifting to Mr Andrew Johnson.' He grimaced, thoughtfully. 'President Lincoln... You know, Mr

James, the scene was heart-rending at his bedside. We were all there; he was breathing only shakily; the bullet, you know, had entered the back of his head, there was no chance that he would survive, but we waited in hope, we mourned. I closed Ford's Theater where he was shot, of course, as a mark of respect. And I was there at his bedside when Mr Lincoln breathed his last. It was then that the words came to me, an epitaph for a great man: *Now he belongs to the Ages*. An appropriate benison, do you not think so? *Now he belongs to the Ages*.'

I had also been told that on that mournful occasion, Stanton had snapped at his subordinates, when the hysterical Mrs Lincoln was sobbing and screaming at her dying husband's side, *Will someone get that damned woman out of here!* Now, his words to me rang with insincerity.

'And his assassin has duly met his own Maker, where he will be held responsible for the great sin he committed,' Stanton murmured, cold-eyed.

'I was at Garrett's Farm when Booth was shot,' I said in an even tone.

Stanton twitched, surprised, hesitated, but regained his composure quickly. 'I think half the world now so claims,' he replied blandly.

'The killing of Booth seemed a rash and unnecessary act. In my view he was about to surrender.'

'The man was a murderer.'

'And now his mouth is closed.' I paused. 'Though I believe there was a diary on the body. It was recovered by Lieutenant Luther Baker.'

Stanton seemed momentarily uneasy, and was silent for a little while; but there was a glint of malice in his piggy little eyes. 'Enough of all that. Why have you requested this interview, Mr James?'

He knew full well the reason for my presence, but he wanted to make me squirm.

'The last time I was in this office, Mr Stanton, you made me a proposal. You suggested that if I were to help Colonel Lafayette Baker in his endeavours, I would in return receive your support for judicial office. I did all you asked: I infiltrated the Fenians in New York–'

'And enjoyed yourself in the taverns, I understand,' he smirked.

I ignored the comment. 'And when that task was completed I agreed to assist the Colonel once more in the trapping of the Secessionist conspirators. I provided you with a report,' I thought I detected another uneasy glint in Stanton's eyes at this point, 'on which for reasons known only to yourself no action was taken. And I was drawn into your service again when the president was assassinated.'

'Into Colonel Baker's service,' he contradicted me. 'Not mine, sir.'

I allowed the point to pass.

'The reason for my presence here now, Mr Secretary, is to request that you fulfil your promise to assist me in my seeking a judicial position in New York.'

There was a short silence. Stanton sat there, not looking at me, stroking his beard thoughtfully. Behind his pince-nez spectacles his eyes glinted maliciously. At last he stirred awkwardly in his chair.

'You know, Mr James, there are many who thought my service would end when Mr Lincoln was murdered. It is well known that the new president, Andrew Johnson, has no great liking for me. And yet here I am. Still with the reins of power in my hands. President Johnson is, of course, a drunken incompetent, but not so foolish as to throw me out of office. He knows what I know... But I am also a realist. I am fully aware it will not be long before the president feels strong enough to dislodge me. And then, well, perhaps I will call in the many favours I am owed and seek my own nomination. Or failing that possibility, a judicial appointment for myself in the Supreme Court.'

Stiffly, I remarked, 'It's *my* future I'm here to discuss, sir.'

'Your future... Hah, yes. But you come at a difficult time, sir, seeking favours.'

'I seek only fulfilment of a promise!' I

flashed angrily.

'You must understand that this is a difficult time,' he continued smoothly as though I had not spoken. 'We are in a time of transition, with the development of a new administration, the ending of the war between the States... Can you not see I don't have time for such trivialities as these? I'm sorry, Mr James. You have been paid for the time you spent in the service, albeit secretly, of the War Department. I really cannot be called upon to pull strings on your behalf at a time of national emergency. Besides, I think you overestimate my powers. Washington is Washington – but New York is a different ball game. Tammany Hall rules there. I have little influence among those damned Democrats! And judicial appointments well, let's see. I understand your own legal practice staggers along rather than races ahead of the competition. And you must realize, whatever the system might have been in England, in New York judicial appointments are of a political nature, and in New York the support of Tammany Hall is critical. The powers of preferment among the Boss Tweed crowd at Tammany are wide-ranging ... one might almost say, exclusive. Rather than turn to me, you should be seeking entry into the good books of that corrupt animal Tweed and his crew.'

'So there is nothing you will do for me.'

'There is nothing I *can* do for you, Mr James.'

At that point, I have to admit, I lost control of myself. And in my anger at what I saw as Stanton's betrayal in casually reneging on his promise I said more than I should have done. 'There is, at least, one thing you can do for me, sir. Explain to me why all roads were blocked to John Wilkes Booth when he rode from Washington ... all roads except the one he took, which was the *obvious* route for his flight!'

Stanton's head came up. He was silent for a while, his mean little eyes glittering at me from behind his wire-rimmed spectacles. At last, he grimaced and said, 'I can assure you, sir, that all attempts were made in due order to capture the villain.'

'Then why did you delay informing the public of the identity of the assassin? I was at Ford's Theater: I recognized Booth, as did many others.'

Stanton's head was lowered. His hand was shaking slightly and he seemed short of breath. 'I think that's enough, Mr James.'

'And what about Garrett's Farm?' I insisted, far from finished with my tirade. 'Why did the pursuit end there, in the hands of your own trusted lieutenant? And why was Booth not brought back alive?'

Stanton was always a coward; now he was trembling, and his voice was shaky. 'These

272

are wild words, Mr James, and I choose to ignore them. This interview is at an end!'

And rather than wait for me to leave he rose and without a backward glance walked out of the room through its rear entrance. He was tottering slightly, but he closed the door behind him with a bang.

What? You appear bemused, shaking your head. You find my accusations far-fetched, beyond reason that I should attempt to suggest that Secretary of War Stanton was part of a conspiracy to murder the president? That he had been providing Booth with funds, was fully aware of the conspiracy to kidnap the president – which would have left Stanton in full control of the reins of power at that crucial juncture in the war?

No, don't deny it. When I was at the Bar I could always tell what a man was thinking when he was in the witness box. It was the key to my success. And I see in your eyes now, my boy, your disbelief. But let me put it to you like this. I would dearly have loved to face Stanton in a witness box and put to him arguments that would have made him wriggle like a stranded fish in a net. Quite apart from the closing of the roads – except the one that permitted Booth to escape – I would have asked him about Officer John Parker. Why was that man not shot for dereliction of duty? In fact no action was taken against him and he was even *promoted*. Why did Stanton tell Grant not to go the theatre, thus disobeying what was in effect an order from his President? If Grant had been there, Booth's mad endeavour would probably have failed. Why did Stanton deny the president the additional guards he requested? And after the death of Booth, why were all conspirators, once arrested, silenced by unusual methods, banishment, or death?

And why was Mary Surratt, essentially innocent of involvement in the plot other than providing a meeting room, subsequently hanged? Oh, yes, my boy, she was executed. And I think I know why: it was Mary Surratt who was Stanton's spy. That's how Di Rudio and I obtained easy access to the house in Surrattsville. And after arrest, she took her incarceration with tight-lipped equanimity because she was convinced it was all for show, hiding her spying activities, believing all along she would eventually be released. Only when she faced the hangman did she realize Stanton wanted her silenced. And then it was too late!

You still seem unconvinced. Well, as I say, if I could have got Stanton into a witness box, I could have put these questions to him, insisted on his answering them on oath, and I would have torn him apart!

And there's one other thing. Colonel Lafayette Baker was another who suffered from Stanton's failure to keep promises. After the trials of the conspirators he was rewarded with promotion to Brigadier General ... then sacked again. A little later he wrote his book, *The History of the Secret Service*. You've not read it? Well, he had some sensational things to say about the diary of John Wilkes Booth ... you'll recall I had seen the diary taken from the corpse by Luther Baker, in the burning shed at Garrett's Farm. Well, that book naturally fell into the hands of the War Department. But when it was finally produced two years later at the Inquiry – Stanton at first denied he had even seen it – it would seem that some eighteen pages had been removed while it was in Stanton's custody. Why would a man's diary be so mutilated? The only answer must be that those pages contained damning information. Damaging to whom? Clearly, the person who held it under lock and key.

Yes, that's right. Edwin Stanton, Secretary for War.

We'll never know what Booth had written in those missing pages. My own suspicion is that they disclosed the extent to which Booth's activities were financially supported by Stanton: it was rumoured he supplied him with money through the medium of a company of which he was director. You pull a face at me, sir: you ask why would Stanton have wanted Lincoln kidnapped? Hah! I would have got *that* out of him in the witness box, believe me!

It's well known that Stanton hated Lincoln, did all he could to undermine him, or belittle him. He pushed Lincoln hard on abolition of slavery and when the president demurred and hesitated, Stanton was infuriated. He wanted retribution against the Southern leaders but Lincoln wanted peace and for-giveness. Stanton also thought that with the president out of the way – kidnapped – his own power would increase, and he would have a fair prospect of himself becoming President at the next election. But Booth's mad, melodramatic adventure destroyed that hope. All he was supposed to do – all Stanton *expected* him to do – was to kidnap the president, not *murder* him!

Yes, yes, all right, I agree that perhaps I exaggerate – yes, I admit I disliked Stanton, I was infuriated by his treachery and false promises, and perhaps I am biased in my opinions. Let it be. It's a long time ago, and I'm in no mood for disputing the matter with you. I am just telling you how I saw things.

In any case, Stanton would do nothing for me and when I went back to New York a few days later, nursing my contempt and fury at Stanton's behaviour, I found that no easy ride awaited me in that great city. I am now of the firm opinion that forgiveness never comes to a man who has erred; whatever ease he might achieve with benedictions from friends and even enemies, the misdeeds are never truly forgiven. At least, not as far as the reverberations caused by past errors continue to shake a man's life. Such certainly was the case with me. For it was on my return to my Broadway office that I discovered the shadows of the past had risen up once more to put me in peril.

I opened my office door that day to find a man ensconced behind my desk. His billycock hat was perched on the back of his head; his soiled, booted feet were crossed at the ankle, reposing on my desk and he was clearly enjoying the fat cigar that was clenched between his bearded lips. He raised a hand as he called to me, fanned away the blue curling smoke and invited me to enter my own office.

His tone was jovial and confident. 'Mr James! Back from great deeds in Washington, no doubt! Sit down, my friend, sit down. We have things to talk about.' He tipped his hat forward so that it jauntily covered one eye. 'You'll remember me, of course! You appeared before me a couple of times, when that rogue minister the Reverend Pease was preaching sedition in the Five Points! We clashed, as I recall, you and I.'

'He was preaching temperance,' I growled. 'Not sedition. And of course I remember you, sir. Matthew Brennan. Police court judge and a favoured man in Tammany Hall circles.' My tone was surly, for I was out of sorts at his manner.

'The very same,' he agreed cheerfully, in no manner offended. 'The man you humiliated with that Supreme Court appeal. But I was never a man to hold a grudge, if it suits me. So sit down. We have things to discuss. And I have a proposition to make to you.'

With a sinking heart, I listened to him, and as he spoke the almost forgotten shadows of my past in England arose once more to confront me and threaten my very existence.

PART 5

1

Matt Brennan. I knew him to be a typical product of the Tammany Hall system developed in New York by the Democratic Party. He was Irish, of course, born and raised in the Five Points. He had begun his rise in the same manner as so many others: making use of boyhood contacts, frequenting the saloons and gin palaces, rising to become a shoulder-hitter at political rallies, using his nailed boots and his fists to ensure a high turnout of voters of the right colour and eventually paying to join one of the fire brigades that were scattered around the city, competing with each other, fighting their own corner and galloping around in their horse-drawn machines like embattled knights of old.

He set up his own saloon in due course, naturally: Monroe Hall, one of the most successful saloons in the city, close to Niblo's and the other Bowery theatres, and competing fiercely with Barney McGuire's network of opium houses, hop joints, junk shops and pawnbrokers. He was closely allied to Bridget McCarty – who procured so-called young virgins for the well-heeled politicians – and he soon wormed his way into the Tammany Hall set-up by way of alcohol, opium, bribes and prostitution rackets. The natural prerequisite to political advancement in New York at that time was by way of service in the fire department and the police, so Brennan's next step was to join the police force – when he could afford it because the entry fees were considerable – and then found himself able to profit from the graft that every officer was expected to indulge in. It meant turning a blind eye to gangs who made a living by burglary – for a cut of the profits – and even protecting them by keeping watch while they entered a house, and then causing confusion by running noisily in the opposite direction in a supposed chase after the guilty villains, once the alarm was raised.

Brennan's rise in the ranks was assured by the favours he provided to the pothouse politicians: free drinks, complaisant girls and shares in the proceeds of graft. By the late 1850s, he had become Police Captain Matt Brennan. When I came into his arena – courtesy of Mrs Grimshaw's pressure to defend the Reverend Pease and his Temperance Movement preaching – he had recently been appointed to the police court as judge. Knowledge of judicial procedures was an unnecessary qualification for such elected office; indeed it was probably a handicap.

And now here he was in my office a few years later, leering at me knowingly as though he was aware that, somehow unknown to me, he had me over the proverbial barrel. He chomped at his cigar, and scratched at the thick mat of hair protruding above his open shirt collar.

'I been learning quite a bit about you, James. And in spite of our little clash a way back – I ain't a man to bear grudges, like I said, if it suits my purpose – I believe that in you I find a man after me own heart. You got style, James, and the kind of skills me and me friends can put to good use. I'd like to put some work your way.'

'In your police court?' I asked, surprised.

'You've not kept up to date, my friend,' Brennan announced cheerily, waving his cigar at me. 'I'm no longer a police court judge! I been elevated. Last week I got elected to the position of City Comptroller. You know what that means? I get to keep up to date the electoral rolls of this great city of New York. And all that it implies.'

I could guess what it implied: electoral control by adding – or removing – names from the list, 'arranging' elections, organizing repeat voting, making sure that Tammany Hall directives were followed to the letter.

'Congratulations,' I said drily.

'I appreciate that! Mr James, you got all the qualities I need in a man,' Brennan said enthusiastically. 'There's still a place for the old ways – we both know Ward Primaries were always decided by knock-down, drag-out brawls, and gangs preventing voters from getting to the polls, getting repeater votes and rigging results. But things are changing, we got to be seen more respectable, so the day of the shoulder-hitter may well be over. On the other hand, these do-gooders who'd clean up Tammany Hall, well, they got to have recourse to the courts, don't they? And that's where you come in.'

'I don't quite understand.'

'I want the dice loaded against them. I want you to become a sort of Special Counsel to me. I seen you in action, James. You got the thunder, the bluster, you got the gestures – I like the white gloves bit of theatre, by the way – you got the temperament and skill to turn a jury inside out. I want you on my side.'

'I'm not sure what–'

'On my side. Not against me.' He chewed on his cigar for a few moments, thoughtfully, moving it from one side of his mouth to the other. 'And then there's the fact you're something of an expert on financial business. Even wrote a book about it, I hear tell.'

Bankruptcy law. It was how my career had started, years ago when I first was called to the Bar at the Inner Temple. I was curious suddenly. Was Matt Brennan in financial trouble? The answer was soon provided. He gave me a cunning glance, and cleared his throat noisily.

'You see, James, certain complications have arisen regarding the setting-up of the Bowling Green Savings Bank. And the Guardian Savings Bank, for that matter ... in both of which I have certain interests. I need sound advice, and I think you're the man for it. Whaddya say?'

I considered the situation carefully. There could be advantage, of course, in being linked to Matt Brennan, and advantage also in scrabbling around in his secrets, obtaining information which might prove useful some day. On the other hand, I was still hoping to make a real career in the law, and to be tied in to such a corrupt individual might serve me ill. Moreover, I didn't like the man.

'I think I need some time to think this over—'

'It's not just advice on the finance stuff I'll require,' he cut in. 'My work as Comptroller will no doubt bring in many court challenges – you know what the Republicans are like. Litigious bastards! I'd want you to be working for me on those matters too – sometimes behind the scenes, maybe, sometimes in court.'

I stared at those scuffed, soiled, arrogant boots still planted on my table. I grimaced.

'As I say–'

'We'd begin by you taking on a little job for me, regarding a certain young Irishman by the name of James Wilson, who's just arrived, fresh-faced and innocent as a babe, from Dublin. Seems he has a considerable amount of money to invest in a suitable project. There's an acquaintance of mine who has various business interests, who would be far from averse to giving this green young feller a hand. Your name has already been recommended to our gullible Irish friend. He will be coming to you for financial advice. When he does, you can recommend the friend I spoke of: Henry Hayward. A businessman of consequence. Things can move on from there, quietly. And profitably. For all concerned.'

I smelled stinking fish.

'I'm not sure I can go along with that.'

Brennan stubbed out his cigar on the surface of my desk. He removed his hat, scratched at his thick mop of black, curly hair and grinned at me, sourly. 'Now, just why would that be the case, Mr James?'

'I don't see,' I said slowly, 'how I can take on as a client a man with money to invest, whom I am then called upon to introduce to an investor about whom I know nothing.'

'Not introduce, my legal friend. *Persuade* to an investment.'

The silence between us extended uncomfortably. At last, I said, 'I think I must ask you to leave now, Mr Brennan. I have been away from my desk attending to business in Washington; I now need to catch up with what's been coming in here.'

Brennan made no move to leave. He caressed his luxuriant moustache with a thoughtful finger. 'From what I hear, you've not been so squeamish in the past, Mr James.'

I felt as though a lead weight had been deposited on my chest. 'I have no idea what you're talking about,' I managed to say at last.

Brennan smiled unpleasantly. 'After receiving certain information, which I'll come to in a moment, I been looking into what you've been up to in New York. Quite the jolly fellow, ain't you! You and some foreign character, once a paid assassin, they say, you spent a lot of time trawling through the saloons of the Five Points, spending time with the Irish immigrants, sighing over their woes, singing songs and trading drinks with them. You got a love for the Irish, seems to me.'

'They're hard to avoid, in New York,' I replied defensively.

'But you seemed to be *seeking* them out,' Brennan smirked. 'Right in the middle of revolutionary talk, wasn't it? What was you up to, James? Little in the Five Points passes my notice. I was born and bred there.'

'It was just a period in my life. My early days in New York.'

'Before your divorce. Caused quite a stir, that, in some circles. But none of my business, your marital problems. No, what I find surprising is that you seemed to be seeking the company of the Irish. Surprising, in view of your previous history.'

Under my breath I cursed my involvement with Colonel Lafayette Baker and his damned Secret Service. Because I was beginning to guess what was coming.

'I don't really want to continue this conversation. We're getting nowhere, Mr Brennan. And I have work to do.'

He chuckled. 'You telling me you don't remember a man called Patrick O'Neill?'

I felt my fingers stiffen. I would have enjoyed wrapping them around Brennan's hairy throat. 'O'Neill is a common enough Irish name.'

'As is Patrick, I'll admit. But this man, O'Neill, well, we're not talking about the Five Points. Patrick O'Neill, I'm led to understand, went to London: when was it? I'm told it was 1860. Would that be right?'

'I've no idea. I never came across such a man.'

'Now, is that the God's truth! That's interesting, because from what I heard this man O'Neill arrived in London from Cork – a

Cork man he was, like me family – in search of certain information. It was in relation to a great scandal of the day throughout England and Ireland. I don't recall the details meself, because we have enough to be getting on with here in New York, but it seems there was a famous Irish member of your Parliament, a financier who set up his own bank and used it to swindle maybe thousands of small tenants in Ireland out of the little money they'd earned by the sweat of their brows.'

I was beginning to feel sweaty myself.

'Now, after this swindler of a banker died by his own hand, so it's said, the gentlemen of Cork decided to set up a society to enquire into the whole matter. It's the bane of old Ireland, is it not, the spread of secret societies? But there you are, we're not much different here, with the Molly Maguires and *Clan na Gael* and suchlike. Anyway, to stick to the point. This society of Cork gentlemen, they gave the task of making particular enquiries of a certain delicate nature – and in a certain direction – to our Patrick O'Neill. Whom you tell me you've never met.'

He paused, eyeing me quizzically. When I made no reply, he went on, 'So our Patrick proceeds to London, and we don't know quite where his investigation into the doings of this deceased banker took him, but the rumour is that they was somehow directed in your direction, Mr James. Now, what do you say to that?'

He locked his hands behind his neck in mock triumph, leaning back on two legs of the chair. I was hoping it would skid and he would crack his skull. I remained silent. It was the best defence, until I knew what the challenge might be.

'Trouble is,' Brennan sighed, 'poor Patrick O'Neill never made his report. Seems he was found floating in the Thames some little while after, with his throat cut. Or was he dredged up on a mudbank? No matter, details are unimportant. And you say you never come across this unfortunate patriot from the Old Country.'

He regarded me with a malevolent confidence while I still retained my own counsel. At last he sighed, rocked the chair back into position and rose to his feet. He went to the window, looked out onto the bustle of Broadway and grunted. 'Aye, it's a grand life one can make for oneself in America. Land of opportunity. Streets paved with gold, if you ignore the pigshit. A haven for many who want to seek a new identity, a new life, an escape from the mistakes of the past. But opportunities must be grabbed while they're there, Mr James. However, you need time to reflect. You've heard my offer. I'll give you a day or so to think things through. I'll say goodday to you now.'

He straightened his hat, brushed a hand through his tobacco-stained moustache, gave me a malicious smile and thrust past me on his limping way to the door, striking my shoulder, almost accidentally, as he did so. My heart was thumping unnaturally, and my fingers were tensed tightly. In the doorway, he paused, as though taken by an afterthought. He stood there, looking over his shoulder.

'Me family, they're originally from County Cork, as I said. Still have cousins there. In fact, it was one of me cousins who gave me name to a recent visitor to New York from the Emerald Isle. Name of Seamus O'Gonagle. It was Seamus who was tellin' me the story about that swindling banker. Can't recall the fraud's name...'

I recalled it well enough. John Sadleir. I had identified the corpse in the Dead House.

'Mr O'Gonagle, now, he's a top man in that secret society I was telling you about. The Cork Revengers. Still making enquiries, it seems. Still wanting some sort of recompense – money or blood, he wasn't clear about that – for the losses they suffered at the hands of that dead man. I sympathized with him and his friends, of course. But I had to point out to him that while the Five Points is crammed with immigrant Irishmen and Tammany Hall is awash with Irish support, we have our own way of dealing with things here in New York. The writ of the Cork Revengers don't run here – unless, of course, we choose to so allow it. And we don't allow it, not against our friends...'

His meaning was crystal clear to me.

Next day I sent him a note to the effect I would be happy to deal with the client who had been referred to me.

And that's how another phase of my life began.

It was how I came to defend in the police courts a series of Bowery saloonkeepers, brothel madams, petty crooks and fraudsters, opium den owners and concert hall proprietors. I became a go-between for the police and Tammany Hall officials, and I became a conduit for the covering-up of payment of bribes and protection money throughout the city, along with the collection of 'taxes'. A certain movement of vice had begun from the Five Points around that time, at the end of the Civil War: a number of the red-lanterned bagnios paid taxes to Tammany Hall in order to open up in better districts uptown. And they changed their style. The most expensive brothel was Seven Sisters House – they demanded evening dress and flower bouquets from their visiting clients, but there was also a rash of lower-class establishments. It was said that uptown now had as many whores as Methodists. I was kept busy collecting dues from these establishments, to secure them from police raids. But I was also kept well at arm's length from the men of political influence in Tammany Hall: Matt Brennan wanted me as *his* creature.

It all started with my involvement with James Wilson; almost immediately I was in trouble.

The young man from Dublin arrived in my office later that week. Brennan had been right: there was something innocent and trusting about James Wilson. He had an open, clean-shaven face, pink cheeks, and eyes that twinkled on the world, seeing only the good in men. He would soon learn otherwise in New York, was my guess.

'I'm staying at the Albemarle for the moment,' he announced enthusiastically, 'until I find my feet in this great city, and then I'll wish to buy a property, maybe in Manhattan. Perhaps you can advise me there, sir, since you know the city well, so it's said. Meanwhile, I need to seek advice on the investment of my liquid assets – the product of my father's life's work as a timber merchant in Dublin. He died recently, God rest his soul, and somehow I felt that after that, for me Dublin had changed, and I wanted a new start.' He smiled, confidentially. 'And there was the matter of a certain young lady, I confess, whose attentions were becoming too pressing.'

I didn't doubt it: a presentable young man of means was always a clear target, in Ireland as much as anywhere else.

'How liquid are your assets at the moment, Mr Wilson?'

'Ah, well, there you are! I have a certain amount in cash – dollars and suchlike – but the larger part is in specie.'

'Gold.'

'That's so.'

I took a deep breath, considered the matter. 'Then the first thing you need to do is place it where it is safe. Not all the banks are as reliable as one would wish.'

'You could recommend a safe haven, until I decide upon a project for investment?'

'Safe as houses.'

It was as simple and straightforward as that. Within three days he had handed into my safe keeping some thousands of dollars' worth in gold. I placed the gold in the keeping of the Bowling Green Savings Bank: Matt Brennan had assured me all was well and financially stable there. I had already looked at the bank assets and all seemed well. On the face of it.

Over the next three weeks, I saw quite a bit of James Wilson. I showed him some of the more salubrious saloons and concert theatres in the city, and he came to me with various proposals regarding the best way to invest his specie. I found reasons to dissuade him from several of these, until finally – albeit reluctantly, but under pressure from an impatient Matt Brennan – I brought up the name of Henry Hayward.

'He's a man of some consequence,' I announced, following the brief given me by the City Comptroller. 'He owns a slice of the equity in a number of riverside projects, he has city and government contracts for the redevelopment of run-down areas in the Five Points, and I am aware that at the moment he is seeking investors to come in with him on a new project, one which should be after your heart, since it is of a kind you are already familiar with. You see, now the war is over, the demand for building materials, consequent upon war damage, is considerable and Mr Hayward has the concession to construct a lumber mill on the banks of the Potomac. It seems to me to be a sound enterprise. You could look it over for yourself, and make your own decision, but I feel I can recommend it as a rewarding investment.'

All right, all right, you look at me askance, my boy, but let me hasten to add that I *had* looked at Hayward's papers and figures and projections and I *was* satisfied that the project looked sound enough. I was aware, of course, that graft would be involved: anything Matt Brennan had his fingers on would have elements of corruption, but that was the same throughout the city in those days: police, politicians, judges, lawyers, builders, they all had their hands in somebody else's cashbox.

Hayward came into my office to meet Wilson the next day, and they shook hands on a deal. I didn't like Hayward from the moment I saw his bloodshot eyes and sagging jowls, his meaty hands and crocodile smile. He was well dressed of course, apart from the billycock hat, and he had the confident swagger of a New York businessman. But he spat tobacco juice too often, and not always in the spittoon provided. Still, he seemed to impress young Wilson and they talked business for an hour.

Thereafter, I drew up the papers, which promised Wilson a percentage share of the profits as well as an immediate regular monthly income and employment as a manager once the lumber mills were constructed. I was also entrusted for the moment with the continued holding of the specie still deposited in the Bowling Green Savings Bank.

Once again, I see a distrustful and cynical gleam in your eye, young man. But you have to appreciate the position a lawyer finds himself in. I had done all I deemed necessary, in checking the papers Hayward waved in front of my eyes. I had given advice to young Wilson, but I deemed that advice sound, even if it was backed by the corrupt

Matt Brennan. But I was just the middle-man, I was merely there in the transaction as a bond-holder, if you will. I wasn't really *part* of what was going on.

It's what I tried to explain to young Wilson three months later. The business he had entered into with Hayward was nothing to do with me.

'But you *advised* me!' Wilson expostulated.

'In good faith, I assure you.'

Wilson was enraged. 'But I have waited for three months, and I find that while large sums of my capital have been drawn from the bank in Hayward's name, I have re-ceived not a single cent by way of the pro-mised monthly payments, and when I visited the Potomac site, I discovered no building work has commenced! Indeed, no one I spoke to seemed to be aware of any such activity being projected!'

I spread my hands helplessly. 'Mr Wilson, these are not matters I am involved with. I have placed your money securely. You have entered a business transaction on your own account. You must take these matters up with Mr Hayward, not with me.'

His eyes narrowed: I realized that while he might seem young and innocent James Wilson was also a man of dogged will. 'I want my money back,' he snarled.

I shrugged. 'You have a contract with Hay-ward. You might have a problem obtaining what is left of your assets at the bank, since they are subject to that contract. Hayward has a lien upon them. But that is where your route lies: with the bank, with Hayward ... not with me.'

You smile. I can see what you're thinking. Lawyers! But I was speaking legal truths in the same way I had done after the Horsham election years earlier, when that damned solicitor Padstone had tried to dun me for the money I had offered on behalf of Sir John Jervis. I wasn't personally liable then – for I was acting merely as an agent – and I wasn't liable now.

Wilson wasn't convinced. He took me and Hayward to court.

He was never going to succeed against me, of course: I knew my law. But the affair caused a certain noise in the press, and I still had enemies back in England. One of them caused an article to be published – inevitably – in the *Manchester Guardian*. It gave a somewhat garbled account of what had happened, claimed I had been arrested on grounds of fraud, and spent a night in prison in the notorious Tombs. From whence I had been 'mysteriously' released by influential friends in Tammany Hall.

When I heard about the article I knew I needed to act. Fortunately, the judge who was supposed to have released me from the Tombs was named in the article: Judge

Connolly. I immediately brought suit in Connolly's court, for libel. All I needed was a statement in my favour – because of course a New York court had no jurisdiction over the *Manchester Guardian*, but that's what I obtained. Connolly was as incensed as I and announced there was no truth in the allegations and that I left the court with no stain on my character. *That* decision was never reported in England.

What happened regarding Hayward and Wilson? Well, sad to say, Wilson lost a large part of his money and emerged a poorer but wiser man. Hayward was arraigned for fraud – there being no lumber yard under construction and no city contracts – and it turned out he was not a businessman but a confidence trickster. He was never tried for the offence, however: bail was posted in the usual farcical way and he immediately disappeared. Matt Brennan seemed pleased with the result.

As for me, well, there were some mutterings around the city precincts. And I continued to handle work in the police courts. But my associate, Tom Dunphy, was getting restless: he was not happy with the way our partnership was going, and though we still had some notable cases to handle such as the Conner murder trial, and Supreme Court hearings such as the Gowan fraudulent divorce matter – in which John Cowan found his father-in-law had brought false proceedings to enable his daughter to divorce, and get alimony from him – there were still too many Brennan-sourced briefs for Dunphy's liking.

'Look at this defence of Officer Busted you've recently taken on. He was charged with not paying for pawn tickets! Is this really the kind of work we should be seeking?'

Officer Busted was, of course, one of Matt Brennan's minions. And Tom Dunphy was right. In his position I imagine I would have felt the same. But I had little choice, with the threat of Seamus O'Conagle and the Cork Revengers hanging over my head. So, I suppose it was with a certain sense of relief on my part that Tom Dunphy finally suggested we should break up the partnership.

I was soon enough approached by another lawyer, Charles Blandy, with even greater Tammany Hall connections. But I held fire for a while. I was still hoping to make my own way, in spite of all these problems. I had achieved great things in England on my own: I felt I could still rise to the top without the support of a partner in New York.

But things only stumbled onwards and the work seemed slow in coming in. I felt dispirited, trapped by the past, and I began to lose confidence in my prospects. That was the time when I felt I was hitting rock bottom; Matt Brennan put me in touch with a certain Charlie King. He promised me that if we went into partnership we could do well in prize cases before the courts. I had already built up a certain reputation with the shipping companies in my early days in New York – though much of that work had drained away in the Hudson River – so I complied willingly enough.

And at first it seemed to go well, until I realized just what Charlie King was up to. He set up a firm of bankers and brokers and listed me as Special Counsel. And I soon found myself bringing a series of claims against ships arriving in New York for non-fulfilment of contract. The claims were largely settled out of court, because the ship-owners did not wish to go to the expense of a lengthy trial in the Prize Courts. When I looked more closely into these so-called con-tracts I realized they were a figment of Charlie King's fertile imagination. And the shipowners – well, they saw the whole thing as a form of blackmail, but with discharging their cargoes and wishing to turn around quickly, they felt it wiser to pay Charlie King off, settle out of court and be on their way. Blackmail, insurance, a Matt Brennan tax, it depends what you want to call it.

And I was supposed to provide the legal muscle to back Charlie King's claims.

I wasn't happy. I soon broke off the con-nection. As for Charlie King, a few years later he was charged with murder, for killing his father-in-law, who had assisted in the seduction of Charlie's wife: a curious business and somewhat complicated. Charlie was bailed, naturally enough, and disappeared, of course. It's the way things operated in New York in those days.

I seem gloomy as I tell you about those times? Well, yes, I suppose it still affects me. My high hopes were being dashed, I was floundering at the edges of my legal career, I was under the pernicious thumb of Matt Brennan, my reputation was sliding and it was becoming clear to me that the glory days of the Old Bailey were long gone, and not to be repeated.

But I wouldn't want you to think that all was gloom. After all, this was the period in which I made the closer acquaintance of your mother. She's never told you how we met? Ah, well, I *first* met her when she was acting as a public lecturer for your father's show in London: the Diorama of India, which drew large audiences. That would be about 1852. She was twenty-two years old then, and quite beautiful. The money she and your father earned was frittered away, of course: your father, J.H. Stocqueler, he always lived beyond his means, much of his activity was on the shady side, there was all the whoring, the doubtful financial deals, and he was bankrupted several times. He had abandoned his first wife and child in India, and when I met Eliza for the second time, years later in New York, he was in the process of leaving her – and you – in the same manner.

Drilling whores, actresses and would-be cavalrymen for the war was his proclaimed forte in New York but he was soon off to Canada, and then England, while your mother was left kicking her heels in New York and you were off on your first sea voyage.

Yes, in my dark days Eliza was a beacon to me. How did we come to meet again in New York? Hah, it was when I was in the employ of Colonel Lafayette Baker in the Five Points, before Lincoln's assassination, during the Draft Riots. I had taken to carrying an Equalizer at that period, whenever I made a foray into Hell's Kitchen and Satan's Circus. An Equalizer, you know ... a Sam Colt revolver.

And it was just as well that I was carrying it under my frock coat that evening when I heard the screams from the alley near the Coloured Orphans Asylum on the junction of 5th Avenue and 47th Street...

2

Colonel Sam Colt.

Americans always loved awarding themselves military titles. I met Sam Colt, you know, when I was still living in London. He'd set up a pistol factory near Vauxhall Bridge to make and promote sales of his 'impossible gun', a pistol that could fire five or six times without reloading. He was actually a farmer's son who laboured for a while as a laughing-gas demonstrator, before he worked out his revolving principle after watching the helmsman on a ship he worked on for a while.

He came to me for advice regarding his patent – which he managed to get at last from the government – after he had exhibited his wares at the Great Exhibition of 1851. He presented me with a sample of his revolutionary weapon. But Palmerston didn't approve of his factory so Sam Colt went back to the States after four years and awarded himself military rank while he busily promoted his guns. In 1860 he was selling the weapons to both North and South. Businessman, you see, taking no sides, concentrating on profit. He died of gout, I believe...

Anyway, I became an *aficionado* of his weapon. That etching I showed you – the one made by Frank Vizetelly when we were in Italy with Garibaldi – it has me with a brace of pistols stuck in my belt. I was in a war, after all. But they were one-shot pistols, and when I first handled a Colt 1851 Navy revolver I knew it was the weapon for me.

It had provided a necessary insurance also when Di Rudio and I were working in the Five Points for Colonel Lafayette Baker's Secret Service: we were spending time with belligerent, drunken Irish supporters of *Clan na Gael* and among the Jolly Fellows there was always the likelihood that a bout of drinking and gambling would be followed by a general brawl; someone would draw a knife, and chaos would ensue. Carrying an Equalizer gave me confidence that I could get out of any scrape that we got caught up in. Indeed, Di Rudio also carried one of those potent weapons. When we rode in the hunt for John Wilkes Booth we each carried a Navy Colt. It had certainly proved necessary that particular day when I found myself cut off from Di Rudio in the Five Points.

We had decided to part in order to cover a couple of separate meetings of the Jolly Fellows that afternoon. You know, New York was not unlike earlier days in London as far as links between concert saloons, bars, billiard rooms and brothels were concerned.

In London, the Seven Dials area and St Giles rookeries teemed with low life, just a few yards from aristocratic houses and clubs. So it was in Five Points: there were almost four thousand Irish families crammed into garrets and damp cellars, living abject lives of poverty where vice and crime flourished. Many of the houses doubled up as taverns, while roaming pigs and chickens were underfoot everywhere. That particular day we drew straws, Di Rudio and I: he went off to the Clifton Shades and De Soto's; I plunged into a couple of the gin palaces and gambling saloons in Madison Square and then into Izzy Lazarus's dive for a while before taking a drink at Country McCleester's in Doyer Street. It was a normally a popular place with its bar, exhibition ring for pugilists, dog pit and faro table, but there were few men there that day. I put one foot on the bar rail and looked at the faded fighting prints on the wall, and talked about old pugilistic encounters with the former knuckle-fighter who owned the bar. But as I drank, I let my frock coat swing open so that anyone who was interested could see that I had arrived duly defended.

You raise your eyebrows!

Now don't get me wrong, my boy! I've never laid claim to being a hero, or a man of heroic tendencies, even. But I knew how to use a pistol and I'd spent enough time in

Norfolk country houses in the old days winging partridges to be confident of my skill. And I was fully aware of the state of tension that existed in the city, and the reason why McCleester's was virtually empty that day.

It all started with Lincoln's Emancipation Act, freeing black slaves who had already left the South. That piece of legislation didn't go down too well with the immigrant Irish, who saw the blacks as competitors for their menial labour. Then came the Draft Act, which led to a great deal of further resentment because Blacks, as non-citizens, were exempt, while exemption could be bought only by whites who could raise the necessary $300 to provide a substitute. You can imagine the outcry *that* piece of legislative folly caused: one law for the poor, another for the rich!

Quite a rallying cry. And I happened to be in Five Points that July day when the resentments boiled over.

I realized there was going to be trouble, when the saloons started emptying, and there were hordes of men and women armed with staves and brickbats in the street. I soon guessed that the trouble would not occur in the Five Points as a location: the mobs were streaming towards Broadway and Fifth Avenue. So, as McCleester's emptied, I decided to stay where I was for the time being, and spend a little leisure time with Lizzie Williams. That's right, the very same whore that Officer John Parker arrested after failing to protect the president some time later.

Lizzie was not a stupid drab: she had conversation, and a nice line in tassel-swinging, a skill with which she used to entertain her customers while they were getting rid of encumbrances such as knives, guns, swords, boots and pantaloons. She also kept the large toenail of her right foot longer than normal and filed to a sharp point: with that implement she could, at the height of your passion insert–

What? Sorry. I'm digressing again.

Yes, I'll get on. Well, there I was spending an agreeable period with Lizzie – not discussing the weather exactly, although it was hot and muggy – and it was about four in the afternoon when I finally left her to make my way back to Broadway. The Five Points streets were largely deserted, but I could hear the distant hubbub of the battles that were going on up towards 3rd Avenue and 47th Street, and see the pall of greasy black smoke that drifted near where the draft office was located. I heard later they took out the draft officer and beat the hell out of him for just doing his job. I gave the area a wide berth and sought a quieter route back to my office.

Over the next few days – for the rioting went on for almost five days – the newspapers were full of reports of the carnage caused by the mobs, made up mainly of Irish immigrants hurling paving stones through windows of public buildings, killing tramcar horses and burning the cars, cutting telephone lines and looting and torching brothels, dance houses, boarding houses and tenements catering for blacks. The white owners of these establishments were stripped naked in the streets, but the occasional black who got caught by the mob was hanged from a lamp post and his body burned.

It had all started as a protest against the draft, but it soon turned to an ugly, racist riot: the Irish saw the emancipated blacks in New York as a threat to their own slim employment opportunities. And after they had burned down the Bull's Head drinking house on that first day, they turned their attention to Protestant churches, homes of known abolitionist and Secessionist sympathizers – and then moved on in a drunken rage to the Coloured Orphans Asylum.

Yes, I see your eyes widen in surprise. But you have to realize that by that time all sense had left the minds of the mob. They were on the rampage, and their attention became fixed on the black community. As for the Asylum, well, the logic seemed to be that since it was supported by white charities it should be attacked as a privileged location. The Irish poor got no charitable handouts, so why should black orphan children be given special treatment?

Unfortunately, my route back to Broadway that afternoon, trying to avoid the disorder, landed me directly in the path of the disorderly, rampaging mob.

I had got to know the back streets of the city during my saloon-bar wanderings with Di Rudio while working for Colonel Lafayette Baker and I made use of that knowledge to good effect to avoid the noisy, violent crowds. A pall of dark smoke lay over Fifth Avenue and there was a constant noise, cheering, screaming, breaking glass, the roaring sound of pitched battles between the outnumbered police and fire-brigade men who sought to hold back the mob. When I came out into Fifth Avenue itself, I found I was able to witness the scene while skirting at the edge of the crowds. There were men and women – mainly of the lower sort – thronging the sidewalks, brickbats were flying, hammers and clubs flailing, and windows were being broken in order to assist in the looting. It was far from a peaceful demonstration against the Draft Act, I tell you!

I was managing, successfully, to sidle along at the edge of the mob until my attention was caught by the turmoil that swirled around the entrance to the Coloured Orphans Asylum. The children had been ushered outside and were standing, crying with fear, in disorderly lines under the care of increasingly frantic female orderlies who were attempting to organize them so they could be taken to safety. The doors of the Asylum had been thrown open by the mob and crowds of men and women were thrusting their way inside to loot the building. There was an acrid smell in the air, a hint of smoke, and I knew then that a fire had been started on the premises. I was edging myself carefully away from the turmoil. The children themselves seemed not to have been harmed: the mob was at least that controlled, wreaking no vengeance on innocent orphans. But when some idiot Protestant preacher cried out, 'Leave the children, at least!' he was savagely set upon, his clothes torn, hat ripped off his head, and when he went down on the cobbles boots went flying in as he was savagely beaten.

Then, as I edged towards the corner of 47th Street, I heard a scream.

It's strange, isn't it, how a single noise can draw your attention in the middle of a maelstrom of sound. The roaring of the bullyboys, the crazed yelling of termagant women fighting amongst themselves to get the best pickings, the crash of glass and the stamping of feet created a wave of furious sound about my ears and yet I still heard that single scream, and my attention was drawn to the sight of three men dragging a woman into a nearby alley. And it's equally strange that in the middle of all that hell I caught a glimpse of the struggling young woman's features.

Eliza Stocqueler. That's right. Your mother.

I've often enough asked myself whether I would have acted as I did if I had not recognized her. Would I have plunged into that slimy, smoke-darkened alley if it had been some other woman, a stranger? Would I have overcome my natural fear and reluctance to get involved in violence, for the sake of an unknown woman's honour?

I can't say, and I've told you several times that I have never seen myself as a courageous man. Nevertheless, that sight of Eliza being dragged into an alley gave me no opportunity for thought, or discretion, or careful withdrawal. They had vanished around a corner, that struggling group, and without hesitation I plunged into the lane after them.

I cannot say, even now after all these years, what I had in mind. But there I was, recklessly running into the alley until, turning the corner, I caught sight of the group again. And a furious rush of blood surged into my head and chest, leaving me almost breathless. Two of the men were fairly young: one was holding Eliza pinned against the wall, while the other tore at her clothing with violent hands and a wolfish grin. The third man had his back to me, one elbow against the soot-stained wall, leaning casually, taking pleasure in merely watching what was transpiring. Eliza's face was soot-blackened, she was screaming and the clothing from her upper body was already torn while the grinning man grabbed at her skirts, attempting to drag them up over her head. I caught sight of her eyes, almost crazed with terror.

I shouted.

'Leave her alone, you damned ruffians!'

Time seemed suddenly to stand still. The two younger men turned their heads, looked at me, and then glanced at their companion, as though seeking leadership. The third man stiffened, turned his head, took his elbow from the wall and looked back over his shoulder. Then he turned further, to face me. He had a shillelagh in his left hand.

He was a man of about fifty. I can still see him clearly, in my mind's eye. He was of my height, moose-jawed, thickset, burly and dressed in an outmoded fashion, with his tattered frock coat, gaudy neckerchief, and trousers tucked into heavy boots. His billy-cock hat was perched arrogantly on the back of his crop-haired head. Many rough-necks had dressed like that, twenty years earlier, swaggering the streets of the Five Points, in the heyday of the 'Bowery B'hoys' when they ruled the roost, fighting and drinking and gambling in the gin palaces and saloons, dressing in what amounted almost to a uniform, but those days – and that fashion – had given way to the 'jolly fellows'. This man, with his blue-stubbled face and malicious, drunken eyes, had not kept up with the times: he still lived in that mindless, violent past, the days of his wild, knuckle-bruised youth.

He stared at me, and a wide smile came to his ugly mouth. I caught a glimpse of blackened teeth as he snarled, 'Leave off here, little man, if you don't want crippling.'

I was incensed. *'Leave her alone, you filthy scoundrels!'*

The ageing Bowery B'hoy straightened, squared his shoulders and casually slipped his right hand into his belt. I caught the glimpse of a knife blade as he swaggered towards me, calling out over his shoulder as he came, 'Carry on, lads, I'll deal with this.' He stood some twelve feet from me, a vicious snarl on his ugly, pock-marked features as he eyed me up and down in clear contempt. 'I'd ruther foight than fuck, any day!' he grunted and he began to advance further upon me.

I held my ground, though my heart was racing madly. I slipped my right hand into the wing of my frock coat, swung it back to reveal the Navy Colt in my belt. It produced no effect on the big man: he continued to advance, knife in one hand and the shillelagh in the other.

I drew the revolver from my belt.

His piggy eyes widened as I levelled it in his direction. He seemed surprised but not intimidated. The sight of the Colt did not deter him in his drunken determination. He came on, swinging the club. I hesitated.

You know, my boy, if you've ever used an Equalizer you'll be aware that it was never the most accurate of weapons. At a distance of six feet, I guess, you'd never miss a barn door. Beyond that it's luck not good judgment, whatever the penny dreadfuls might write about the remarkable skills of Bat Masterson, Wild Bill Hickok, Wyatt Earp and Billy the Kid. I reckoned myself a good shot, after my experiences in England, shooting at grouse and crows and pheasant, not to mention the scarce bustard. But I had never fired at a man before, though some had fired at me when I was with Garibaldi in Italy.

This man provided a big target.

As he came on, I stood my ground, levelled the pistol and his mouth opened in a violent, mindless gape as though he hardly believed I would press the trigger. But press it I did, and the sound of the shot echoed around the alley. His eyes widened further and he let out a roar of surprise and anger and then he clutched at his kneecap, staggered, fell back and went down onto his back, yelling obscene imprecations. At a distance of twelve feet I'd hit him in the right knee.

To be honest, I'd actually aimed at his belly.

As the smoke drifted from the muzzle of the Navy Colt I looked past the roaring, writhing man on the ground and saw that I had caught the attention of the two young thugs attacking Eliza. They were staring at me as though I was mad, and I could see that they were not only scared, they were *impressed* at what they regarded as the accuracy of my shooting. So I waved the Colt in their general direction and they rapidly released Eliza so that she slumped to the ground. I affected a bravado I did not really feel: my pulse was racing, and I was shaking at the knees. But I managed to hold the Colt steadily enough.

'Get out of here, and take that piece of ordure with you!' I commanded, waving the Colt shakily in the direction of the howling man on the cobbles.

Under the muzzle of the threatening Colt they complied, dragging their leader by his armpits, edging away from me, deeper into the alleyway. I could still hear him roaring in pain after they had disappeared and I went forward to assist Eliza to her feet.

She was trembling, shaken, almost unable to stand after her ordeal, and she allowed me to half lift, half carry her back into the main street. Fortunately the mob was moving on, away from the Asylum, which was now wreathed in smoke and the children were being ushered away to safety.

I knew where safety lay.

I took her back into the streets of the Five Points.

It's odd, Joe, how things can affect you. I knew these streets pretty well, and yet seemed to have paid little enough attention to them before that day. But now, as I half carried Eliza to safety, it was almost as though I became aware for the first time of the pullulating atmosphere, rotting dog carcases in the gutter, the crust of horse manure, dog turds and pigshit baked hard under the summer sun, that the mob had further trampled into a concrete mass under our feet. I saw with new eyes the decrepit, tilting houses with the soot-stained washing hanging from broken windows, the sagging boardwalks, the scrawny pigs and chickens creeping back to forage in the slowly swirling rivulets of slimy, soiled water that trickled along the length of the gutters. I'd seen the poverty and vice of the London slums and their counterpart here in the Five Points, reeking and smoke-darkened and soiled, and yet with Eliza at my side it was as though I was becoming *aware* of the nature of the area for the first time. And it shamed me that men and women could bear to live in such conditions.

We were deep in the Five Points. The mob would not be rampaging here: they *lived* here.

I thought first of taking her to Kit Burns's Sportsmen's Hall where I was well known, but guessed she'd be offended by the smell of the rat pit there. Water Street was a dive location frequented by 4th Ward gangsters, but surprisingly John Mien's saloon held prayer meetings on certain days, for whores, bartenders and musicians, but unfortunately not on that day. So we took some quiet back streets towards Paradise Park and then when we reached the south-west corner of Water Street we made our staggering way down the few steps from street level to push open the battered doors of the Crown Grocery Store.

It was not just a provisions store, of course. It doubled up as a saloon and a whorehouse in addition, like most such establishments in the Five Points. I led Eliza past the miniature mountains of cabbages, eggplants, potatoes and other commodities and found a chair for her to sit down. She stared dumbly at the upright casks of rum, whisky and brandy that ranged the walls beside her while I ducked my head under the hams and tongues, sausages and onions that hung from the festooned ceiling while I sought out Susan Crown. Her husband had been an Irish immigrant who had established what had become a neighbourhood institution: he had profited greatly but could not resist the spirits he peddled. Mrs Crown had been running the combined grocery and groggery since her husband died, of intemperance it was said, five years earlier. I found her, standing somewhat disconsolate, behind the long, narrow bar at the end of the room. It seemed the usual denizens had gone to join the rampaging fun uptown. I approached Mrs Crown and told her I needed a room, a couple of glasses and a bottle of her best brandy. She raised no eyebrows, asked no questions: she gave me a room number – one of the five or six narrow, appropriately furnished rooms on the first floor where she spuriously advertised virgins fresh from the country for the knowing and selective client – and I assisted Eliza to the designated space under the eaves, where I poured her a stiff shot of brandy.

She was still shaken, and somewhat dazed. She drank the tumbler of brandy, shuddered and sat silent for a little while. Under the warm influence of the liquor she slowly came to her senses, focused her gaze on me, and after a few minutes her brow cleared, she blinked, and murmured, 'Mr Edwin James.'

I was flattered. 'You remember me.'

'We were introduced at the Great Exhibition. You were a famous man in 1851. And you became even more famous later. I used to follow your career, in the newspapers.' She hesitated, her voice a little shaky. 'How could I not remember?'

319

'And I remember you from hearing you lecture at your Diorama.'

She was silent for a little while, then sighed. 'That would have been in the same year. The Stocqueler Diorama of India at the Regent Street Gallery. It was very popular, for a while. But we made no money out of it. At least, what money we made was all spent, faster than it came in.'

She fell silent again. I considered it wise to keep her talking. I gave her another shot of brandy. She sipped it slowly, almost dreamily as her mind dwelt upon the past.

'What were you doing, walking in the neighbourhood of the Coloured Orphans Asylum?' I asked.

She took a deep, shuddering breath. 'I help out there occasionally, with a little teaching. When my husband is away – which is often – time drags on me since we no longer operate the Diorama in New York: it did not prove as great a success as in London. Americans seem to have little interest in India. So I give of my time at the orphanage, since my son Edgar is also away now, gone to sea. It passes the time... I was working at the orphanage today, but then, when that mob arrived I thought it best to try to return home. Before I had gone a few yards I was trapped by those villains...' Her eyes widened at the memory and she picked helplessly at her torn clothes. Her cheeks began to redden with shame.

To take her mind from her ordeal, I asked, 'Where is your husband at the moment?'

She shrugged. 'Mr Stocqueler? In Canada, I believe. Doing what, I am not certain. Recruiting soldiers. Journalism. Writing a book. Who knows? At least it keeps him away from the New York theatres.' She glanced at me, sadly. 'Do you know Miss Agnes Cameron?'

I frowned, hesitated. 'An actress, I believe. She's given some benefit performances in aid of wounded Union troops, according to the *New York Clipper*.'

Eliza nodded. 'She is nineteen. I am past thirty. These things are important to Mr Stocqueler.'

I had heard so. Your father had a *penchant* for young girls. There seemed little I could say further on the topic. We were silent; while refocusing, she at last gazed around the room, noting her surroundings. She took in the sight of the sagging bed with its single blanket, the grimy washstand, the faded pornographic prints on the wooden walls. Her eyes turned to mine.

'You know this place well.'

I shrugged. There was no point in dissimulation. 'I have rarely been here, but it is one of the establishments where women can appear at the grocery downstairs. Most saloons are masculine retreats.' I looked about me. 'There are many such groceries in this area.

321

My work ... it brings me into the Five Points from time to time. But you will be safe here for a while. The mob won't attack their own rat holes.'

'Your work?' she asked, puzzled.

I could not elaborate too much. Colonel Baker's was a *secret* employment. 'My work in the police courts necessitates my talking to people in the Five Points. Much of the city crime emanates from this area.'

'I can believe it.' She shuddered.

We stayed at the Crown Grocery, Eliza and I, for almost two hours. Downstairs, Susan Crown, drawing her own conclusions about our stay, must have marvelled at my stamina. But we just talked, Eliza and I, about the old days in London, the theatres, the success enjoyed for a while by the Diorama, and we got to know each other better. She spoke little of your father, but I knew his character well enough, and I felt sorry for her. I could guess where his regular absences were leading. It had happened before: he had left a wife and child behind him in India, before marrying Eliza Wilson. I wondered if he had ever divorced...

Then, in the early evening, I heard gusts of wind rise against the leaking old roof of the Crown Grocery and a brief hammering of rain on the grimy window. 'That'll cool things down,' I opined, and after a little while I suggested we might venture out into the streets again.

The rain did what the police and firemen and militia could not do: it dispersed the mobs, who began to stream back into their rat holes in the Five Points. We managed to make our way back uptown with little difficulty, apart from the sludge we were forced to trudge through, the hardened cake of faeces in the streets soon turning to filthy mud under the rain. I took your mother to the door of her home but did not enter. Nor did she invite me, as I now recall.

After that, well, I didn't see her again for ... what? ... two years or so. At least that. Our paths did not cross again until one day I met her as she came out of Judge Barnard's court, as I was going in on Matt Brennan business. She seemed distressed, so I invited her to a nearby tearoom, where I learned she had that day obtained a decree of divorce on the grounds of adultery and desertion. Your father was back in England by then and I believe you were on your third voyage to South America. So I suppose one should not be surprised that your mother and I began to meet from time to time; innocently enough, I assure you. After all, we were both divorced, leading rather lonely lives – I was getting rather too old to continue cavorting with the Jolly Fellows and my work for Colonel Lafayette Baker had ended. I was finding my legal practice was beginning to have a somewhat disreputable reputation because of the stream of Matt Brennan clients who dragged me to defend them in the courtroom and when I finally agreed to go into partnership with Charles Blandy it did not seem to work out well. He was a jealous man, retaining the more interesting cases for himself, and I suspected he wanted me in his office merely for the Matt Brennan connection.

I was able to talk freely about such problems with Eliza. You know, I found her, right from the beginning, a woman in whom I could confide. Not everything, of course…

So, yes, that's how it came about, really. We married … when was it? That's right, 1868. I don't know where you were at that time … Melbourne, was it? Anyway, the marriage has proved to be a comfortable one: there have been none of the tumults of my time with Marianne, but perhaps that was inevitable since I was leading a quieter life. But both your mother and I, well, we each felt a longing to return to our roots: America had not come up to our expectations.

And it was not long after our marriage that the past loomed up against me once more. I found myself face to face at last with my dreaded Nemesis.

The leader of the Cork Revengers.

3

'So, how's your eyesight now, Mr James?'

As I've explained to you before, a good lawyer never asks a question to which he does not know the answer. Don't press a question on a witness if you aren't certain what he's going to reply. Trap him by all means, lead him into an indiscretion, or a downright lie. But be always on your guard: you might hear something that could blow your case apart. And it's the same in life outside the courtroom, that's my contention, and with answering a question you don't quite understand. Consider the motivation behind the question before you answer it – and if that motivation is not clear, prevaricate until the clouds of indecision clear.

'My eyesight...? It's well enough, sir.'

'The eye surgeons in Europe, then, they know their business.'

'They have the highest reputation,' I replied carefully, not knowing where this conversation with a stranger was leading.

We sat there in my office in Charles Blandy's premises and looked at each other silently for a little while. I wondered what on earth he was talking about regarding my eyesight. But overriding that question was the more dangerous one: why was this man here in my office?

My mind drifted back to the day when John Sadleir had asked me to assist in his death. I could smell again the stink of the Dead House where I went to view Sadleir's body and agreed, lied, that it was indeed his corpse. The money he paid me had helped me into Parliament, but then there was that evening of my inquiry before the Benchers of the Inner Temple when I received the message from Ben Gully.

'*Get out of London. NOW.*'

The Cork Revengers were seeking me ... and in the dark London streets there had been the scuffling, the throat-cutting, the dumping of Cork Revenger Patrick O'Neill into the stinking sludge of the oily Thames.

At first sight, my visitor Seamus O'Gonagle did not present a threatening sight. He was about my age, thick at the waist, dressed in a somewhat outmoded fashion with his yellow waistcoat and pale-grey trousers. He sported a black satin cravat and a breast pin that glittered in the slanting sun that filtered into the office. His features were ruddy, mastiff-jowled, his stubbly beard greying, and if his gnarled knuckles, tightly gripping the heavy-knobbed stick he carried, were thickened from old battles his body, slumped in the chair facing me, was relaxed, legs crossed at the ankles in casual fashion. But I was never a man to be misled by casual appearances. There was a hint of steel in this dandy Irishman's eyes. O'Gonagle, Matt Brennan had assured me, was the acknowledged head of the Cork Revengers, the group of Irishmen determined to avenge – with blood if not monetary compensation – the frauds of the swindler John Sadleir ... and anyone who had conspired with him to avoid his deserved end. Which, as far as *I* knew, deserved or not, happened to be a comfortable and obscure retirement in Venezuela or some such place.

'You are intimate with my friend Comptroller Matt Brennan, I understand,' O'Gonagle said at last.

'I have undertaken many briefs in his court,' I agreed carefully.

O'Gonagle nodded. 'I understand you were a great man in England, sir, a decade ago. But fortune does not seem to have smiled on you to the same extent in the United States.'

'I am not unhappy with my lot,' I lied. 'And I am happily married.'

If I was hoping to soften his steely glint with a mention of my marital state, I failed. He grunted, nodded again, grimaced. 'I'm not a married man, meself. Though that does not mean I am not an admirer of the female form.' He glared at me as though daring me to contradict him. Perhaps his mother in Ireland had wanted him to do the traditional thing and become a Catholic priest.

We sat once again in a strained silence. O'Gonagle continued to observe me, but the steely glint was fading and an odd sadness seemed to appear in his face. He shook his grizzled head after a while, and sighed.

'There is *one* woman I *would* have married, without a single moment's hesitation had I obtained the opportunity. I remember when I first saw her – the perfection of womanhood. She was dressed in boyish fashion but there was no hiding the sublimity of her figure, and the flashing of her eyes struck at me heart, I have no hesitation in telling you. And she bestrode the stage as no woman has ever done before – or could ever do again, in my opinion. Later, in London and in Paris and in Albany I saw her again and again – yes, I travelled like a besotted swain – just for the thrill of seeing her and enthusing over her performance and her beauty. I was overcome by her performance on the back of that galloping steed, her seemingly naked body, her agonized features, the way she held her arms to the skies ... thrilling, thrilling... And to think, at the end, she left us so young, and with no Dumas, no Swinburne, no Barclay, no Menken, no Newell, no husband, no lover at the graveside to mourn her passing. Deserted by the world.'

Silence fell once more between us as he

grieved. I had stiffened. I now guessed who he was talking about ... but why was he discussing her death with me? The last time I saw her, it was when I arranged for her passage to London after her attempted suicide.

'You knew her ... intimately, of course,' O'Gonagle said with a slight edge to his tone that I understood instinctively.

'We were ... we were close *friends*,' I stammered.

'Closer than many,' he replied, and the edge to his tone faded, softened. 'And, I understand, the only one who was loyal to the end.'

I was staggered to see that his eyes had misted over again, this violent Irishman, head of the Cork Revengers. And you know what happened then, my boy? This murderous Irishman thrust his hand into the breast pocket of his yellow waistcoat and drew out a ragged pamphlet, which he began to *read* to me! I listened, stupefied, still not understanding what on earth this interview was all about. But the pamphlet – I was so taken aback that later, I obtained my own copy. I have it here somewhere, still ... let me think, the drawer over there, yes, that's it! Listen to this! Seamus O'Gonagle sat in front of me in Blandy's office in New York and read out this passage from the pamphlet. Let me read it to you now from my own dilapidated copy.

'*I was losing my sight through an incurable*

affliction of the eyes, contracted while going to the funeral of Harry Lazarus, who was murdered in New York by Barney Friery. I went to Europe to seek a specialist who might save my eyesight. It occurred to me that the trip might be made commemorative by placing a monument over the remains of Adah Isaacs Menken, who died a few months previous. The great heart had passed away and neither Dumas nor Swinburne, nor any of the thousands of leeches who drank her champagne in life and revelled in her society and manifold charms, knew her in death!'

'So true,' O'Gonagle sighed, 'so true!' Then he continued reading.

'It was with the greatest secrecy and difficulty I managed to carry out my plans as it is strictly against the Jewish customs ever to remove the dead once buried but I finally accomplished my object. The day set apart for the exhumation began with a heavy rainstorm but at eleven the sun shone out in a blaze of glory and at 12.15 I set out from the old cemetery for Cemetiere Mont-parnasse and the coffin was lowered into the vault. I placed two little mementoes in glass cases a pansy and a forget-me-not – on the granite cover and arranged about the monument and railings. I arranged, in compliance with her last dear wish, for the inscription...'

At this point O'Gonagle stopped, his voice breaking slightly, while I remained silent and still bemused. His eyes were glistening with tears.

'The inscription,' he said at last, 'was *Thou Knowest!* You, Mr James, you will know what that means, and I will not intrude upon your patent grief over the loss of a dear friend to enquire of you its meaning!'

He droned on for a while longer but I hardly heard him. I did not know how to react to his sentimental outpourings about the woman I had known briefly – well enough to cause the breakdown in my first marriage, but nevertheless briefly. When he had finished, he leaned back in his chair, folded the pamphlet, replaced it with exaggerated care in his coat pocket and wiped the back of a knotty-knuckled, hairy hand over each eye, blurred with tears. As I sat silent, stunned with continued incomprehension, he went on.

'When I first read what you had written, Mr James, I was overcome. The way the world treated her! I had seen her in triumph, the glorious Adah, the wonderful, courageous Mazeppa! She had stormed New York, Baltimore, London, Paris ... the whole world was at her feet! Loved by princes! Befriended by high society! She had Mark Twain and Bret Harte as her admirers, and Dumas, Swinburne and Dickens were held in the palm of her tiny hand. And I *adored* her! A distant swain! An unrecognized lover! But for all that, she was destined to die alone in a Parisian garret, to be interred without cere-

mony, disregarded by those she had rewarded. Disregarded, forgotten, ignored by
all ... except by *you*, Mr James.'

Then the light slowly dawned upon me.
And believe me, my boy, I was so shaken at
that stage that I was on the point of opening
my mouth to explain his error, the mistake
he had made in identities, when I remembered my legal training, my years at the Bar,
my understanding of human nature and my
appreciation of the weaknesses and foibles
that can drive a man to decision. So I closed
my lips tightly, and did not explain Seamus
O'Gonagle's error to him.

He thought it was I who had written the
twenty-four page pamphlet, *The Life and
Times of Adah Menken*. I had *not*.

You see, when I became an associate editor
of the *New York Clipper*, engaged to produce
sporting and theatrical pieces, *I was not the
only Ed James on the staff!* There was also the
deputy editor, of the same name! Normally
known as Ned James, twenty years younger
than me, a follower of pugilistic endeavours
and an acquaintance, like me, of John
Heenan and Tom Sayers, among other fighting luminaries, he had from an early age been
afflicted with worsening eyesight – he ended
up blind, in fact, for no European ophthalm-
ologist could do anything for him – but he
had one thing in common with me. In the
1860s he had been swept off his feet by Adah

Menken – I told you she collected admirers. Indeed, I understand he carried on a long correspondence with her, much more extensive than mine, and even acted as a sort of press agent on her behalf, placing notices in various newspapers, eulogizing her performances. I never doubted that he wanted to be her lover, but though she used him, she never admitted him to her boudoir. Nor for that matter did I achieve that honour, I admit, though there was that one time when we came close...

But O'Gonagle was not a close reader of the *New York Clipper*... I doubted whether he was inclined to read anything other than accounts of pugilistic endeavours and reviews of his adored Mazeppa. And he had not realized he was talking to the wrong man: it was Ned James who had written Adah's life story, not I.

So I sat there, tight-lipped, as the head of the Cork Revengers mopped his glistening eyelids and sighed.

'Your account of her passing affected me deeply, Mr James. Your loyalty, your affection, your love over the years ... all this spoke to me from your account of her life and death. It's why I still treasure your account, keep it close to my breast, read it in the twilight hours, over and over again... It moves me, sir, it *moves* me!'

The Irish were always a remarkably sentimental race. All those sad songs about the Old Country even while they were battering someone with boots and fists and shillelaghs. All those missing Marys, half-remembered hills sweeping down to the sea, sparkling streams and lonely valleys, and their ridiculous beliefs about the Little Folk... Sentimental, but still addicted to murderous violence, rampaging drunkenness, and a deep-seated desire for revenge against the English lords who had trampled on them for centuries ... and the swindlers of their own kind who had ruined thousands of tenant farmers' lives... Like John Sadleir.

O'Gonagle straightened in his chair and fixed me with a clear glare, from which all moisture had now been erased.

'So there you are, Mr James, it's all over, so it is. Adah... A beautiful life, finished, extinguished before it had given all it could have done to the world. Her inestimable poetry ... her stage performances...' He paused, nodded slowly. 'An immeasurable loss. The light of the world – snuffed out!' He paused again, sniffing, his eyes welling once more with tears. Then he straightened his shoulders, seemed to regain control of his emotions. 'You will be aware, sir, I don't doubt, that we are still on the trail of James Sadleir, for we are certain he was involved with his swindling brother in the destruction of hundreds of livings in Cork. He has disappeared in Europe, but we shall find him one day. And when our sadly-lamented colleague Patrick O'Neill was carrying out his enquiries in London, in 1861, eight and more years ago now, he did transmit certain suspicions to the brethren regarding *your* role in the business...'

I was again tempted to speak, but frantically resisted the temptation as my panicked fingers curled around the Navy Colt I carried under my tailcoat.

'We've followed your career in New York with a view to one day getting from you the truth – whatever it is – of your association with that scoundrel John Sadleir. But Matt Brennan ... well, his interests did not coincide with ours and he kept you at arm's distance from us, for you've been useful to him. And now ... well, I've thought long about the matter, and reflected upon it, and I tell you true, Mr James, a man who could write what you did about Miss Adah Menken, the trust and truth and *loyalty* that shines from those pages, the fact that even though half-blind from your own ocular weaknesses you yet found the time and energy and *devotion* to seek her out, to retrieve her remains, to arrange for her proper burial... Such behaviour tells a great deal about a man.'

I sat almost gasping, waiting for the words that I hardly dared were now to come.

He sighed, almost theatrically. 'I consider

myself a man of perception where character is concerned. Adah Menken was the light of my life, and that light still burns in my Irish soul. I cannot believe that the man who went to Paris, the man who wrote this pamphlet,' here he touched his breast, 'is the kind of man we've been looking to exact revenge upon.'

He paused, affected, but then some of the previous glint returned to his eyes. 'And even if that man is someone we've been looking for, it is my considered opinion that the time for revenge is over. Forgiveness should take its place. Forgiveness, and absolution.'

Suddenly, he lurched to his feet. I guessed he was overcome by the emotion of the moment. He held out his gnarled hand. I rose, took it, carefully. His grip was firm and determined.

'Next week I return to Ireland. I'm glad your sight has returned, Mr James, and the affliction has gone. You'll be hearing no more from us ... even though Mr James Sadleir must still cast a glance over his swindling shoulder. And should you return to England – or even into our own jurisdiction in Ireland – you'll not be bothered by us.'

He stared at me for several seconds, still gripping my hand fervently and then, releasing me, he turned abruptly, and left the office. I could hear his heavy feet clumping down the stairs. I sat down, shaken but mightily relieved. I could hardly believe it, but the danger and the threat, after almost a decade, had been finally lifted. The Cork Revengers were no longer seeking to question me regarding my relationship with the swindling banker John Sadleir.

I never saw O'Gonagle again: he was as good as his word. Naturally, I never disabused him or any of his followers – or anyone else – of his mistaken belief. But I privately blessed the half-blind pugilistic writer, my namesake, who had kept the flame of Mazeppa burning in his little biographical pamphlet. Last time I heard, Ned James had retired, completely blind, from his editorial work with the *New York Clipper*, and spent his time writing accounts of famous pugilists like Heenan, and Morrissey and Hyer.

So there you are. A cloud had lifted. A year or so later, chance put me in the way of a lucrative brief. I received quite a windfall from that representation, I can tell you. What? No, no, the details won't interest you, but enough to say that when the money came in, with the threat of the Revengers lifted, Eliza and I packed up swiftly to make the unhindered crossing back to London.

I was finished with America. And now I was clear of hindrance or threat from mad Irishmen I was determined to storm the portals of the English legal establishment all over again.

4

Of course, I failed.

The hoped-for success eluded me, as you will already realize, as you cast your eyes about this grim little tenement that houses your mother, me and the single, simple little servant girl, Sarah Lewis.

I had high hopes when I reached London. I returned to a certain acclamation, to be sure. My brother Henry assured me I still had friends in England. Much had changed in London of course, since Eliza and I had separately left for America. The Metropolitan Underground railway had been constructed, the Albert Memorial unveiled, the Albert Hall founded and a new bridge erected at Blackfriars.

Many of the old faces had gone: I remember going to see the gun-carriage procession for the funeral of the Duke of Wellington in 1852, but I didn't manage to turn out for the funeral of the pugilist Tom Sayers: he died when I was in America. I would have liked to see that turnout: they say 100,000 members of the Fancy had lined the roadside on the route from Camden Town to Highgate. The hearse was drawn by four horses and followed by Tom's phaeton with his dog sitting in the driving seat. The mongrel was followed by cabs, farm wagons, costers' carts, a brewer's dray and a donkey cart. I'd like to have seen that! But apart from Tom Sayers others had gone: Lord Palmerston and Tom Duncombe were dead, as was Dr Thomas Wakley; my Marylebone stablemate Lord Llanover had shot himself; several of the judges I had faced, like Cresswell Cresswell and Pollock, had passed on and so too had Joseph Tallents, the solicitor who had given evidence against me at the Bencher's Inquiry. Dickens and Thackeray were no longer with us, of course. Even Simon Bernard, whose cause had helped me to a seat in the Commons, had breathed his last: he was made a fool of by a woman, lost his reason and died in an asylum. As for my old friend Alexander Cockburn, he was still active, now Chief Justice of the Queen's Bench. We did not meet. We now moved in different circles. My enemy Inspector Redfern had retired to grow roses in Kent. As for Ben Gully ... well, I made enquiries, but it seems he had simply disappeared. I learned by discreet inquiry that he hadn't been seen in his old haunts since shortly after the killing of Patrick O'Neill. I wondered whether the Cork Revengers had found him but I doubted it: Ben was a resourceful man with many friends – and many enemies, to be sure – and I was convinced he would have found a new haven for himself. I never found out, of course, but I didn't expect to.

One thing had not changed much: the entertainments were much the same. Leicester Square was still the hub of the nightlife, whores still prowled around the Haymarket, though Cremorne Gardens had been closed. Highbury Barn, Kate Hamilton's Night House, the Alhambra and Mott's were all still in business. As was the brothel reserved for parliamentarians in Lupus Street. That old hypocrite, Gladstone, night-street wanderer and self-abusing collector of whores, gathered a deal of criticism when he later closed down that establishment in Lupus Street. It was such a convenient berth for parliamentarians after a late-night sitting: indeed I had introduced young Lord Worsley to it, years ago... Not that the establishment was available to me now, of course; not that I went back to my old ways: I was now a respectable – if impoverished – married man! But I was aware that the brothels at the Prussian Eagle and the White Swan in the Ratcliffe Highway were still booming as were the Stepney opium houses; the homosexual brothel in Oxford Street remained popular with its particular clients and Madame Rachel's Arabian Baths in Bond Street were still offering beauty treatments as a cover for

340

discreet liaisons and blackmail. The police reckoned there were still four hundred whores working between Piccadilly Circus and Waterloo Place, parading from 4 p.m. till 3 a.m. And the dance floors, galleries and curtained alcoves of the Argyll Rooms still provided a thriving marketplace for amateur dollymops. Soldiers' whores continued to frequent Wapping and Whitechapel, and Knightsbridge and Birdcage Walk were still thronged with ladies of pleasure. As for Swinburne, he was still getting his personal pleasure from erotic flagellation at 7 Circus Road while others of his ilk were known to get their stimulation at Mrs Potter's in Chelsea and Soho.

Yes, the shops, cafés, Turkish cigar divans, assembly rooms and concert halls were still much the same as when I had left England ten years earlier, but in my wanderings around the West End – merely curiosity-driven, I may add – I came across only two familiar faces: Lascar Lily and Swindling Sal. Lily had specialized in erotically imaginative hair-plucking in the intimate regions, but advised me she had now become an establishment madame. Sal was a tall, muscular whore, stoutly built with a fist like a hammer, who was well known for cracking the occasional rib during sexual byplay. She had always been popular with the pugilistic fraternity. She recognized me in the street, offered me the welcome of her open arms, but I backed off, concerned for the welfare of my now well-fleshed ribcage.

I soon got up to date with the current legal appointments. It was with some chagrin I learned how lesser men had taken the posts I had coveted and almost won: that idiot Gillory Pigott was now a Baron of the Exchequer; my old adversary Bovill was now Chief Justice of the Common Pleas. The incompetent Roundell Palmer had climbed the heights and was now on the Woolsack as Lord Chancellor Selborne. I had bested them all in my day, in forensic debate; and there they were now, high and mighty while I was struggling to make a successful return to practice.

I could have been one of those five ex-Lord Chancellors receiving £5,000 a year pensions. As I complained to Eliza, if only my luck had held, if only Lord Yarborough had died earlier in 1861, if only Fryer could have been persuaded to hold off, if only the malice and jealousy of my rivals at the Bar had been less virulent, I could have been with Thesiger and Wood and Bethell and the others, and perhaps still a force in Parliament.

But, I also told Eliza I was convinced I could do it yet. I started by writing a book: it was published in 1872 as *The Political Institutions of England and America*. There's a copy of it over there, on that shelf... And I announced my arrival back on the London scene with a public lecture at St George's Hall in Langham Place.

A good crowd turned out to welcome me that night; there was a huge burst of applause when I appeared, and my speech was punctuated by cheers as I spoke warmly of the relationship between England and America. It was just like the old days! I still had my adherents in Marylebone, and I made some criticisms of the corrupt American legal and political system, but I also scattered my talk with amusing anecdotes, as usual. And as I did in my speech in Dr Bernard's case, I ended on a rabble-rousing, jingoistic note by castigating the current movement for the introduction of republican institutions. I sat down, flushed and hoarse, among wild cheering, and I knew I was back and in contention!

But somehow, that was really the high point. Thereafter my support seemed just to ebb away. I managed to place a few short stories in *Temple Bar Magazine*, including *Reminiscences of the American Bar*, and Eliza and I, we kept our heads above water for the time being with my savings from my last success in America. But I was now sixty, disbarred, and still unable to follow the only profession in which I could make a good living. I needed to make my appeal to the judges for reinstatement and so I turned to

George Lewis of Ely Place to prepare my case. Since the days when he had brought me briefs, he had gone up in the world: a friend of royalty now and recognized as the leading solicitor in London, slippery rogue though he was. Still, what attorney was not? I thought using him would be to my benefit, but in the event I still decided to speak in my own cause on the day: there was no barrister in whom I had greater confidence! Moreover, I still had many enemies among the Inns of Court and I did not know whom I could trust to speak on my behalf. So, I made my application. Then I waited.

As the weary days passed by, there were echoes of my past all around me: Lord Huntingtower, whose bankruptcy had helped launch me on the legal scene, was dying, and W.J. Ingram, Herbert's son, was standing for the Boston seat. I didn't pay too much attention to such events for I eagerly awaited the hearing of my appeal, scheduled for February 20th. It was finally held at the hall of Serjeants Inn, Chancery Lane.

A large, curious crowd had gathered, but most were denied entry: the judges told me they had decided a private hearing would be more satisfactory in view of the disclosures that would necessarily have to be made concerning the financial and other affairs of the former Lord Worsley, now Earl of Yarborough. The public was, therefore, barred, with the exception of a shorthand writer for the judges, and my faithful brother Henry. I suspected at that point that the dice would be loaded against me!

When I stood there in the hall the faces looking down at me from the Bench were familiar enough: I'd known them as juniors, as QCs, and socially, as well as in the House of Commons. But their features were expressionless: I could have been a stranger. President of the Court was the Lord Chief Baron, Fitzroy Kelly, whom I'd routed in *The Queen v Bernard*; Bovill was there too with Baron Martin, who had presided at the *Running Rein* case and Russell Gurney who had spoken against me in 1861 at the Benchers' Inquiry. These were men I'd known well on circuit as QCs. Justice Blackburn was present: I never thought much of him, a jumped-up nonentity whom I was surprised to see had risen to the Bench; and otherwise there were only Justices Quain and Grove, apart from Justice Keating, the man whose promotion had left the post of Solicitor General open to me in 1861, when my luck had finally run out.

And there was not one among them I could count on as a friend, or even one willing to give me a sympathetic hearing.

And that was what happened. They listened to my side of the case but their eyes were hard. The first step I took was to request that

Justice Bovill stand down on the grounds that he had been Ingram's counsel in *Scully v Ingram*. They agreed, and a grumpy Bovill stumped out of the hall. It was my only success. I began my speech in that long, almost empty, echoing hall. It lasted throughout the day.

It was useless, of course. My main argument was that no specific charges had ever been levelled against me as a result of that Benchers' Inquiry in 1861, and I could see that when I began to put my side regarding the financial transactions, *private* financial transactions which should have been of no concern to the Inner Temple Benchers, their eyes did not meet mine.

I remember stating, 'I am not seeking to avoid responsibility, but I *did* pay all interest and premiums due on the loans, and on the last advance of £13,589 made by the Eagle Office there were no previous liabilities...'

And all would have been well, I insisted. Even up to the time of the Benchers' Inquiry all could have been salvaged if only I had been left alone. The Benchers had condemned me for not reducing Lord Worsley's involvement out of the Eagle loan, but I insisted that this was never the agreement I had made with Lord Worsley. The Benchers had interfered without jurisdiction.

I dealt with *Scully v Ingram*, and the loan I'd received from Herbert Ingram as a fellow

Reform Club member. But I soon realized all this was to no avail. I could not tell them the real reason for my leaving England while the Inquiry was still sitting, and I knew they still felt that desertion had been a sign of my guilt.

I didn't even bother turning up for the second day of the hearing. George Lewis spoke on my behalf. I knew the outcome was preordained.

I was there again on Saturday morning, for the verdict. But it was all a waste of time and effort, and my hopes were quickly dashed.

Things might have been different if I'd led a quiet life, I admit. But the judges could look back over the years and recall the events of Horsham; Fitzroy Kelly could remember the facts that came out in *Newmarch v James*; there had been the rabble-rousing defences of Dr Simon Bernard and the black slave Anderson and the indiscretions of the *Café Chantant* affair. They could recall the curious Dickson business, and my later espousal of the American cause in the controversial arrest of the Confederates Mason and Slidell in the seizure of the *Trent* on the high seas and then there were all the damaging rumours thereafter that had crossed the Atlantic, published by my enemies at the *Manchester Guardian*: the Hayward business, my work for the *New York Clipper*, and my relationships with pugilists and sensational actresses and the low life of New York. They were determined to avoid scandal, wanted to maintain a high moral ground ... in spite of the *facts*.

In their eyes, I was a man who seemed to attract scandal: and they felt the Bar should not again be forced to accept an individual with such a doubtful, tarnished reputation.

Their statement, when it came, was hardly surprising.

They refused to readmit me to practise at the English Bar.

I don't deny it was a crushing blow, for me and for Eliza, who never lost her faith in me. I'd felt confident that since my creditors had allowed me to return I could have won back my right to practise, but the hope was now dashed. What was left for me now?

I sent short stories to the *Temple Bar Magazine*: one successful one was entitled *Next-Door Neighbours*, an account of a confidence trick with a twist in the tail; and then I looked around for other possibilities. In September 1873 the seat at Marylebone fell vacant and I immediately tried to put the clock back by offering myself as a candidate for my old seat. But I had no money to pay bribes and other election expenses and the electorate displayed a humiliating indifference to my oratory. Simon Bernard was just a memory and Reform no longer a burning issue. The

Marylebone Mercury, once my champion, described me as an ageing roué who lacked neither the money to buy Marylebone nor the fame to persuade it. I realized that a renewal of my political life was just a pipe dream. *Running Rein*, Horsham days and Marylebone triumphs were just a distant memory.

So finally, I took the bitter step of approaching an old enemy: the attorney Mr Parkes, who along with Mr Tallents had persuaded Lord Yarborough to press the issues which led to my resignations from my clubs, Recordership and seat in the House of Commons. Mr Parkes heard me out, and took great pleasure in offering me a final humiliation – a seat in his legal office, with the intention that I should become a solicitor at his office in 46, Moorgate Street.

Should I have been surprised at the resultant uproar? Perhaps not. The Law Society demanded to know why I could be admitted without first passing the required examinations. Me, Edwin James, the QC who had terrorized witnesses and counsel in some of the greatest cases of the day! I needed to take examinations?

It was a humiliation too far.

I returned home to Eliza, then cocked a snook at both Law Society and Bar and placed an advertisement in the London press.

'*Mr E. James may be counselled preparatory to the commencement of legal proceedings upon questions of American and English law by parties in financial difficulties and in all matters of a confidential character. 9 New Burlington Street, W.*'

So there you are, my boy. For the next few years I eked out a precarious living in this manner, on the fringe of the legal world. And I saw with frustration great cases that would have been meat and drink for me in the old days. I tell you, I *lusted* for some of those briefs – what a stir I would have made in the Tichborne Case – the claimant ruined by the hysterical outpourings of Dr Kenealy for the defence! What I could have done in the Chetwynd divorce hearing regarding the numerous female servants kept in the household as mistresses, or in defending Colonel Baker when accused of lifting the skirts of Miss Dickinson – an overheated, hysterical young woman – in a train carriage! And as for Lady Aylesford, when she and her husband were in the Divorce Court, what could I have not drawn out regarding her fast life at hunt meetings, racecourses and other locations where the loungers and butterflies of high society fluttered away their lives – while her husband favoured resorts of harlots and other dehauchees of his own stamp!

Such cases were custom-made for me! But I was denied them by the jealousy of Temple barristers. And in my reduced practice, my clients were inevitably poor, or ignorant, and the only way in which I could make any sort of return from the business was by spinning out my involvement with them as long as possible before I was forced to take legal action on their behalf ... when I would be forced to hand them over to someone with a right of audience.

But I struggled on, dealing with disreputable clients, producing an odd article for the magazines, and writing to the newspapers in defence of Garibaldi. But I was getting old.

You know, I used to go out early each morning, walking to the City from the lodgings Eliza and I had taken at 11 Bayley Street. But I attended the courts only as a spectator. I was now virtually penniless, and all but forgotten. I often considered how far away was my present address in St Giles from Berkeley Square. I no longer wore my once famous coat with the astrakhan collar; I took to a worn, threadbare old Aberdeen to keep out the cold on my morning walks to the City. I passed the occasional old acquaintance: few acknowledged me.

And as for this last winter, it's been bitter. It's when I contracted this damned cough ... bronchitis. Then there's the kidney problem.

The year before, the damned fogs and snow saw off my old friend Alexander Cockburn. So I've outlasted him, anyway. What a claim to fame!

Hah! The bitterness of age and defeat.

What? Yes, my boy, of course I've often reflected on my rise and fall. My glittering success, and my martyrdom.

I tell you, Joe, martyrdom can do wonders for a man. Or at least, for his reputation. Take President Lincoln, for example. Nowadays it's fashionable to laud him to the skies as a great president, the Emancipator, the man who freed the slaves. But what was the reality, as I recall it? Many in his own party, the Republicans, derided him at the time for his indecision, his ineptitude, his gawky appearance, his unfitness for high office, his refusal to outlaw slavery in the Southern States. He couldn't control his cabinet, Secretary of War Stanton held him in easy contempt, and the generals – McClelland, Grant, Burneside, Hooker, Halleck – all ignored his orders.

I think I told you that shortly after my arrival in New York in 1861, I paid court to Judge Daly's wife, a snobbish, gushing, sharp-tongued woman who had little love for anyone but her immaculate husband and who openly detested Abraham Lincoln for his lowly beginnings. 'Old Abe,' she freely announced to me, 'or King Log as I call him, is mentally and physically long and loose in the joints. He is unfit for high position, unaware of the peril in which the country finds itself, merely content to be president, tell risqué stories and have Mrs Lincoln dress herself up in an undignified manner and hold *levées.*'

I remember how Mrs Daly preened herself, smoothed down her voluminous skirt as she spoke.

'She bullies him unmercifully, you know: that's why he's so meek. They say when he started his political career he tended to stay out late at meetings and return home somewhat the worse for wear. His wife would lock him out and tell him from the window that he could not come in. And there was the occasion when he called out in the street, "My dear, let me in I have something important to tell you."

'"I don't believe it," Mrs Lincoln is said to have replied.

'"I have indeed," pleaded the poor ungainly man in the tall black stovepipe hat. "I have something astonishing to tell you. I have been nominated for president!"

'"Pshaw," Mary Lincoln replied in disgust. "Now I *know* you're drunk!" and slammed down the window, cutting short his protests.'

But in 1862, when I talked with Mrs Daly, I think she spoke for a great number of people in New York and Washington. They saw Lincoln as a second-rate Illinois lawyer and his wife as an upstart, affected, almost comical *parvenu* who was raised far above her real station in life.

Getting himself assassinated changed all perceptions about President Lincoln, of course: it was perhaps the best political move in his career.

As a martyr he became a national hero: North and South joined in reviling his murder and re-establishing his reputation and he was looked back upon as a sage and honourable president. Mind you, that was helped by his having been preceded by an incompetent in James Buchanan and followed by a corrupt idiot in Andrew Johnson. Martyrdom worked for Lincoln...

But for me, martyrdom didn't quite work out like that. I was a martyr to the moral panic that swept over the Inns of Court in the 1850s. But why was I treated so severely? There were others who were attacked for worse, *professional* sins, like Kenealy in the Tichborne Case, and Kennedy in the Swinfen hearings, and even the Lord Chancellor, Lord Westbury, managed to survive financial scandal and claims of nepotism ... but I was the one singled out for *special* treatment. So why me, when they couldn't even prove any professional misconduct, merely unwise private behaviour?

My guess is that I'd made just too many enemies. Maybe it was because I'd become too friendly with Lady Palmerston and a few other political wives, and tongues wagged; there were many at the Bar who envied my rapid rise and the huge fees I was winning, together with my prospective elevation to a knighthood; politically I was too radical in my views for many of the old fogies in Parliament, not least in my support for the unions in the building industry.

So I was singled out to be punished. The charges were trumped up, of course: the Benchers at the Inner Temple could not point to any *professional* misbehaviour, the only area in which they had real jurisdiction. No, I was made a martyr to hypocrisy and self-seeking aristocrats and jealous, small-minded men.

So, for me, martyrdom brought no rise in esteem, however. Unlike Lincoln. That's one of the injustices in the world, don't you agree? When the full facts were known about my disgrace, when I finally returned to England and personally stated my case, no one – apart from my close friends – seemed to want to know. And yet in my own way – on a smaller stage than Old Abe, admittedly – I had every right to rehabilitation. I had every right to have my merits recognized, my achievements lauded, my political and legal talents rewarded.

Instead, well, I was caricatured by Dickens in *A Tale of Two Cities* and by Trollope in *Orley Farm*, my achievements were glossed over, my name no longer heard in polite society and here I am now, years later; well, you see my condition and circumstances. A humble, mean dwelling, a single servant, a back-room desk in a minor attorney's office ... all a far cry, a great distance, from the Old Bailey successes, my home in Berkeley Square, my early days at Cobham Park, and the drawing rooms of the Upper Ten Thousand...

Or am I deceiving myself? Am I ending my life, as many do, in a whimper of self-deceit?

Hell and damnation, is *that* brandy bottle also finished?

AFTERWORD

It is almost twenty years now since my stepfather, Edwin James, passed away. His death occurred shortly after our last conversation in 1881, just before I married Mary Ring.

Oddly enough, my natural father died about the same time: he had managed to marry his thirty-year-old actress Agnes Cameron, and sire another two children before expiring. It was the only time he had ended a marriage in a natural way, I suppose. I did not attend his funeral: he was really a stranger to me. After that, well, I was involved with my sea voyages to Australia and South America, and my wife bore me several children and with the money she brought to our union – she was a wealthy young widow when we married – I set about establishing my shipping business, but it was hard work. All of this activity drew my attention away from the remainder of the story Mr James had narrated to me: I was a busy man.

But I am forced to admit I was also reluctant to put pen to paper once more, in recounting his history, for I feared that during his time in New York he had become infected with that disease to which Americans are particularly prone: the telling of tall stories. I felt unsure whether I could believe his account of his involvement with Colonel Lafayette Baker and the Secret Service, and his pursuit with Major Charles DeRudio (as he now styles himself) of the fleeing John Wilkes Booth. And his views about Secretary of War Stanton's involvement in the assassination of President Lincoln seemed to me to be somewhat far-fetched. As for the Cork Revengers...

However, I recently read that James Sadleir had been murdered in Switzerland. It was put down to an attempted robbery, but I certainly wondered whether the Cork Revengers had at last found their man. Moreover, last year my business expanded so well overseas that I found it convenient to open an office in New York. While there I was able to find some leisure time to browse in the archives of the *New York Times* and the *New York Clipper* and I discovered that many of the events Mr James described were true: the John Heenan case, Mary Real, Henry Hayward, the police corruption, the scandals, the Draft Riots and the political personalities like Matt Brennan, who ended as Police Commissioner in New York and was himself jailed for corruptly allowing a murderer to escape custody. And, to my surprise, I learned Mr James had not lied about his namesake who had, inadvertently, drawn the fangs of the Cork Revengers as far as my stepfather was concerned: there had indeed been another sporting editor at the *Clipper*, called Ed James, who wrote a number of accounts of his pugilistic heroes – such as *Fistiana*, and *Life of John Heenan* ... and penned, in addition, *The Life and Times of Adah Menken*. He went blind in the 1860s, but lives still.

And when I came across the published reminiscences of Colonel Lafayette Baker I began to think again about Mr James's account of his involvement in great events in the 1860s. The book made no specific mention of Mr James – but then, why should it if my stepfather was, like Charles DeRudio, in fact working as a *secret agent?* However, I was surprised to learn that Mr James's account of the hunt for John Wilkes Booth was circumstantially correct and his views about Secretary of War Stanton were not entirely fanciful: they were echoed in Colonel Lafayette Baker's own account – where the existence of the damaged diary of the assassin is revealed, and Stanton's conspiratorial involvement with Booth is hinted at. Colonel Baker died shortly after publication of his book; it is rumoured he'd been poisoned by arsenic-tainted beer provided, some say, by his brother-in-law at the instigation of the War Department. Stanton's arm was long.

I had hoped to talk with Major Charles DeRudio, in order to confirm Mr James's account of their adventures together in New York and Washington, but that sturdy soldier, one-time assassin and survivor of the Battle of Little Bighorn was in service with the 7th Cavalry at Fort Meade in the Dakota Territory and not available to me. Though he did write to me a courteous letter, in which he complained about lending his Austrian binoculars to General Custer, a loss he has, it seems, neither forgotten nor forgiven!

So perhaps it was not a simple matter of tall story-telling on Mr James's part...

But my final decision to tell the story arose out of the recent publication of the autobiography of one of the most successful fraudsters of our time: Austin Bidwell, one of the four men who robbed the Bank of England in 1872 of the massive sum of £100,000 by the cashing of forged bonds and bills of exchange. When I perused this published account I was taken aback to discover that in the late 1860s the Bidwell brothers, in carrying out extensive forgeries and frauds in the United States, had actually used Mr James as their legal adviser!

When he was telling me his story in those miserable lodgings in Bayley Street years ago, Mr James had seemed open enough about his various activities, even of a doubtful moral kind, but on one matter he remained somewhat reticent. Shortly before he returned to England, he said, he had gained a 'windfall' from some legal representation, but he declined to explain this in detail. Now, in reading Austin Bidwell's *From Wall Street to London Prison*, I discovered how he had obtained that windfall, if the forger Bidwell is to be believed: Edwin James obtained the huge fee of $5,000, enough to enable him to return to England and try to resume his legal career in London, by working with Austin Bidwell and his brother George in a complicated swindle that targeted New York banks!

When I read Bidwell's account I could understand why Mr James had been reluctant to discuss the source of that $5,000.

According to Austin Bidwell, when he and his brother attempted a massive $240,000 fraud on the Jay & Cooke Bank in New York they used Edwin James as their lawyer to provide them with a respectable 'front'. There can be little doubt that he was fully aware of what they were up to, in using forged bank bonds, but when the scheme collapsed because of an eagle-eyed detective called George Elder, Mr James was questioned by the banks but protested that he was merely the Bidwells' lawyer and negotiator, quite innocent of their nefarious intentions. A defence he had used on several occasions! No action was taken against him; the Bidwells fled to Europe, where they launched numerous frauds culminating in their 1872 attack upon the Bank of England which led to their imprisonment in Newgate – but at that point my stepfather, with the money he had received from the Bidwells, deemed it appropriate to return to England and escape the suspicions which were swirling around in New York with regard to his behaviour.

This surprising account was enough to encourage me to go back to Mr James's story, if only to round off some of the edges and expose some of the weaknesses of that remarkable man by way of independent sources rather than his own conversation.

I did of course ask some questions of my mother but although she confirmed his account of his saving her during the Draft Riots she seemed reluctant to provide any other information, certainly nothing about his adventures with Colonel Lafayette Baker, or Charles DeRudio, and later, the Bidwell brothers. As for the Cork Revengers and Seamus O'Gonagle, when I mentioned the actress Adah Menken, she merely rolled her eyes. On the other hand, she remained stubbornly proud of Mr James's former status as a leading Queen's Counsel and it seemed she never lost her faith in my stepfather. I remember on one occasion, becoming irritated by some glowing comment she had made to me regarding his personality and achievements, I rounded on her, my patience snapping. I demanded of her – how, after experiencing one marriage to a shady swindler like my natural father Joachim Stocqueler – how could she have chosen for a second husband a rogue such as Edwin James?

My mother looked steadily at me for a few moments, and her blue eyes widened as she said quietly, 'Don't you understand?'

'I do not.'

'He saved my honour. He saved my life.' And then she added, 'He was my *hero!*'

To that I found little response. There seemed little more I could say in considering the life of Edwin John James, former QC, MP. So...

Requiescat in pace.

Joachim Edgar Stocqueler
Managing Director
Stocqueler Shipping Line
1897

The publishers hope that this book has given you enjoyable reading. Large Print Books are especially designed to be as easy to see and hold as possible. If you wish a complete list of our books please ask at your local library or write directly to:

Magna Large Print Books
Magna House, Long Preston,
Skipton, North Yorkshire.
BD23 4ND

This Large Print Book, for people
who cannot read normal print,
is published under the auspices of

THE ULVERSCROFT FOUNDATION